Thrace Talmon

Heroine of the Revolution

Or, Captain Molly, the brave woman

Thrace Talmon

Heroine of the Revolution
Or, Captain Molly, the brave woman

ISBN/EAN: 9783337185107

Printed in Europe, USA, Canada, Australia, Japan

Cover: Foto ©Andreas Hilbeck / pixelio.de

More available books at **www.hansebooks.com**

HEROINE OF THE REVOLUTION;

OR,

Captain Molly, the Brave Woman.

BY

THRACE TALMON.

Why should I fear a foe, a beast, an arrow, or a lance? We are assaulted by the more noble part of Nature itself; by the heavens, by the seas, and the land. He that fears not death, what does he care for either fire or water: the very dissolution of the universe?—SENECA.

WITH ILLUSTRATIONS.

NEW YORK:
DERBY & JACKSON, 119 NASSAU STREET.
1860.

The following Pages are Inscribed,

AS A TRIBUTE OF FRIENDSHIP,

TO

MARY DEVENS BALFOUR,

DAUGHTER OF THE LATE REV. MR. BALFOUR:

AND TO

CARRIE LOUISE BUTLER,

DAUGHTER OF THE LATE HON. JUDGE BUTLER.

PREFACE.

The title of Captain Molly is derived from an incident in the history of the American Revolution, a sketch of which is inwoven with the eighteenth chapter of this volume.

If it be thought that the life of the heroine is too dramatic to be natural, let it be remembered that in the period when she lived, eventful experience was much more frequent than in later times. Then, life-scenes were characterized for *masterly expression*, as were the pictures of Raphael, and not for the mellow tone of *perfected color* attained by Titian.

While we believe that courage and patriotism are commendable in woman, and that she should endeavor to be equal to whatever exigence may arise before her, we no less believe that she is especially designed by her Creator to hallow and make beautiful the sphere of home, rather than to flourish on the arena of strife and illustrious events.

CONTENTS.

CHAPTER VIII.

CHAPTER IX.

CHAPTER X.

CHAPTER XI.

CHAPTER XII.

CHAPTER XIII.

CHAPTER XIV.

CHAPTER XV.

CHAPTER XVI.

CHAPTER XVII.

CHAPTER XVIII.

CHAPTER XIX.

CHAPTER XX.

CHAPTER XXI.

CAPTAIN MOLLY.

CHAPTER I.

THE GOLD CASE.

BACKWARD through the years, go with me, gracious reader, to the winter of 1760. It is not, perchance, too far, for do we not remember our grandfathers' tales of this and even earlier time ! They live in our memory like the odorous leaves of evergreens, while other leaves fall to the ground, decay, and are forgotten.

The place is a venerable mansion, near the heart of the old Bay State. The particular time, early evening in the New Year. About this spot was a stateliness, an indescribable impress of power, that betokened superior life. The house was irregular and rambling, but it had been built on the liberal scale of the wealthy landed proprietors of that period. One might easily fancy that its wide hall-doors of unpainted oak, had erst unclosed to portly personages in gold laced hats, embroidered velvet coats, and long powdered queues, who, with uncommon dignity, had struck the lion-headed knockers, and stamped their high, military boots upon the steps of white marble. The ancient trees, ranged unevenly before the house, whispered mysterious tales of the past. They wound their strong arms together, and pointed upward, as the winds soughed through them prophetic peans of future strife and triumph.

On this evening, as usual, some half dozen servants were grouped before a huge fireplace in the entrance hall, engaged in various occupations. In an adjoining front-room, before another hickory fire, was a middle-aged man, who had just thrown aside his military cloak, and settled himself in his large arm-chair of solid mahogany. This was Colonel Epps, the head of the house. Upon a settle, cushioned with embroidered leather and bound with brass nails, sat a pale, matronly looking lady, with sufficient mark in her bearing to inspire respect, but with such a sweet smile habitually hovering about her lips, as more often to win love than fear. She was knitting a white silk stocking, with scarlet clocks, while upon her lap nestled the fair head of a little girl, who was amusing herself by dropping chestnuts upon the shaggy back of a large Newfoundland dog, reclining at her feet. Beside a ponderous table sat a boy of some ten years, reading, with absorbed passion, from an old book under the flaring, unsteady light of a brace of candles in holders of carved silver. Upon the sideboard were baskets made of varied colored shells, filled with waxen flowers and fruit. A sword in a gilded scabbard, which was an heir-loom in the family, hung conspicuously over the chimney-piece. Several ancient portraits of Mrs. Epps' family were ranged along the walls.

The Colonel took the newspaper from one of the capacious outer pockets of his coat, and began to read in silence.

Presently, the attention of all was arrested by the sound of footsteps without the house, advancing up the avenue, over the hard crust of snow. In a moment Lion was on his feet, his hair erect, and with a low, sharp growl evincing his displeasure.

"Reuben," said the Colonel, without lifting his eyes from the paper, "tell Peter to open the door and see who has come."

But this order was scarcely spoken before they heard a noise, as of a person falling heavily against the door, with a groan. The dog now sprang forward, barking violently, and following closely upon Reuben as he went out.

Upon the step he discovered the figure of a woman, who was too much exhausted to enter without assistance. She was speedily brought in, and Mrs. Epps commenced vigorous exertions in aid of the stranger, while the Colonel added another hickory log to the already glowing fire, and opened the live coals wide upon the hearth. Emerging to the changed atmosphere, the stranger fainted in the arms of Mrs. Epps, and became wholly insensible. On removing her cloak, great was their surprise to discover a little girl asleep, bound closely to the woman's bosom by a shawl.

The child was not very cold, and soon awoke, apparently much interested in the new scenes around her. She was consigned to the care of Reuben, who held her carefully upon his knee before the fire, while little Mary looked on, almost overcome with astonishment.

The stranger was borne to a bed in the adjoining room, and no exertions were spared for her restoration.

"I fear that she is frozen to death," said Mrs. Epps, "for all I can do is in vain."

But she had scarcely said this, when the woman unclosed her eyes, and looking wildly about her, moved her lips in an earnest whisper.

"She calls for her child," said the Colonel.

The little girl was brought to the bedside, upon seeing whom, the mother groaned aloud, while an expression of the deepest sorrow settled upon her face. "My dear child! Alas! who will shield her when I am no more?" she murmured, as she pressed the little head to her bosom. "If I could have only reached him!"——Vainly she strove to speak more. The words of importance, which evidently labored upon her mind, died upon her lips.

"Dear mamma," lisped the little girl, "it is warm and good out there before the great fire. Come and sit with us —do, dear mamma."

Tears now stole out from the mother's eyes, while she looked earnestly upon the sympathizing face of Mrs. Epps.

"Your child shall not be forsaken," responded Mrs. Epps to this appeal, "she shall live with us as our own."

She saw that the stranger had not long to live ; her eyes were glassy, her lips rigid and white, and the death shadow was falling over her brow.

"Reuben says that he will take care of me, mamma," said the little girl ; "I love him, and you, too, and I will be so good if you will talk to me once more."

The mother closed her eyes, and pressing her child's hand to her lips, while her arm encircled her neck, she lay motionless, and moved her lips as if in prayer. A few minutes later, she looked upon Mrs. Epps with an expression of earnestness, and placing the little hand she held in hers, closed her eyes, sinking apparently into a quiet slumber.

The little girl was closely interrogated, but nothing could be ascertained which gave a clue to her former history. She could only tell that her name was Mary, and that she had come a great way from her home with her mother. That she had been accustomed to superior style of life, was evident ; her clothing, though much worn, was of fabrics more elegant than Mrs. Epps had ever seen before, as was also her mother's. Her dark hair was bound from off her high brow with a fillet of silver, and there was an air about her which revealed that she had not been accustomed to humiliation. In Reuben's arms she soon fell asleep, and was allowed by Mrs. Epps to share the same bed with her own Mary.

"What a dear child !" whispered Reuben, as he watched her sleeping with her rosy cheek nestled in the pillow. "As pretty a Mary as ours."

"Poor thing!" said his mother, brushing away her **tears,** "in the morning she will have no friends but us."

"And we will love her and take good care of her!" said Reuben, proudly.

"I hope so ; and, if ever hereafter, you are disposed to feel angry towards her, remember this night, Reuben," said Mrs. Epps, very solemnly.

Although the Colonel and Mrs. Epps were desirous to learn something more of the child committed to their care, it was impossible, for the mother remained in a state of insensibility till she expired, about midnight. She was evidently a victim of disease, which had been suddenly terminated by her late exposure to the inclement weather. Concealed carefully upon her person, was found a richly chased gold case, which they supposed was designed for a locket, but being unable to open it, they could not ascertain its use. This they laid aside, to be given to the child in the future. No other article of value was found upon the stranger, and nothing which bore a name or place of residence.

In the morning, little Mary was for a time inconsolable when told that she could not see her mother, but the presence of the children served gradually to divert her attention from her grief. While Mrs. Epps and her housemaids were occupied with their duties, and relating meanwhile in mysterious tones the singular events of the preceding night to a few neighbors who had been summoned in, Reuben employed all his skill for the amusement of little Mary and his sister. Wrapped warmly in a blanket, she was taken in his arms to see the wonders about the homestead, and when at length a handsome cat with her well-grown family were discovered, inhabiting cosily a warm nook in one of the out-houses, the child was wild with delight. Reuben immediately gave her the kitten of her choice for her own, which she was permitted to carry in her arms to the kitchen, and this, with the companionship of the other Mary and her kitten, proved a source of varied amusement for hours.

Early that morning, the Colonel mounted his fleetest horse, and started for the Bald Eagle, a tavern situated a mile or two distant, which was well patronized by the people in all that region. He had now news of importance in his keeping, and not even the rigor of the morning could induce him to remain quietly at home. He learned that a lady and her child had stopped there, early in the preceding evening, to inquire the distance to the next town. They had endeavored to persuade her to remain over night, fearing that she would freeze to death if she went farther ; but she could not be dissuaded from her purpose, although evidently in feeble health, and she had refused to answer any questions respecting her destination or from what place she had come.

So much had the Colonel to communicate, such a variety of questions to answer, and surmises respecting the affair to settle, that he did not return till toward the middle of the day, when he entered the house curiously to survey the progress of affairs in his absence.

"Where is the child ?" he inquired of his wife, as he glanced about the kitchen, and saw only his own Mary.

"She is near, somewhere," replied Mrs. Epps ; "I have not missed her before, for she has been playing with the children, and seems already quite contented."

Little Mary Epps now abandoned her play to seek her companion, but soon informed her mother that the little girl was nowhere to be seen. Reuben was next summoned, and sent in search of her, but returned unsuccessful. Mrs. Epps joined in the quest, and uneasiness was felt by all, when it was declared that the child was nowhere about the house.

"It cannot be possible she is in there ?" suggested the Colonel, pointing toward the door which opened into the "great spare room," where lay the corpse of the stranger.

Mrs. Epps, who was a courageous woman in everything save when her superstition connected with the dead was excited, now turned pale, and refused to obey her husband's suggestion. On examination, the Colonel found the little Mary lying over the cold bosom of the dead, with her arms about the neck of her mother ; she had evidently wept herself to sleep. With tears in his own eyes, he bore her out of that drear room, and held her in his arms till she awoke.

This circumstance contributed to throw an increasing sadness over the family. Mrs. Epps confidentially declared to her husband that she should not shut her eyes to sleep that night, and the servants scarcely dared leave the kitchen singly, in their affright. Such was the superstition of those days, that a woman was less afraid to face a cannon, or a catamount, than the presence of a corpse ; and even the sterner sex were strongly influenced by the traditionary waifs of the unaccountable and supernatural.

That night the Colonel and Mrs. Epps sat late before their huge hickory fire, after all the household were sleeping in their beds. The next day was to bring the funeral of the stranger, and they had much to talk over in low, solemn voices, of the singular circumstances in connection. Thus they remained, held fast by the mysterious influence of the thought of the dead in the next room, until the candles all burned low, when, throwing on extra fuel, to keep the fire till morning, and covering the coals, the Colonel declared that he should no longer sit up to keep watch with ghosts. His wife turned pale, and gladly would have remonstrated, had she not been well aware of the futility of such a proceeding.

But long after her husband slept soundly, she lay awake, watching the glimmering shadows on the white wall of her bed-room, as they came in through the open door from the smouldering fire, and thinking of the rigid form in the spare room, till its exact impression seemed stamped ineffaceably upon her excited imagination. At last, she fell asleep, lightly, to dream the same scenes over in greater intensity, and was shortly awakened by the slow, heavy sound of the house clock, striking the hour of midnight.

"Now I shall sleep no more to-night," she sighed to herself, " and gloomy indeed it will be thus awake alone till the morning ! "

She had scarcely said this, when she heard a singular noise, which seemed to proceed from the "spare room." It was as if a person had fallen heavily to the floor ; then all was silent as before, save the loud ticking of the clock.   Too much frightened to compose herself again, Mrs. Epps continued breathlessly listening, when she was certain she heard the door of that room slowly open, and footsteps advance lightly over the sanded floor—so lightly as to be heard only by keenly excited ears—in the direction of her bed-room door.   Nearer and nearer they came, often, indeed, pausing, as if gathering strength to proceed, when, in a state more dead than alive, Mrs. Epps called faintly to awake her husband, at the same time lifting her head above the pillow, and fixing her eyes, through the glimmer of the firelight, upon the entrance to her room.

"See there !" cried Mrs. Epps, seizing her husband's arm.

"What is the matter ?" responded the Colonel, in no quiet mood at being thus unceremoniously awakened in the first round of his sleep.

At the same time he sprang up, and thus became conscious of the presence of a white figure, standing directly before the foot of the bed.

"Who is this ?" demanded the Colonel, springing to the floor.

Both hands of the white figure were now lifted menacingly, and it retreated a pace backward.

"Are you not really dead ?" he asked, huskily, for he recognized a general resemblance to the appearance of the corpse, and suddenly thought that the stranger had revived from a trance which they had mistaken for death.

"Dead ! dead ! dead !" pronounced emphatically a hollow voice, which proceeded from the figure.

"A ghost !" gasped Mrs. Epps, now overcome with fright.

"Yes," continued the figure, shaking its white covering violently, "I return to warn you to befriend my child ; and, as you live for happiness hereafter, I charge you to deliver me the gold case which is in your possession."

The Colonel now stood thoughtfully a moment, when, turning as if to obey the request, he brought out from his bed's head a loaded gun, and aiming it directly at the head of the figure, said coolly, yet with the determination of a resolute man :

"Throw off that sheet and show yourself, or I shoot you dead !"

The figure now uttered a deep groan, and retreated several steps, into the darkness of a corner, till it wholly disappeared. The Colonel dropped his gun, and in a single leap brought the hidden spectre to the floor, while in an instant, he tore its cover into strings. A voice, entirely unlike what had before proceeded from the visitant, now sued loudly for mercy.

"Ha, ha !" shouted the Colonel, "I have my ghost that demands the gold case ! I have seen you, Button Husley, before to-night."

The man, as now he was disclosed to be, affected to change the scene, by protesting stoutly that he was only enjoying a clever joke at the Colonel's expense.

"Joke !" returned the Colonel, "I remember now, when

I was down to the Bald Eagle yesterday, telling the story of the strange woman and of her heavy gold case, the look of your eye, villain! This is not the first joke of yours where gold is concerned."

By this time, the disturbance of the scene had attracted the terrified servants from the chambers, who entered the room, screaming in consternation. Mrs. Epps had fainted. The Colonel, with his man under his grasp, was reflecting summarily on the expediency of what was to be done next. He knew well the character of Button Husley, as indeed every man, woman, and child knew him, in all that region. He knew him to be the incarnation of evil, and he did not like to think that his purposes would be bent against him in the future. Beside, the protection of all law, but military, was not so strong and direct as in later times, and if he should proceed to lodge his ghost into custody, the chances of failure were decidedly against him. Quickly revolving all this in his mind, he sprang to his feet, ordered one of the servants to light a candle, and saying to Button, " Jokes don't suit me, sir, at this time of night. Begone with your shroud, and be thankful that you carry a head on your shoulders ;" he appeared to receive the whole thing exactly as Button would have it.

The released man gathered himself up without delay, and with a leering grin, skulked quickly out of the house, and was saluted violently from the premises by the enraged Lion, who had just effected his escape from his kennel.

The next afternoon, at the funeral of the stranger, appeared conspicuous among the assembled neighbors, Button Husley, in the character of mourner in general. Reverently, and with tears in his eyes, he listened to the lengthy sermon of the parson on the occasion; and, after little Mary had been brought to take her last look of her dead mother, he took her in his arms and kissed her till she cried to be released.

The procession to the burial-ground was formèd by the Colonel, with great deliberation; for, being one of the most important men in those parts, and strongly imbued with a love of military parade, he evidently felt it incumbent on him to have this unusual event pass off with the greatest credit to his arrangements. After the hearse, which was not, indeed, quite so suitable a vehicle as the model of later times, being rudely constructed, and without sables, he appeared upon his favorite spirited horse, which he invariably rode on extra occasions. His dress was rather showy than otherwise, for that day, being in full military suit, with the addition of white silk stockings and knee-buckles. About midway of the long procession of people upon horseback and on foot, walked Button, with an acquaintance.

For some distance, the road being very nearly level, the procession proceeded at a regular and comfortable pace, amid the noise of which, Button took occasion to exchange a few words in a low voice to his companion.

" What should you say," he remarked, " if I should tell you it's my secret opinion that this ere strange woman isn't really dead—that is, she is alive as much as ever she was ?"

" I should say that you are a fool, Husley," quietly replied the other.

" Do you know it's hinted round that the Colonel and his wife saw an apparition last night, just after twelve o'clock ? Did you mind how pale Mrs. Epps is to-day ?"

" Faugh ! they say, Husley, that it was you who started up the Colonel with your ghost fixings, and that you came near losing what few brains you have."

" I !" sneered Button, in profound surprise.

" Yes, Button Husley, *you.*"

" And that's—fine. I wasn't within three miles of Epps Hundred after six o'clock last night, till to-day, and I can prove it. The truth is, as I have it from a reliable source, that the dead woman really appeared to the Colonel and' his wife, and he thought it was a thief who had broken in; then, who should the thief be set down for but me—of course ? I am the very Evil One always."

" Didn't know as you could speak so much truth."

" Look here, now; I tell you that this ere woman is super-nat'ral. Goody Wythe, who you know can tell all such things, says that she won't go to her grave in peace to-day; for she didn't want to die here. Believe it or not; watch close, and see if something don't happen."

Button subsided into silence, and his face wore a deeper shade of gravity than before. The foremost of the procession had now come to a steep hill, and this soon caused the whole body to fall into a walk.

No sooner had the hearse gained the steepest ascent of the hill, than the coffin slid out to the snow, which was succeeded by a sudden halt and great commotion in nearest proximity. At this unusual and seemingly miraculous event, every face was blanched, and the story which Button had industriously circulated, respecting the dead stranger, rapidly gained credence. It was afterward declared by the sexton, that the confinement behind, which held the coffin within the hearse, had been secured as always before, notwithstanding the two wooden pins used for the purpose were gone, and were nowhere to be found on the way. If they had searched Button Husley's pocket, the mystery could easily have been understood.

But the matter did not end with the slide of the coffin to the ground. The horse which was rode by the Colonel, being nearest to the hearse, took fright at such a remarkable object appearing suddenly at his very feet, and after plunging violently to the right and left, started off up the hill at the topmost speed, so that the Colonel lost all control, and could only cling closely for his seat. Neither the Colonel nor his horse were seen more that afternoon. The dead stranger was at last decently interred; but very few, however, could persuade themselves to look into the open grave after the lowering of the coffin, for many believed that whoever did so would be strangely influenced during the remainder of life.

Late that evening, the Colonel rode into his yard, after a variety of misadventure, much the worse in temper and outward appearance, for his silk stockings were fatally rent, and his scarlet coat was transformed thoroughly into a coat of many colors.

CHAPTER II.

Mumford Epps, usually designated as "the Colonel," was a gentleman of the old school which flourished a century since. He ordered his servants, devoted himself largely to military and other public affairs, and was a generous liver, after the customs of the Old Dominion, in which he had been educated. A rigid disciplinarian in his family, his word was law, and that law was sure to be euforced in a way so direct, as to be usually effective. To his wife, indeed, he confessed tacitly and half unconsciously, some influence, for she was one of the best women of that generation of good wives and mothers. Her heart was as sound and benevolent as though it were a golden bowl filled to the brim with Heaven's goodness. She had been, also, superiorly educated for her time, having been allowed extra advantages by her father, who was one of the wealthiest men of the State.

Accompanying her father southward, on a tour of business, she had met Mumford Epps, a native of Virginia, and they were subsequently married, and settled in Mrs. Epps' paternal home. Upon the death of his wife's father, the Colonel became possessed of a fine estate, which, he named Epps Hundred, partly in remembrance of his birth-place, Bermuda Hundred. There were but two children, who have already been introduced to the reader.

Notwithstanding their ample means, the habits of this family were not ostentatious, though superior to those around them. Their hospitalities were proverbial ; their charities, munificent.

The stranger child was soon domesticated in the home where her lot had so singularly fallen, and, under the excellent care of Mrs. Epps, and in the pleasant companionship of Reuben and his sister, began to thrive and develop her character like a shoot in the spring sunshine. That she was uncommonly active and precocious was evident, for she made rapid progress in familiarity with all the new scenes by which she was surrounded. In the warm season, she was out in the open air with the children much of the time, passionately engrossed in sports and the light labors, such as children were then often required to perform.

In the winter, she went to the hills in the vicinity of their home, where she enjoyed swift rides with Reuben upon his sled. It was not then the mode to confine children within warm rooms, even in weather which was colder than the coldest of the present time ; but they were sent out to brave the keen, frosty air on the hills and ice-bound streams, which inured them to hardship and confirmed the excellence of their constitutions.

"We must find a name for you, to mark you from our Mary," said Reuben on one such occasion, when he had fully tested the inconvenience of the same name for both the little girls.

"Call me anything you like, Reuben.   I think your father has the best name of any of us all," was the reply.

"Why?" continued Reuben.

"Because 'Colonel' sounds so high and brave, like the top of this big hill."

"That is not his name," said Reuben, laughing wildly. "It's only a title which people call him, because he trains and commands a company of soldiers."

"Let's ask mother what to call Mary," said Mary Epps.

That night when they went home to their supper of mush and milk, Reuben proposed the question to his mother.

"I'll tell you what to call her," said old Peter, one of the "help," who was passing through the room.   "The child has so much smart to her, it strikes me her name should be Molly."

"I like that!" exclaimed the little girl, clapping her hands; "it sounds just as I feel."

"How is that?" inquired Mrs. Epps, with a smile.

"Why, Mary seems like Reuben's sister—soft and pretty as a handful of snow; but Molly seems like the ice when the sun shines on it—hard and shiny, and that is what you must all call me."

"Not 'must,' my dear child," said Mrs. Epps decidedly, but kindly, "I see that such words slip off your tongue easily. You should have said rather, that is what *I should like* to have you call me."

A warm blush now overspread the child's cheek, and she looked steadily at her spoon several minutes without speaking another word.

"It seems to me," said old Peter to Mrs. Epps, when the children had gone to an adjoining room, " that our Molly is mighty grand in her spirit; I've noticed it ever since she was a little mite."

" She is very good-tempered, if rightly directed," said Mrs. Epps.

"Then, the child's fallen into the right hands, exactly."

"I don't know," continued Mrs. Epps, "I hope I shall ever do well by her."

" You couldn't do any less, if you tried," said Peter, who, with the other members of the household, believed firmly in the perfection of their mistress.

When Molly was considered of sufficient age she was sent to school with Reuben and Mary. This was a great event in her young life, which was talked of and dreamed over for some time before the " first day " came. The school-house, a low, square building, painted a dull red, and without shutters to the windows, was situated on the fork of two roads, about half a mile from Epps Hundred. There were no wide-spreading, whispering trees about it, no dreamy coppice to invite summer rambles, or dingles for hiding-places in the sports of the intermission, but it was surrounded by wide, bleak-looking pastures, whose surface was dotted here and there with a thistle or a stunted bush. On either side along the highway in the vicinity of the school-house, were, indeed, evident attempts at play-houses, in the shape of certain cave-like hollows in the banks, and small stone-partitioned squares and rounds of earth ; but these were now covered with snow, and so the house seemed to stand alone on a kind of Siberian plain, which was designed as a retreat for exiles from happier regions.

For the nine preceding winters, the school had been taught by Goodman Hart, as he was called, a man above middle age, who with his family, lived in that neighborhood. But being too severely attacked with the rheumatism to properly discipline the unruly, his place was now supplied by a younger pedagogue, by name Hazor Wilkhurst—a tall, spare fellow, who flourished a conceited looking nose, and a large silver watch with depending steel chain and seals. He was the son of the landlord of the " Bald Eagle."

Little Molly was not awed at the spectacle presented before her upon her first introduction in school. Most children would have hung their heads and merely ventured occasionally a timid glance of observation, but Molly was not intimidated easily. Indeed, the presence of unusual scenes seemed always to inspire her with high fervor and courageous impulse. After the first spell was broken, she sat steadily on one of the front low seats, and looked about her with an evident consciousness that she had an undoubted right so to do.

The seats were closely filled with scholars, who seemed to merit the title of men and women rather than boys and girls.

2*

Some of them seemed old enough to set up house-keeping or school-keeping on their own responsibility. Upon the desk, before a high-backed and flag-seated chair, designed for the teacher, lay a ferule of uncommon length, and a bundle of handsomely cut rods. The use to which these were adapted, Molly could not divine, but waited patiently till the mystery should be solved. In the rear of the room, occupying nearly the whole of one side, was a fireplace, in which blazed and crackled several huge logs, piled transversely against the chimney. Upon the hearth lay two melting balls of snow, which had been placed there to signalize the entrance of Master Wilkhurst.

With strong suspicions of disputed sovereignty, or at least limited monarchy, had the new master entered upon the reign of terror ; and he soon announced, with fiery eyes, that he "meant to begin as he should hold out," a metaphysical expression, the tendency of which was not definitely under-stood before practical illustration.

Molly lost not a word which was said, or a move of the performances, until at last she was called out before the master to read. She stood alone, for she was the youngest of all the school, and Mary Epps, being a year or two older, had been assigned to another class.

"What's your name, girl ?" inquired Master Wilkhurst, with great sternness, for he did not like the tranquil look of her eye upon one whom he intended should be so formidable as himself.

" Molly," she replied in a clear voice.

"Molly what?"

"Molly—nothing."

"What!" exclaimed the master, sharply, while suppressed laughs fell upon his ear from all directions.

"Molly *nothing*," was again promptly answered.

"Do you see this?" said Master Wilkhurst, taking his ferule in hand.

"Yes, sir."

"Then give me your name—your whole name, or I shall bring it out of you with my ferule."

Molly now began to tremble; the color deepened upon her cheek and her small lip quivered, but she still kept her black eye fully fixed upon the green and grey one of the master.

"Are you going to tell me?" demanded the inquisitor, in growing passion.

"No, sir," replied Molly, quickly, "I've told all I can tell."

"You have, eh?" said Wilkhurst. "Hold out your hand."

"Please, sir, may I speak?" now asked Reuben, who had been an excited observer of this scene.

"Sit down," answered the master, believing that he was interrupted with the purpose of annoyance. At the same moment a strong, sharp blow fell upon Molly's little palm, succeeded by a passionate scream, which made Reuben leap from his seat in a moment.

"Molly hasn't got any other name, sir," he said, with a

tone of suppressed feeling, " and that was what I was going to tell you."

Master Wilkhurst, who was now flourishing his ferule irresolutely, struck it against his desk, and it fell to the floor. He bent forward to recover it, when, swifter than an arrow, Molly darted upon his head, and, thrusting her aching hand into his locks, while with the other she held his neck downward, in a desperate energy, brought out a lock of his hair, which, when he had risen again, she held up in triumph to his bewildered recognition. In another instant, she rushed to the door, and without stopping for her hood and blanket, was on her way home.

" What is it that brings you home in this way ?" inquired Mrs. Epps, in surprise, at her singular and unseasonable appearance.

Molly burst into tears, but remembering what she still held in her right hand, said—

" Haven't you got some of my dead mother's hair laid away ?"

" Yes ; but why do you ask that now, child ?"

" I want to know what you keep it for ?"

" That you may have it to look at in memory of your dear mother, Molly."

" Is that what they keep folks' hair for ? Then I shan't keep this !" she exclaimed, discovering her collection to Mrs. Epps' astonished gaze.

" Where did you get that hair, Molly ?" inquired Mrs. Epps.

Molly darted upon his head, and, thrusting her aching hand into his locks, while with the other she held his neck downward, in a desperate energy, brought out a lock of his hair, which, when he had risen again, she held up in triumph to his bewildered recognition.—PAGE 36.

"At school, out of the master's head," replied Molly, unflinchingly.

"Have you gone mad, child ?" said Mrs. Epps, in increased wonder.

"Yes, ma'am, I feel very mad," answered Molly, "and this hair I am going to burn."

So saying, she threw it over the forestick of the fire, and watched it carefully till it had all disappeared.

"Now just look at my hand, mother," said Molly, showing Mrs. Epps the marks of her punishment, which were very decided.

Mrs. Epps made Molly sit down, and gradually elicited the whole story from her. When she had concluded, Mrs. Epps took her smarting hand in both of her own, and saying only, "I wish you to think this all over, Molly," sat thus for some time, without saying more.

This was the way of Mrs. Epps in the hour of excited passion. Her own temper was mild and equable, and the more clearly she could understand the lack of self-control in others. There were, also, several of the household present, and she never reproved before a spectator. But, that night, when Molly had gone to her pillow, Mrs. Epps joined her to listen to her evening prayer. Then she talked kindly of the effects of such a spirit as Molly had manifested that day, and of the blessedness of forgiveness. The little girl listened thoughtfully, yet silently, for Mrs. Epps never sought to extort promises of amendment for the future. The hallowed influence of that hour Molly could never afterward wholly forget.

Nor was this the sum of Mrs. Epps' effort. Unknown to all save Reuben, whom she took for a companion, she walked that evening a distance of two miles, over the cold snow, to see Master Wilkhurst. Gladly would Mrs. Epps have persuaded her husband to have taken her place, but she knew the attempt to do this would be utterly vain, and even worse, for the very knowledge of Molly's offence would have incurred his displeasure. The Colonel had little mercy for transgressors against authority, especially that delegated to the master of a school, which, in those days, was considered almost infallible.

With the new teacher Mrs. Epps talked alone, for a long hour—it seemed to Reuben, who waited for his mother—relating the circumstances of Molly's history and the peculiar nature of her disposition, even condescending to entreat him to deal with her gently in future. An affair of great importance it must have been considered by Mrs. Epps, to have induced her, with all her long established power in her position at Epps Hundred, and in the whole vicinity, thus to supplicate a young man who had no claim to her friendship or respect, after the commission of such an unmanly act. But she did this cheerfully and patiently, carefully guarding all knowledge of the deed from Molly. Master Wilkhurst received her sullenly and interrupted her often by allusions to his " position," and also seemed desirous of impressing her that he was " a man who should begin as he meant to hold out."

It was noticed, however, during the remainder of that

winter school, that he avoided further collision with Molly, although, indeed, she scrupulously abstained from offering him cause of offence. But it was not less evident by a hundred trifling proofs, that Master Wilkhurst disliked her from the depths of his small narrow soul. He never forgot or forgave. The roots of his hair which Molly had torn out, were springing up anew, to become serpent's heads.

CHAPTER III.

Molly was an ardent worshiper in the great temple of earth and air. There was an indivisible communion between her soul and the majestic trees, the cloud-laurelled summits, the melody of flowing waters, the purple and rosy gloaming, the night with its depth of silent and subdued beauty, and whatsoever else was sublime or picturesque in nature. In the spring she often took long rambles over the lands of Epps Hundred, with Reuben and Mary, and accompanied by old Peter for their guide and protector, when going at some distance. Each carried a small basket, which was usually filled with wreaths of wintergreen, pine buds, curious leaves, and sometimes with spring flowers. Peter would frequently stop to point out some spot marked as the haunt of Indians in former time, and to relate long stories in connection, which invariably proved of intense interest to his listeners ; and Molly, who was remarkably pervaded with a liking for the traditionary lore of the time, and for all

40

that was wild and wonderful, was never wearied with their repetition.

"Some day when I get time," said old Peter, "I will take you, children, into what we call the Dark Woods, and show you Cave Rock."

"Cave Rock! what kind of a rock is that?" inquired Molly, with breathless interest.

"It's a high, curious ledge, with a cave in one side, over the water, where the Indians used to hide when the white men were hunting 'em," said Peter, marvellously.

"How did they get in there, if it's over the water?" pursued Molly.

"Oh! they got there with canoes, and climbed up on the side, I s'pose."

"How grand it will be to see it!" shouted Molly; "and I shall want to crawl in, so as to know what it looks like in there."

"And see if there are any bones or tomahawks," said Reuben, laughing at her enthusiasm.

The children were so delighted with the proposition, that old Peter was persuaded to promise an early day for their gratification. A short time after this, the Colonel having gone to attend a muster, and some idle hours being thrown upon Peter's hands, he announced to the children that he would go to the Dark Woods. The very name fell upon their ears like a magical word, and wild with anticipated pleasure, they sat out, inhaling the fresh spring air like an exhilarating potion, and bounding over the ground with the impulse of the elasticity of their spirits. After a long and circuitous route through glens, copses, over rude bridges, and finally amid the trees of the dim old forest, they reached the spot.

It was truly a gloriously wild scene presented to their view on all sides ! A black, swollen stream divided the heart of the woods, dashing over jagged rocks and about clumps of underbrush, till, a short distance below, it formed a cascade, with a base of beautiful foam, like thousands of white birds, forever aspiring upward. On either side and opposite the water, were the dense fastnesses of the wood· Before them was a mass of rock projecting out into the stream and connected with the bank by a pass, so narrow as to admit of the step of but one person.

Upon this rock, Peter conducted the children, who were delighted to find themselves in such a singular spot, far above the water. Under their feet was a rich carpet of green and silvery moss, with its tiny red blossoms, more beautiful to them than the softest and gayest fabric from Persian looms to the children of the present day. Down on one of the shelves of the rock, they could descry the entrance to the cave, which was now nearly overgrown with brushwood and gnarled roots of vegetation. It was altogether a dark and fearful-looking place—the mouth of that cave, which seemed only fitting the lair of a wild beast or of some other hideous thing.

" Oh, this is grand !" exclaimed Molly, as she knelt upon the moss and looked all about her in serious, rapt admiration ; " I would go to sleep forever, as my mother did, on this rock."

" What a thought !" said Reuben.

" It is so dark and wild and awful !" continued Molly.

" That is what makes me want to go-home," said Mary; " I am sure I should be afraid to stay here alone a minute."

" Afraid," repeated Molly, " why, I am not afraid of anything. I should like to live here a long while without anybody but myself."

" What would you do ?" inquired Reuben.

" I'd watch the water running under the rock. I'd try to climb down and see what is in that dark cave, and if I found it a good place, I'd make it my bed-room, and sleep there every night. And I'd sit here for hours, looking at these great trees, and hearing the deep, far sound of their roar in the wind. And "——

" Perhaps you would be called to see visitors, too," said Reuben, laughing.

" Yes; I hope you would come and see how I got along, dear Reuben."

" Do you ?" said Reuben, pleased with this, for it was not often that Molly spoke such words.

" I meant the bears, Molly," said Reuben, pointing mysteriously into the woods.

" Do the bears ever come here ?" inquired Molly.

" Not a great many years ago, I killed one nigh this very spot," said old Peter; " but I guess the critters are skass now in these parts."

" I should like to stay here," said Molly, "when the clouds roll themselves all up thick and dark with thunder, to hear the drops of rain patter down on this water, and see the lightning shoot big guns of bright light among the trees."

While Reuben and Mary amused themselves by throwing leaves and pebbles into the stream, Molly sat quietly studying the prospect about her, with an intensity of enjoyment, of which her companions had no knowledge. It was only with the promise of soon bringing her there again, that old Peter could persuade her to leave for home with any degree of pleasure.

That evening, when the Colonel overheard Mary and Molly talking of their excursion, he said.

" Those woods are not the place for you, children; I forbid you going there again."

" Is there danger ?" asked Mrs. Epps, in alarm.

" It is only safe for a man with a gun," he replied.

" Then," said Mrs. Epps, "I must tell Peter never to repeat his visit to the place with you. He was not aware of danger, I know."

Molly heard this silently, but there were sobs in her heart, and she murmured to herself, " I know there is no harm in going to that beautiful spot. Father only says so to keep us at home."

A few days after this, Mrs. Epps left home for a visit, accompanied by the Colonel ; and, unknown to any of the household, Molly started again for Cave Rock.

She had marked the way closely before, and it was with but little difficulty that she came once more to the spot. Again there, and alone, she threw herself on the rock and shouted aloud with exultant gladness. The freedom, the novelty of her situation, inspired her with keen satisfaction. There was a far-reaching light in her eyes, evolving illusions, of which the surrounding scenic features were only the basis.

From the gigantic forest trees, which had stood there in tempest and calm through hoary centuries, arose aspirations indefinite, oppressive, gloom-empurpled. In harmony with the flow of the stream, thoughts, dreamy and most musical, swept through her soul. Exquisite traceries of fancy poised lightly here and there, and all through the intertangling boscage of long-leaved shrubs—of vines entwining the gnarled trunks, and sending forth delicate, spiral streamers to the breeze—of curious parasitical plants, epiphytes, and the wintergreen, pencilling over the ground figures of matchless grace—the wild blossoms, the grasses, the fragrant mints, fringing the banks and the narrow strip of everglade—the white and golden-colored lilies, flecking the water amid their large leaves—were so many linked threads, on which she strung unwritten idyls of natural beauty.

"For all this grand scene," she mused, glancing about her more soberly, "I am not so happy as I thought I should be. I wish that I had asked leave to come."

The first feeling of triumph gone, came another thought, which brought no joy. She was soon conscious of weariness, for the excitement accompanying her efforts to seek her way alone, left her quite breathless and exhausted, and she half reclined upon the rock to rest awhile, while she listened to the sound of the flowing water below. Her head gradually sunk upon the soft bed of sun-warmed moss, and next she was quite asleep. Her slumber was deep, her breathing calm, and her fair cheek was rosier even than usual. Her red lips, just parted, disclosed the even pearls between. Her head lay upon one uncovered arm, lightly shaded, also, by her falling hair ; and her pretty hands, clasped together, rested in the soft, green moss. The natty, scarlet-colored tunic she wore, was unbuttoned and thrown open just below the necklace of almond-shaped pearls that circled her neck and strayed into her bosom. Her high-heeled and pointed-toed shoes of blue kid, clasped with silver, she had suffered to escape from her feet, which rivalled a fairy's made expressly to " trip it on the light, fantastic toe."

It might have been, as she thus slept there, the white wings of her angel mother hovered over her slight form, exposed unconsciously to whatever of peril was lurking near. For, a large white and yellow water-spider, which had sallied out from its den for prey, crawled directly over her hands, but paused to leave no trace. A bee flew so near her face that his wings brushed the tip of her nose, but he did not alight till he reached the tiny cup of a wild flower. The birds cast down upon her side-long glances, then talked together in their own language of the marvel of such a spectacle in that lonely place. Thus the minutes grew into hours.

Molly awoke with an indistinct impression of having heard the report of a gun. A dream of the Indians had thus been suddenly terminated. She sprang up quickly, and in surprise recognized her present situation. The sight of the dark expanse of forest on all sides about her, did not now inspire her with the sublime courage which her childish enthusiasm had pictured. She had just decided to return as quickly as possible, and was gathering up a few curious pebbles, which she had collected on the rock, to carry home with her, when her attention was suddenly arrested by a rustle in the thick bed of leaves near her. She paused, motionless with affright, for she perceived approaching upon the pass which led directly upon the rock, a huge snake, rattling loudly at every motion !

With a wild cry of terror, she made a movement with her slender arms to frighten the monster to retreat, but raising his head some inches from the ground, he ran out his scarlet tongue rapidly, while he gazed defiantly upon her eye. The snake then slowly advanced along the narrow pass, while Molly fully comprehended her danger. There was no hope of escape, for the rock was surrounded by water on all sides save one—and that was blockaded by the snake. Passing rapidly from one side of the rock to the other, and screaming violently, she abandoned herself to frantic fear.

"Reuben ! Reuben !" she cried, in the unconscious impulse of the moment.

Then, remembering the perfect isolation of her situation, she said to herself, in a tone of bitter reproach :

" Oh, if I had only stayed away from here ! Horrible ! horrible !—this death of all others !"

The stories which she had heard of snakes winding themselves about the bodies of persons, more vise-like with every convolution, till they had finished their work, stood out in her imagination with an intense distinctness.

The rattle-snake, for such it was, whose home was afterwards discovered to be shared with several others in the cave under the rock, continued his progress toward his victim, but so cautiously that it was scarcely perceptible. He seemed to comprehend that she was in his power, and meted his work with a leisurely triumph far more terrible to endure than a swift destruction.

Molly began to yield to her overmastering terror. Sinking down upon the rock, she clenched her hands together in the passion of horror, and breathed a wordless prayer to God. From the instant that she had first perceived the monster, she had not moved her eyes away; now they were riveted upon the small, sharp, basilisk eyes of the snake, with a power that appeared indissoluble. Her heart, which had beat so swiftly that it had almost choked her breath, now sunk within her, for fear had settled upon it like a heavy weight of ice, crushing out her very life.

Yet nearer the snake approached, till the distance between them was greatly lessened. Molly shrunk back to the farthest edge of the rock which overhung the water.

Crouching there like a doomed thing, she began to tremble in every nerve, and her face was as pallid as that of a corpse in its tomb.

The snake now ceased to advance, and, as if satisfied with his position, commenced to wind his first coil, in preparation for the fatal spring, when a crackling of the underbrush near the rock arrested Molly's attention. Quickly springing to her feet, and summoning all her remaining strength, she gave one long, appealing shriek, which smote through the heart of the forest like a mortal wail of anguish.

"Thanks to Heaven!" a voice responded.

"What's the trouble there?"

"The snake! See! Oh, save me!" Molly replied, perceiving the figure of a huntsman approaching among the trees.

The echo of her words had not died away, when the snake suddenly rolled backward, rattling and writhing, which was instantly succeeded by a deafening explosion, that seemed to Molly like the bursting of the ledge beneath her into fiery atoms. But it proved that the snake was only wounded.

With maddened venom, he now upraised his head, fastened his eye anew upon his aim, and attempted a swift and certain spring. Molly darted aside; then, throwing her arms aloft with a last cry of frenzied despair, leaped off into the dark water below!

Once—twice—thrice, she arose to the surface, struggling to keep her hold upon the side of the rock, when losing her grasp, she went suddenly down and the water closed over the spot.

CHAPTER IV.

WITCH HAZEL HOUSE.

WHEN Molly was once more conscious, she found herself upon a bed in an unfamiliar room, with an old woman, whom she had never before seen, watching over her.

"Where am I ?" she inquired, confused.

The old woman, who sat on the foot of the bed, glanced upon her over her spectacles, shook her head mysteriously, but said nothing.

Molly thought now of her late terrible adventure, and seeing no face about her which bespoke security, began to cry.

"All's right, gal," spoke the voice of a man, whom she did not see; " so jest take it easy, if you don't want to pop off again."

But Molly could not compose herself to ease, as long as she could see directly before her the old woman, who continued knitting incessantly, occasionally turning her eye between the plaits of her cap border, with a glance upon her, which sent the blood from her heart. That she was the most singular old woman in the world, was Molly's foregone conclusion. There was a look about her small black eyes, closely set together, and shaded heavily, that made Molly remember what she had heard of witches with the evil eye, and little accustomed as she was to fear of any human being, she could not help wishing that she was safely at Epps Hundred.

When the old woman arose and moved across the floor, Molly was more than ever impressed. She was very tall, with a gaunt, bony, and slightly stooping figure, which gave her an air of one who is on the watch even to the darkest corner ; with an aquiline nose, thin and compressed lips, as if they held within a world of mystery, and a step as noiseless as a cat's—which was partly owing to her peculiar carriage, and partly to the Indian moccasins which she wore on her feet. About her person was a loose jacket, or tunic, of home-spun linsey-woolsey, while under this was a skirt of black crape. She wore a cap with an enormously high crown, upon the base of which was set a bow of rusty black ribbon. Sometimes she came to Molly and examined her pulse, then nodding her head with an air of mystery, left her again to her wild conjectures.

At length another face looked upon Molly, the face of a man, with large, round eyes, which were ever as wide open as possible, seemingly to frighten children and curs, and, if possible, people of greater consequence. This face was quite hedged about with plentiful, bushy hair, which stood out stiffly in every direction. It was, altogether, an evil face ; and, but for Molly having seen it before, would have frightened her sadly.

" Is this you here, Button Husley ?" cried Molly.

" Yes, chit, I'm the critter that jumped into the water arter you, when you seemed clean gone, and fetched you out by the neck, like a drowned chicken."

" Oh, dear, that was dreadful !" exclaimed Molly, shutting her eyes.

" Where do you think you be now, gal ?" asked Button ; " in that are place they call heaven, eh ?"

" I don't think heaven is much like this," said Molly, glancing about her, on to the low, smoke-browned rafters, and the small, old windows, so grimed as to cloud the light.

" Don't you ?   May be it's t'other place, then."

" This won't do," said the old woman, motioning Button away.   " Stay there till she gets better," she added, pointing to the farthest side of the room, where was some work upon which Button had been engaged in tinkering.

" Look here, Goody," replied Button, " this ere gal is my property, and it don't hurt her a bit to hear me talk ; does it, Molly ?"

" On, no," said Molly ; " and I am so thankful that you saved my life."

" Be you ?   Well, then, I s'pose you won't mind doing what I want you to.   You see," he continued cautiously, " I know that your mother left you a gold case, which they save for you, over there at Epps Hundred. I want you should let me look at it some day."

"I will," said Molly, "any time that you will come to our house."

"No; that won't do," continued Button, shaking his head, and opening his eyes wider than ever, if possible. "Harkee! now if you tell your folks that I want to see that are case, I'll "——

He stopped and looked so fiercely, and flourished his clinched hand with such a purpose, Molly trembled violently.

"I will do what you wish me to, I am sure," said Molly, with great earnestness.

"Sartin!" said Button; "you couldn't think of doing less, when you know I've risked my own precious life for yours. You must bring it over here some day."

"How can I ?" said Molly; "the case is always locked up in Mrs. Epps' desk."

"I'll tell you how to do," said Button; "take a time when the folks are gone, to get the key and bring it away. You can put it back again, and they never will know."

"I shouldn't like to do that," said Molly, firmly; "it wouldn't be right."

"You jest said you would do what I wanted you to. Is't right to tell a lie ?" pursued Button, warily.

"No ; but you must not bid me do that."

"Look here," said Button, in a softer tone, " I'm one of the sort that likes to do about right, as well as you ; and, on the whole, I think it would be a better way to let the thing alone. But, mind now, if you tell the first word of what I've said to you about it, you'll be sorry."

"I never will, certainly," said Molly ; "but I'm sure I wish you could see it, if you want to so much."

"You say," said Button, indifferently, "that it's kept in Miss Epps' desk—down stairs, or up ?"

"Oh, it's in her room down stairs," said Molly ; "I know just where it is."

"Maybe you know where she keeps her keys ?"

"Yes, they always hang on the first nail, just inside her closet door ; and it's the littlest one that unlocks the drawer where my case is. I've seen it many a time."

Button listened to these words with his head slightly averted, lest Molly should discover the keen interest he felt in that moment. But Molly, on her part, was entirely innocent of having communicated anything which could be of such interest. Her heart, ever alive to the noble impulses of generosity, was now so filled with gratitude, that she never paused to reflect upon the wisdom of giving her preserver whatever information he desired, especially upon anything which so exclusively concerned herself, as the gold case.

"Am I not going home soon ?" she inquired at length of Button.

"Not to-night," he answered.

"I must go," said Molly, "for when they know that I am gone they will feel dreadfully about me."

"Let 'm worry," said Button, "they will find out how to

set by you, so as not to let you go off into the woods again alone."

" I went myself," said Molly, " and they didn't know about it. I know that the blame all belongs to me."

Her lip quivered and the warm tears rushed to her eyes.

" Jest you keep still," said the old woman, now coming from an adjoining room in which she had been during the chief of their conversation, " or you'll be sick. And you, Button, I say, hush !"

" Well," said Button, " I feel well paid for my ducking to-day, by hearing you talk so woman-like and sensible, Molly. In the mornin', if you are well enough, I'll take you to Epps Hundred. I ain't got any horse, but maybe you can walk."

Night approached early, for the sky was heavy and the rain began to fall in great drops against the little diamond shaped window-panes and on the low roof overhead. Molly, somewhat reconciled to her situation, remained quietly and watched Button cook some wild fowls which he had shot that afternoon, while the old woman bestirred herself in and out of the room to accomplish other domestic preparations for supper.

"Does this woman live with you ?" inquired Molly, when she was alone with Button for a moment.

"I guess she does, when she isn't nowhere else," said Button.

" Is she your mother ?" continued Molly.

"Not quite, though a' most as nigh, all things considered."

"What is she, then ?"

"Hain't you never heard of the old witch, Goody Wythe ?" said Button.

"Oh yes," answered Molly, "but this isn't her, is it ?"

"Hist !" said Button, hearing the hand of the old woman upon the door. "Don't you think I'm a handy cook, Molly ?" he added, as Goody Wythe made her appearance.

"I think you must be used to it," said Molly.

"I rather think I be," said Button. "Yes, I'll bet all I ever laid my hand on that I've cooked more game than I could stuff into this ere house, chimbly and all—and cooked it good enough to make a body's mouth water, too. Some folks think I ain't good for nothing, but what I shouldn't be ; but you don't think so, Molly, eh ?"

"I think you are good for saving folks' lives," said Molly.

"Humph !" now uttered the old woman in a voice which seemed between a groan and a growl.

"That depends on how I take a fancy," said Button, turning a curious eye upon Goody Wythe.

A deal table, which stood against the wall, was now laid with dishes from an open dresser, without a cover or other appendage than what was strictly necessary. In the centre, upon a large pewter platter, Button set his birds, which he had brought to a perfection of culinary skill, and plentifully dressed with golden butter. A generous bannock of barley-meal, just taken off an iron plate over the fire, and some potatoes from the bed of hot ashes, were soon added by Goody Wythe, all which, with a small jar of cream, and another of molasses, for the pennyroyal tea, afforded a sense of comfort by no means disagreeable to Molly. Sugar and imported tea were too precious, then, for common use.

"Do you feel as if you'd like to try a wing of one of these ere birds, Molly?" said Button. "If you do, I'll lift you up and put you here in Goody's great chair quicker than I took you out of the water to-day."

"Though weak and exhausted, Molly suffered herself to be placed beside the table. She now perceived that the garments she wore were not her own, but were so large and odd she scarcely could identify herself. Her own, which were placed to dry, had been exchanged for a suit improvised for the occasion by Goody Wythe.

They had scarcely seated themselves around the table before their attention was arrested by the sound of a horse's feet approaching the door. Button arose and looked from the window.

"Somebody has come," he announced.

"Who is it?" inquired the old woman.

"Anybody come for me?" asked Molly.

"Don't know who 'tis," answered Button. "A mighty fine stranger, though."

A knock with a riding stick now sounded heavily against the door. Button, stumbling over chairs and some other articles, proceeded to open the door, and thus disclosed a noble looking man in the garb of a traveller, holding his horse, a large, fiery animal, mounted with a rich housing, over which hung saddle-bags.

"Is this the direct road to a tavern called the "Bald Eagle ?" he inquired.

"No, stranger," said Button, with some hesitation, " you are pretty considerable wrong for that are part."

" How far ?" pursued the gentleman.

" Oh, you'll have to go back the same way you come till you reach a road that runs south and then strikes off to the west agin. It's a matter of four or five mile out of your way in all."

"To where does this route lead ?"

" Nowheres, only to some housands on the heights."

" Isn't there a tavern nearer here than the Bald Eagle ?"

"Why, this ere place is a sort of one," said Button ; " we keeps strangers here often. It's known in these parts as the Witch Hazel House, for my aunt in here tells fortins. You'd better conclude to stop," urged Button, seeing the gentleman hesitate. It'll sartinly set in to storm for the night, and gut a supper all ready that's good 'nuff for the king."

During this speech the stranger had glanced past Button, into the room, where he saw a cheerful fire glow upon the low walls, and little Molly with her sweet face fastened upon him with a lively interest.

" As I find myself so far off the right way," said the gentleman, " I believe I will stop, for it isn't very comfortable riding in the rain when one has been travelling fifty miles."

" Sartin, true," replied Button ; " step right in and make

yourself at home, while I take your horse round to the barn."

"I will look to him myself," said the gentleman, "for it is an animal too valuable to me to neglect."

"I am glad that he is coming in," exlaimed Molly to herself, "for it does seem so pleasant to see his face and hear his voice !"

" You shall be well paid," concluded the stranger in his conversation with Button, when they reappeared.

" Don't talk about that," rejoined Button, with an air of great magnanimity. " I'm the sort of man that don't live by gittin' all out of folks I can."

Bowing to Goody Wythe and smiling upon Molly, the gentleman sat down by the fire, placing his saddle-bags on the floor beside him.

" Well, little girl, what shall I call you ?" he inquired, when he had rubbed somewhat of the chill out of his hands.

" My name is Molly, sir."

" And you live here, do you ?"

" Oh, no, sir, I was never in this house before to-day. I live at Epps Hundred." Here Button began to relate an account of Molly's encounter with the snake, and of her rescue by himself, bringing out every detail with great distinctness, and concluding with a strong declaration that Molly would have been as dead as a bat by that time if it hadn't been for him.

Goody Wythe having replenished some of the articles upon the table, they all sat round and commenced eating.

"Where do you come from, stranger ?" inquired Button, after studying the gentleman covertly for a few minutes, as he sat opposite him.

"I'm now on my way from Boston," was the reply.

"Belong there ?" pursued Button.

"No ; I reside in New York."

"On your way home, then ?"

"Yes, I had business at several places in this vicinity, so I took this route."

"Agent for the Indians, or something of that sort ?"

"Not at all," rejoined the stranger with a smile, for it was plain that he was not accustomed to being thus catechised.

"Trader, maybe ?" Button went on indefatigably determined to find out the whole story.

"Yes."

"Business pooty brisk in New York, aint it ?"

"Yes."

"Do you go to school Molly ?" the gentleman now inquired, with the evident purpose of changing the conversation.

"No sir, not now ; but I went last winter."

"Very pleasant—going to school, isn't it ?"

"I don't think so," said Molly.

"Indeed !" rejoined the gentleman, "I thought you might be one of the little girls who love their books."

"I like to read, very much, but I don't like Master Wilkhurst,"

" That is it, then.   I have got a little boy at home, who is but little older than you appear to be, and he will read all the books I can get him," said the gentleman.

" I should like to know his name," said Molly.

" Hollis Rushton," replied the gentleman, in a tone modulated to new softness, betraying his love for the absent.   "I guess he is much like our Reuben," observed Molly.

" Then you have a brother, Molly ?"

" He's not my brother, sir, but just as good, for I have lived with him ever so long."

" This ere gal," now interposed Button, " don't know much about what she's got for 'lations.   You see, when she's a little bit of a thing, her mother died and left her with a man they call the ' Colonel,' about here.   And they've fetched her up ever since, jest like one of their own."

The stranger looked kindly upon Molly, but with the politeness seemingly instinctive to him, forbore to ask the questions which naturally occurred in connection.   When the meal was over, he persuaded her to come and sit upon his knee, while he told stories of Hollis and his home, till Molly seemed almost transferred to the scenes which he described.   Then unlocking one of his saddle-bags, he produced a beautiful book which he designed as a gift for Hollis, and permitted her to examine it, while he instructed her in the stories which it contained.   Molly soon became quite familiar with him, and ventured to ask him many questions, the curious originality of which, frequently excited his admiration.

The time thus fled rapidly away, when the old woman appearing with a long, white blanket over her head and in a pair of high boots, announced that she must put Molly to bed, for she was going out and would not be back till near morning.

"What! ma'am, you do not intend to venture without the house in this storm, on foot?" exclaimed the gentleman.

"Sartin," replied her hollow, gruff voice.

"Stranger, you don't know Goody Wythe, seein' you don't live in these ere parts;" said Button, "but if you did, you'd know that a chain of red-hot iron wouldn't be 'nuff to keep her in the house to-night."

"Humph!" responded the same cavernous voice, while the sharp eye of the old woman fell a moment, like fire, upon Button.

"It's jest the sort of night for witches to be out a ridin' their broomsticks, you know," added Button, in a low voice.

The stranger could not wholly conceal his surprise, and Molly instinctively drew nearer his bosom. A thought of the peril which might be concealed like a spring mine under his feet, in that lonely old house by the forest, smote him as with a heavy blow, and he had half a mind · to order his horse, pay his bill, and continue his journey, even at that hour. But he was no coward; and then, the clinging of the little form of Molly to him, as for protection, forbade all further thought of leaving until the morning.

"Come, child," said the old woman, "I can't wait for you."

"It's only right in that small room jest out of this," said Button.

"Good night, Molly," said the gentleman, imprinting a kiss upon her trembling lips.

"Please, sir," said Molly, if I might say one thing more "——

"Certainly, my child," said the gentleman, kindly.

"I wish you would just take me along with you to-morrow, as far as Epps Hundred, and then if you would only stop there to see where I live, I should be so glad!"

"I will do so, willingly, my dear," replied the gentleman.

Being very much exhausted by her recent excitements, Molly soon fell soundly asleep, and did not awake till far into the watches of the night, when she was aroused by a singular sound in the room adjoining hers, succeeded by a noise as of something falling to the floor, when all was still. She listened a few minutes longer, and hearing nothing more, dropped to sleep again.

In the morning, she awoke early, very much refreshed by the night's rest, and looking from the little old window in her room, saw that the storm of the last evening had given place to a bright April sky. Thinking meanwhile of the pleasant stranger, she hurriedly arrayed herself in her own clothes, which Goody Wythe had left there on the last night. Soon hearing some one stirring in the next room, she went out. It proved to be Button, who started violently upon her appearance there, as if she had brought before him a mortal fear.

"It's only me," said Molly, laughing at his affright.

"Who should it be, if not you?" he replied, fiercely.

His appearance was so entirely unlike what Molly had ever seen it before, that she shrank away with the impulse to keep as far from him as possible.

"Did you know, child, that I keep a cat?" asked Button, after he had concluded the lighting of the fire.

"No," said Molly, "let me see it, for I love cats, if they are pretty."

"She's out now, but she was in here last night and made so much noise I couldn't sleep. Did you hear her jumping about?" he added, huskily.

"I guess so," said Molly, "for I awoke once in the night, and heard a noise in the house."

"Did you get up to see if it was the cat?" continued Button, looking upon her intently.

"Oh, no, I fell asleep again in a minute after," said Molly.

"Well, I got up and I found that it was ; if she gets in here again, I mean to kill her," he concluded, looking wildly about him, as if in search of something.

"I wonder if the gentleman has risen yet?" said Molly.

"Didn't you hear him?" said Button. "He altered his plan, and set off at daybreak, this morning."

"He hasn't gone!" exclaimed Molly.

"Don't you believe what I say?" replied Button, with an air of irritability at being disputed.

"Oh ! I am so sorry !" said Molly, going to the window which looked upon the road, with an unconscious hope of catching one more glimpse of him, whom she had so soon learned to love.

"After all," she said, at length, "he may have concluded to stop at Epps Hundred, and wait for me."

"He made up his mind to take the other road," said Button.

Molly now fairly burst into tears for her disappointment, which seemed not a little to increase Button's aggravation.

"I don't see why you need to make such a fuss about a stranger, no way," he said, impatiently. "I tell you what it is," he added, after a pause, "I won't have you here sniffing, so I'll go along home with you, the next thing I do."

Molly was not sorry to hear this, and she made preparations to leave with alacrity.

"Where is Goody Wythe ?" she asked, when she had looked in vain for her bonnet.

"She ain't got home, yet. Why ?" inquired Button.

"Because I can't find my things to wear home."

"I guess you'll have to hunt a good while," he said, "for the last I saw on 'em they were goin' down over the falls, below Cave Rock, as fast as the water could carry 'em."

"Can't I find a blanket to wear home, then ?" asked Molly, approaching what seemed to be a closet.

"Don't go there," shouted Button, at the top of his voice, which made Molly pale with fear. She looked more carefully now and saw a deep, dark door with an iron bolt.

" I keep loaded guns in there, so that if any body tries to open the door, but me that knows jest how, they'll go off and kill a body quick," said Button, with the same fearful look which Molly had noticed before that morning.

Molly started a few minutes in advance of Button, at his request, as he said he would stay behind to see that all was right, for he didn't expect Goody back till the afternoon.

As she passed the little old barn, a rod or two back from the way, she heard what she believed was the stamp of a horse's foot, and thinking immediately of the handsome horse which belonged to the gentleman, she ran around quickly to the opposite side and looked within, between the wide cracks. There, indeed, stood a horse, and so nearly like the one which the stranger had rode, she could scarcely believe that it was any other. But she had no time to continue her inspection, for, fearing that Button would see her, she ran away and was far on the road, before he overtook her. She did not dare to allude to what she had seen, for Button had manifested such anger that morning at the mention of the stranger, she was only anxious to safely escape his presence. But the matter dwelt upon her heart with such a weight of indefinable sadness, she could think of nothing else. Button appeared not less engrossed with his own thoughts, moodily leading the way, and often starting unusually at the motion of a bird or tree beside him.

When they had come in view of Epps Hundred, Button informed her that he would leave her to go the remainder of the way alone.

" Now, child, remember and not speak the first word about the gold case, if you want to see the sunshine hereafter," he said, sternly.

"I have promised ;" said Molly, with a decision which made her seem quite superior to a child of her years ; " but there is one thing, Button, which I would like to say to you now," she added, with a serious earnestness.

" Say on," replied Button, fastening his round eyes steadily upon hers, as if he would read her inmost thoughts.

" Did you ever think that God sees all we do—in the dark, as well as in the daytime ?"

". What do you ask me that for ?" demanded Button.

" Because it has ached in my heart ever since I went away from home yesterday, when is wasn't right for me to go ; and I wanted to know if it ever made you feel so."

" Faugh !" said Button, turning on his heel suddenly, and setting off rapidly on his return home.

To Molly's great relief, she found that the family had experienced no alarm on account of her absence, concluding that she had gone to Parson Willowday's, as she sometimes went, though never before without permission and alone. But a short time before, however, Reuben had been dispatched to bring her home.

Molly hurriedly besought their forgiveness, then proceeded to narrate briefly, an account of herself during her absence, coming as soon as possible to her meeting with the strange gentleman at the Witch Hazel House.' Casting aside the restraint which she usually felt in the presence of the Colonel, she told him of her disappointment at not finding the stranger that morning as he had promised, and, with a breathless earnestness, dwelt upon the fact of her seeing a horse in Button's barn, which, she believed, was the one which belonged to the stranger, as Button had mentioned that he had no horse, himself.

The Colonel listened with greater attention than he was accustomed to give to children, and, after asking some questions relative to the gentleman's appearance, and becoming well persuaded that he was a traveller with money, he announced, to Molly's unlimited joy, that he would take one or two of his men, and go directly to Witch Hazel House, and ascertain for a certainty if the stranger were really gone.

When the Colonel was about setting off, he directed Molly to take her breakfast in her hand and go with him, as he should be unable to identify any of the property of the stranger, if found on Button's premises. To this, Molly gladly assented, and was quickly prepared to be set before the Colonel upon his horse. Behind, rode two of the stoutest farm-help on other horses. On approaching their destination, before emerging from the woods which bounded Witch Hazel land in front, they all dismounted, and the horses were fastened to a tree, to prevent the suspicion of Button. The Colonel then directed them to wait there quietly, while he went forward and explored the existing state of affairs about the house. A little later, the Colonel returned, saying that the house appeared desolate, while he had found a horse in the barn, which he was satisfied was too valuable to have been recently bought by Button. He had descried Button at some distance behind the house, employed in digging with a spade in one corner of his field.

He then ordered Molly and his men to accompany him forward in a direction which would not come under observation, announcing that in right of his office as a magistrate, he intended to make a careful investigation of the premises. On entering the precincts of a deserted home, the first footfall ever brings a presence which chills the soul as with a solemn mystery ; but on this occasion,.the old, silent house, with its black, cavernous walls, seemed more like a tomb, than the abode of living beings. This impression was not a little assisted by the one Idea of Evil, which always hung over that roof, like a boding owl, to warn away the steps of the unwary, for Goody Wythe was a veritable emissary of witchcraft in those days, and was generally supposed to be in the possession of a power which was given her from no good spirit, while Button, from his first introduction in that vicinity years ago, had been marked with a character blackened by sin, although so far undetected as to keep aloof from the punishment of the law.

"Don't go near there !" exclaimed Molly, indicating the closet door from which Button had so decidedly warned her.

"Why not ?" inquired one of the men.

"Because he told me that if anybody opened that door but himself, they would be killed in a minute, for he kept loaded guns in that place."

"I rather think, then," said the Colonel, reflectively, "that is the first place I examine."

Molly burst into tears, for she believed that the Colonel was rushing directly to his death, as she saw him move the bolt.

The next moment, the door opened, and a large body fell into the room, so suddenly, it made the Colonel leap back as if he had felt, in reality, the shot of a gun. All stood aghast, for they saw it was a human form which lay there !

"It is he ! oh dear, it is he !" cried Molly, as the Colonel, with an unsteady hand, exposed the face to sight.

"And here is the mark of a heavy blow on the head," said one of the men, " which, most likely, did the work, and not long ago, either, for the body is still warm."

"This," said the Colonel, "will put a period to that villain's operations in future, for nothing can be clearer than that he has murdered this man."

"What shall we do next to get hold of Button ?"

"Wait here, quietly, till he comes for the body, which he will do, probably as soon as he finishes digging a grave for it. We can take him then without any trouble," replied the Colonel.

Molly stood looking from one to the other, as they said these words, till the life seemed escaping from her body. But waiting to hear no more, she glided out, unperceived, for they were too intent in their examination of the body, to bestow a thought upon her. Darting like a bird over the land in rear of the house, she soon came upon Button.

before he had perceived her approach. He started angrily and lifted his spade with a menace.

"What brings you back again so soon?" he asked.

"Fly from here, quick!" she cried, gesticulating with the passionate earnestness of her words. "You saved my life yesterday, and to-day I will save yours. They have found it all out. Go!"

"Found what out?" demanded Button, now cowering with mortal fear.

"The murdered man in that closet!"

Button paused not an instant longer. Dropping his spade, he leapt like a wild animal over the way which led to the woods, and was soon lost from her sight.

When Molly believed that he had fully escaped, she returned to the house, and found that she had not been missed.

CHAPTER V.

" Button has taken the alarm and is nowhere to be seen !" exclaimed the Colonel, on looking from the window to ascertain if his plan of securing the murderer were about to succeed.

Immediately ordering his men to start off in the pursuit and to gather recruits in their aid wherever it were possible, his next effort was to find some one of Button's old vehicles to attach to his horse, that the body of the stranger might be conveyed away to the public house.

" If you wouldn't like to wait here, you may come out with me," he said to Molly.

" I'm not afraid," she replied, very sadly, " he was so good, and talked to me so kindly, he would't hurt me if he were alive, and I'm sure he can't do any harm now."

" That is right ; never make a fool of yourself as most girls do," said the Colonel ; " you have behaved well in this affair."

While the Colonel was without, Molly sat in the dark old house alone with the body of the murdered man. Marvellous and wild imaginings swept over her thoughts, like fearful gusts of wind which precede the coming of a thunder storm, when the darkened heavens cast an ominous gloom over all the earth.

She was suddenly recalled to a consciousness of her situation, by the sound of a groan ! She listened, trembling with a new fear, and heard another groan. This time, she knew it proceeded from the body before her !

Running quickly out of the house to the Colonel, she exclaimed wildly, "He lives ! he lives ! Come into the house and help him !"

The Colonel followed her in amazement, half believing that she had lost her senses.

"Where am I ?" murmured the stranger, unclosing his eyes upon the forms who were bending over him.

"Safe ! safe !" replied the Colonel, huskily, as he proceeded to throw up the sash for the admission of more air. "Very strange—all this," he said to himself, while Molly ran to obey his direction to bring some cold water.

"Oh ! that hideous dream !" said the stranger ; "and yet it seems so real, I think it was not all in my brain."

The Colonel soon had found a large basin, which, filling with water, he threw with a single dash over the face of the sufferer, saying meanwhile—

"It is not comfortable, but the best thing which can be done   Bear it, sir, and all will come out right."

4

"Don't take it ill," pleaded Molly, tremulously, "he will make you better, and you can then leave this awful place."

The stranger looked upon Molly with that dreamy, uncertain stare, which indicates clouded consciousness.

"Alice! dear Alice! is this really you?" he said faintly.

"It's Molly—don't you remember, sir?" she answered.

"Yes, yes; it's a long time ago, but I thought you had grown to be a woman, and "——

His voice died to a whisper, and he closed his eyes with exhaustion. Molly abandoned herself to a fresh burst of grief, for she believed that the gentleman was now dying.

"His mind wanders," said the Colonel; "I must throw on more water."

Vigorous and judicious exertions made Colonel Epps, till the stranger revived again, and was at length able to be removed. Comfortably established at Epps Hundred, Molly was only too glad to be able to contribute to his wants; and the whole household spared no effort in his assistance. These exertions were soon blessed by the signal convalescence of the stranger. In a week, he was able to converse freely and talked of resuming his journey homeward. On the evening preceding the day he had fixed for his departure, he wished to hear the relation of the particulars of his late misfortune, for he had only been informed that he had escaped some terrible peril, of the definite nature of which he retained no recollection.

"So, then, to you, dear child," he said, to Molly, when

the Colonel had concluded the narration, "I owe my life, after the blessing of a merciful Heaven! Had it not been for you, Hollis, my own boy, would now have been an orphan! Heaven bless you evermore for this."

He then inquired minutely the circumstances connected with Molly's history, and manifested an unusual interest.

"You say," he said to Col. Epps, "that in your possession is a gold case, which was found on the person of the mother. I wish to see it."

Mrs. Epps went for it, but presently returned in consternation, announcing that the case was nowhere to be found. Molly was immediately questioned, but she knew nothing of it. She now recalled what Button had said to her of the case, with an impression of evil ; but remembering her promise of secrecy, made no allusion which might point the suspicion of the theft to him. The servants were all summoned and closely interrogated, but none could give the slightest clue to the mystery, save one, who alleged that upon the night after the gentleman was brought there, he heard the window of one of the lower rooms opened and shut, but supposing it was the Colonel or Mrs. Epps, he had thought no more about it. It was then remembered, that the room in which the case was kept was not occupied during the night, the Colonel and his wife watching by the sick stranger in another part of the house.

"If that villain, Button Husley, had been anywhere about here, I should set him down as the thief at once," said the Colonel ; "but since the fatal morning when he was discovered, he has not been seen.　Every effort to capture him has as yet entirely failed."

"I hope he will live to repent his wickedness," said Mr. Rushton, slightly shuddering at this allusion to his intended murderer.

"He is unworthy to live at all," said the Colonel.

"I regret," resumed Mr. Rushton, after a serious pause, "that I cannot see this case.　I have already conceived a strong interest in Molly."

Molly ran to his open arms, and received his affectionate caress with smiles.

"Do you think that I shall ever be as dear to you as your own Hollis?" she inquired, naively.

"Already, you seem like a child to me," said the gentleman, "and I think," he added, looking at the Colonel and Mrs. Epps, "I shall return and claim you, by and by.　You will go and be a sister to Hollis?"

"No, no, we cannot spare her," said Mrs. Epps.

"We certainly have the best right to her," interposed Reuben, who did not like this sudden transfer of Molly's interest.　He was a boy of fifteen now—proud, brave-hearted, and generally taciturn, but so fond of Molly, he could willingly have laid down his life for hers, if necessary.

"You will never be forgotten by me, dear child, nor yet these generous friends of yours and mine," said Mr. Rushton, "and, were it not for being rifled of my money, I would leave you some substantial token of my esteem. However, you will hear from me again."

When the stranger had gone, Molly scarcely talked of any other subject than the late remarkable circumstances, in which she had been an actor; but as weeks passed away and no intelligence from Mr. Rushton came to Epps Hundred, she grew thoughtful, and even sad. The roses bloomed about the grounds, the grasses waved in luxuriance on the hills and in the meadows, and all the world wore its loveliest aspect, for it was in the month of June, yet Molly was less joyous now than ever before. A little dell behind the house, shaded with lilac bushes and the heavy branches of an ancient tree, with a moss-cushioned rock for a seat, was her favorite resort in the moments allotted to herself. Here she sat late one balmy afternoon, her fingers engaged upon her knitting, and her thoughts weaving fancies about the memory of the stranger, who seemed like a dear relative to her, when Reuben made his appearance before her.

"Molly," he said, throwing himself upon the rock at her side, "I have been watching you some time, behind these bushes. I saw that you were sad. Tell me what troubles you."

"I was thinking of Mr. Rushton, and the thought came that he might be dead—for something must have happened to keep him from his promise," she replied.

"I believe," said Reuben, impatiently, "if that man were to come back, you would leave us all willingly, and go with him. "Indeed, I hope we never shall hear from him again."

"O Reuben!" exclaimed Molly, angrily, and she sprang to her feet to leave him alone.

The boy's arms had quickly circled her lithe figure, and she was compelled to resume her seat, though with but an ill-grace. Her pretty, red lips pouted with vexation, and her foot beat the grass in time with her kindled spirit.

"I shall not let you go," said Reuben, "until you make me one promise."

"I'll not promise you anything, now," replied Molly.

"Yes," said Reuben, "you must promise me that you do not, nor ever will—love this strange gentleman, Molly."

Molly now laughed merrily, and gave Reuben a roguishly triumphant look.

"You mad boy !" she exclaimed, "to think of being jealous of a man who is so much older than me. I love him just as I do your father."

"Then you do love me better—far better than any other man ?" continued Reuben.

"I can't say," replied Molly, with a wise shake of her head. "I haven't seen that boy, Hollis, yet."

Reuben's lips whitened, his whole frame trembled, and his eyes flashed the fire he felt at the hearing of these words.

"What is the matter ?" asked Molly, with assumed simplicity ; "you look as if you really were in earnest."

"Do you think I am playing, Molly ? No, I am very serious."

Here Molly abandoned herself to a fresh gush of laughter. Reuben could not withstand this ; he drew her closer to himself, and his face quickly wore another and tenderer expression.

"I love you and Mary just as well as ever," said Molly, carelessly ; "let me go now."

"Good !" said Reuben. "Remember, Molly, what you have just said."

"Yes—as a brother."

"Not that," said Reuben, disappointed.

"What then ?" asked Molly.

"Better than a brother," continued Reuben, fondly ; "I remember that I have loved you, Molly, ever since that first night when you came to our house, and fell asleep against my heart. You seemed to me like a child-angel, then."

"And now ?" pursued Molly, archly.

"Like an angel-girl. You must be my angel-wife, sometime," said the boy, with a tone of seriousness.

"Never," said Molly, who scarcely understood the depth of these words, but the tone of assurance in which Reuben spoke was sufficient to arouse her opposition.

"And you must love me now, and always," continued Reuben, taking no notice of her last word, "as your life—your heaven—your all."

"That is not right, Reuben," answered Molly ; "your mother has taught us to love no one before God. I shall ask her if such words are not wicked."

"No you mustn't," said Reuben ; "what we say about these things no one must know, not even Mary or my mother."

"Why ?" asked Molly.

"Because—because—they would not understand—they

might think us foolish," replied Reuben, with embarrassment.

"Oh, I shall certainly tell," said Mòlly, divining that she could thus tease Reuben; "that is," she added, "if you will not let me go free in just one minute, I will tell every word you have said."

"Well, Molly," said Reuben, "with all your naughty ways, I love you better than anybody on earth—I worship you. If you will kiss me right on my lips I will let you go."

A heavy step was now heard near the spot, and both saw the tall figure of the Colonel approaching. Reuben greatly feared his father, and Molly had to plead no longer for her release. Like an arrow, she shot off toward the house, while Reuben drew himself up into the smallest possible compass, within the leaves of a lilac bush, till his father had passed on out of sight, when, with a high glow on his heart, he bounded away.

Notwithstanding Molly's perverseness, these words of Reuben did not fall upon her young heart to be lightly forgotten. Many times did she repeat them to herself, and ponder over them with a keen, exultant joy. Yet in the presence of Reuben, she was as impetuous and indifferent as ever, often aiming toward his peculiarities, shafts of wit which cut him to the heart, and made him shun her for days after. Indeed, it seemed that they, even as children of one family, could never agree. Reuben was a natural scholar, and in no pursuit did he delight so entirely as in the study of his books. All his tasks were meted with the promised reward of time for reading, which he never failed to secure to the utmost. But Molly did not love to study ; anything was more congenial to her than the patience and hard study requisite to the mastering of a book lesson. A few old volumes, containing wild and marvelous tales of battles and brigands, powerful to hold the imagination spell-bound, with the lives of certain distinguished warriors, she read and mused over with unfeigned delight. Adventure, such as no other ever thought of, was indisputably the passion of her nature. To explore the wildest and most unfamiliar spots about Epps Hundred, to dare all perilous endeavors, and to be the central actor of the most extraordinary scenes, was ever sufficient to make her entirely happy.

A love for study, however, was in part awakened in her mind, on the following winter, when a new teacher was secured in place of Master Wilkhurst. He was popular with the pupils, and indefatigable in his efforts for their improvement, so that among the many who achieved an unusual progress was Molly, greatly to the delight of Reuben.

"O Molly !" he exclaimed, one evening, when he had concluded hearing her recite a long lesson, to his perfect satisfaction, "I think you will be a learned woman, after all."

"I hope not," said Molly ; "I would rather be a warrior. There is no study I like at all, but history, and I like that because I can find out all about the wars."

"I do not like war," said Reuben, "and I never will be one to take part in it unless, indeed, I were called to fight for my country—to defend it from foreign oppression, as ours is harassed now."

"That is right, my son," said Mrs. Epps, who sat listening; "never cultivate a love for war for the sake of fighting with your fellow-men."

"Then my choice is not a good one," said Molly.

"No," replied Mrs Epps, decidedly ; "it were wiser for one of our sex to aspire to be fitted for a good wife and mother."

Molly shook her head, and something very like scorn darted from her dark eyes.

"It strikes me," observed Reuben, when he had remained thoughtfully silent for some time after, "that you like nothing which other girls do, Molly."

"I know it," she replied. "Now, all the girls I know, like you."

"That's true," joined his sister ; "I have always just as many friends as I want, and I know it is because they love Reuben."

Reuben smiled a little, as most brothers will on such an occasion, but looking earnestly upon Molly, said—

"Remember what you told me, one day, when we sat among the lilac trees. I have hoarded those words as I would gold."

Molly was wholly forgetful, but when her words were forced back upon her recognition, she only laughed and said—

" I have grown older since then.   Besides, I have an impression that I shall see Hollis Rushton yet."

Reuben had also grown older, and he had learned to conceal what annoyance he might feel in return for Molly's words. His years of patient study and reflection, quite unlike the years of other boys, had not left him without wisdom, and discernment ; and long ere this, he knew well that Molly did not speak such words from her inner heart. His gifts were treasured by her as she treasured no others ; she secretly yielded to his influence ; she studied her books to please him ; and, although she openly professed as much indifference to him as ever, he was content with the footing on which he stood.

And Molly ?

She could not deceive herself, however much she labored to delude others as to her real feelings. By nature a veritable coquette, with the inalienable perquisites—beauty, wit and daring—there would have been danger of her being spoiled by so much affection ; had her wild and passionate impulses not been held in check by her secret love for Reuben. She was conscious that his love was no light thing, and she was proudly aware of his superiority over all the other boys she knew. At school and among their young companions, his attention distinguished her, and with triumph, she marked the envy of others. Aside from his position as the only son of the most prominent family in that region, he was noble and handsome as any of the heroes of which she read in her favorite old books of romance. His high, serene brow, shaded with light, clustering hair ; his thoughtful, blue eyes, and his mouth, so lovable when he smiled, and so indicative of an unusual character in repose, were treasured in her young heart, as a talisman against all the ills and darkness of life.

There was yet no awakening to Love's first, bright, beautiful dream of heaven upon earth.

CHAPTER VI.

"I am not glad that people are sick, neither can I regret that we are left by ourselves, this evening," said Reuben to his sister and Molly, as he joined them before a cheerful fire one winter evening, having late returned from driving his father and mother to the home of a sick neighbor, where they were to remain as watchers during the night.

"We won't study at all, to-night, but enjoy ourselves for once in our own way," rejoined Molly.

"What shall we do to-morrow with our lessons not learned?" queried Mary.

. "Don't you remember, it says 'take no thought for the morrow?'" answered Molly, gaily.

"But the master will take thought for us," said Reuben. "I propose that we set to work and learn our lessons as soon as possible, then we can have the rest of the time for what we like. Attention to books; the one who speaks first, after this, shall pay a forfeit."

"What forfeit? demanded Molly.

"They shall—oh, they shall—go to Rome."

"Which means, I suppose, that we must kiss you. I shall do no such thing," said Molly.

"Yes; and if I speak, I must kiss you and Mary," said Reuben; "come we will begin now."

For a few minutes, they sat in silence and quietness, only Molly, being full of fun and mischief, was unable to restrain herself entirely. Now and then an inkling of a laugh burst out between the covers of her book, which she held before her face. When the novelty of the plan had a little worn off, Molly, observing Reuben studying attentively, rose on pretence of getting a pencil, and tripping softly behind his chair, gave one of his back curls a sly pull. This caused him to shout aloud; and throwing down his book, he sprang toward her. But she eluded his grasp and darted out of the room, closing the door behind her. Reuben followed, and after considerable ado, brought her back, and made her resume her place.

"Now be good and learn your lesson," he said. "Shall I show you?"

"Not at all," she replied; "I know everything, already. But I will fix the fire a little; the coals need stirring."

Very demurely she worked over the fire for some time, when, at last, she took up her book and appeared to study in earnest.

For this, Reuben bestowed an admiring glance upon her occasionally, of which she vouchsafed no consciousness.

They sat thus for some time, when suddenly a loud sharp report of continuous explosions began in the ashes, followed by shots of chestnuts in all directions over the room. A hot nut hit Reuben directly in the face and one or two more on his hands, before he was fully aware what was the nature of this strange commotion. Mary, greatly frightened, ran to the kitchen for assistance, declaring that the house would soon be afire.

"Who has done this?" cried Reuben, in consternation, as he saw the chestnuts continuing to pop over the room, carrying ashes and coals with them.

"Who could have done it?" responded Molly, dodging the coals and nuts.

It was some time before the tumult ceased and the scattered relics of the warfare removed. After breathing several long breaths of relief, Mary stole back, and speculations concerning the origin of the affair were rife.

"Molly," said Reuben, looking upon her steadily, "what could put it into your head to play such a sorry joke upon us, to-night?"

"Was it you? Oh Molly!" exclaimed Mary, reproachfully.

"I wish to study," said Molly, "and I shall be obliged to sit in the other room, if you trouble me with questions."

"Look here," said Reuben, "you must come and sit in this chair by me till we have done studying, and behave properly the rest of this evening, or I shall consider it my duty to report your proceedings to the authorities, to-morrow."

Molly meekly obeyed.

"Now," continued Reuben, as he saw her sober looks with a little relenting, "let us *all* see how well we can do for one hour."

"So let us," replied Mary.

But Molly said nothing, looking like a miniature deacon, on tenter-hooks. It is not clear what might have next occurred, for Molly's brain was busy, when they were newly startled by a hard, fluttering sound against an upper pane of one of the windows. Books were once more thrown down, and all were equally interested. The noise continuing, Reuben went to the window and threw up the sash. Directly a bird appeared within the room, and excited by the sensation which hailed his appearance, he flew rapidly from one object to another, finally alighting upon the frame of an ancient portrait of Mrs. Epps' father.

"Now let us capture it," said Mary.

"No, no," said Molly, "do not touch it, for the world."

"Why not?" Mary rejoined.

"Because I feel that we ought not to. There is something wonderful about it," replied Molly, now thoroughly serious.

"Hark!" whispered Reuben, "it begins to sing."

"A clear melodious warble soon filled the room ; the door was opened, and the occupants of the kitchen came to witness this singular night scene. A strange awe crept over the listeners, for there is ever that in such an unusual event, which impresses unconsciously, as if the barriers between

earthly existence and the world of spirits were partially removed.

Presently the song ceased, and the bird seemed to sleep
upon its perch.

"Let it stay here, till father and mother come in the
morning," said Reuben.

It was an impossibility to attempt to study more that
evening, and with lessons but partly committed, the books
were laid away. Reuben brought the warming-pan, in
which to parch corn for their entertainment. But the bird
could not be forgotten, while they were thus engaged, and
the keenest zest of their amusement was gone.

The corn came out, at last, like porous globules of snow,
and it being an occasion extraordinary, it was not deemed
advisable to eat it in the usual manner ; so Mary and Molly
sallied out to procure something to improve its flavor. They
returned with cakes of maple sugar and a pitcher of milk,
which they divided in bowls, sprinkling in the delicate ker-
nals as they ate. While they sat thus, Reuben proposed
riddles, generally proving so mysterious, that he was compelled to be his own expositor. After spelling nearly every
article in the room backwards, and playing a brisk game of
"odd and even" with the kernels which remained not parched, they covered the fire, and dispersed to their chambers
for the night.

Early on the following morning, the Colonel and Mrs.
Epps returned home. The bird was the first thing to which
their attention was directed. But no sooner was it aroused

by their presence, than it began to fly about the room, and, at length, circling over the head of Mrs. Epps, it fell at her feet.

She took it up, unresistingly. It was dead !

Mrs. Epps turned pale and shook her head sorrowfully.

" Nonsense, wife !" exclaimed the Colonel, " you think it is ominous of evil. Don't be led away by old signs."

" What does it mean ?" inquired Mary of her mother, tremulously.

" It means, child," answered the Colonel impatiently, " that a bird flew in here and knocking itself so hard about the room as it flew, it was killed, and so dropped down dead."

Molly stood silently, with wondrous eyes. Reuben regarded the whole thing as did his father.

" Think no more about it, and give it to the cat for her breakfast," concluded the Colonel.

But Molly, unperceived, rescued the dead bird from that fate and laid it carefully under the snow, planting a stick to mark the spot.

Mrs. Epps had taken cold on the night of her absence from home, and was an invalid for some days after. But gradually her health seemed to mend, and with the approach of the following spring she had never devoted herself more zealously for her children and family. With renewed love, they acknowledged her care, and, as she was habitually of delicate health, they strove to dissuade her from such exertion.

One morning, among the latest of the winter, she appeared not among her household as usual. The Colonel said that she was ill, and dispatched a messenger for the physician. When the doctor had made observations, he looked grave, and declared that she must have been suffering for months, for her disease had subtly stolen to the very foundation of her life.

For a week, she rapidly declined. Her children and Molly were inconsolable, and when, at last, she summoned them to her bedside to hear her parting words, their very lives seemed ready to be sacrificed to their anguish. An earnest charge was given to them to love their father and each other.

"To you, my dear Reuben, my first born," said the dying mother, "I especially intrust Molly, because you have an influence over her, such as no other will have. Love her as your own sister, advise her well and whatever may come, be true to the trust, which your mother received from hers."

To her own Mary, she gave many messages of trust and love.

"O! my beloved ones!" she concluded, "trust ever in the good Father, and remember that in keeping his commandments there is great reward. Thus you will meet me again in Heaven."

Then they knelt around her bed, while she faintly prayed. Gradually the words of supplication ceased, and no sound broke the solemn stillness, but the sobs of the stricken hearts.

A second time Molly was motherless !

Great calamities are like the coming of a leaden night. The darkness thickens, till it becomes dense to the senses, as in the days of the plagues of Egypt,—so dense as to be felt !

A heavy, gloomy night had fallen upon the home of Epps Hundred, for its light had set. Day after day, the loss was more fully recognized by the bereaved family. The Colonel now spent the greater portion of his time at the Bald Eagle, and scarcely an evening at his own home. Sometimes, however, he returned before the family had retired, but then, he was seldom himself.

The demon of intemperance possessed him. It had long been held in check—a dwarf, by the influence of his wife. That influence removed, it was fast becoming a giant ! Sickened and oppressed at heart, Reuben beheld the manliness of his father blurring and blotting out behind the film gathered by the rule of the senses. Sometimes words of warning love trembled upon his tongue ; but such had ever been his fear of his father, he remained silent. In the natural result of this state of things, all the interests pertaining to the prosperity of Epps Hundred were neglected, and hirelings held their sway undisputed. Old Peter, who had grown grey in the faithful service of the family, from the time of Mrs. Epps' father, exerted himself against the stronger current in vain.

In whatever contributed to the gratification of his besetting sin, the Colonel only embarked his attention. Mary

and Molly were left almost entirely to their own companionship, for Reuben was now absent from home during the day.
Each morning he walked a distance of three miles to recite
to the parish minister, with whom he was endeavoring to
prepare to enter college, and returned at night to spend the
evenings in close application to his books. The hearts
of the girls were often filled with grief, for the presence
which had made that home ever cheerful and pleasant, they
missed too keenly at every turn, to look in each other's faces
with their olden joy.

Thus the long days of the summer passed wearily, while
the flowers bloomed and the grass grew for the first time
over the bosom which had once throbbed in love and care
for the youthful mourners.

"Mary," said Reuben, one afternoon, when he had
returned home earlier than usual, and surprised his sister,
weeping by herself, "I am going to be at home all this
coming fall, and I shall be better company for you and
Molly, I hope."

"But why do you not go on with your lessons?" inquired
Mary.

"Because I am needed at home," he said, with a momentary sadness; "the affairs of the place do not go on well
now, and I told father this morning that I would give up my
recitations and have a care till the time of the winter school."

"What did he say?"

"He answered that my care was of no consequence.
Things were doing well enough as they were. But he does

not see as I do." He paused, and a shadow of pain crossed his face

At this moment, Mary was summoned by one of the house-maids to a council respecting the supper ; and a gay voice exclaimed, " O Reuben ! Peter has just told me that you are going to stay at home with us for the present."

Reuben turned, as he sat on a grassy bank before the door, and saw Molly, looking more like herself than for a long time before. Her dark eyes were sparkling with delight, and her cheeks were beautiful in their soft bloom under the shade of her unconfined and flowing hair, which was black as night.

"And you are glad of this ?" responded Reuben, inspired by her presence to smile.

" Perhaps—just a mite," answered Molly, pulling off some grasses at her side.

"Come and kiss me, then," cried Reuben, with the air of one directing a petted child,

Molly pouted her red, sinuous lips, and moved a little fur-ther away.

"Cross so soon ! I think I will not stay at home ; at least, if I do, I'll be careful to keep from the house as much as possible," said Reuben.

"As you like," said Molly, carefully winding a ribbon of striped grass over her fore-finger.

" Now, Molly, don't be so much as you used to, when you wished to vex me. I think you always try to dash cold water over my heart when it's glad."

Molly lifted her eyes to Reuben.   She saw that he looked weary and comfortless, and she relented in a moment. Approaching him with hesitation, she sat down upon the bank by his side.

"Dearest one," he said softly, "I was wrong. You do love me, after all."

"I pity you, dear Reuben," said Molly.

"Pity only ?" asked Reuben.

"No : but we will talk about something else," said Molly.

And so they sat, with his arm about her slight waist, and hers over his neck, talking of the past ; and for once, Molly spoke to him reasonably, soberly.   She promised to aid him and Mary in making their home cheerful in future.   New plans were sketched, and bright schemes of happiness discussed, till the dew began to fall, and Mary interrupted them with a call to the evening meal.

Reuben exerted himself manfully to mend and straighten his father's broken and tangled affairs.   But he had so many obstacles to overcome, that he was often well-nigh disheartened at his prospect.   His father was now in the frequent habit of being absent from home, and his interest seemed entirely transferred from his family.

The landlord of the Bald Eagle had one daughter who was a widow, and this woman, from the time of the death of Mrs. Epps, had exerted herself to acquire an influence over the heart of Colonel Epps, to the end that she might become his second wife.   Such was the power which the father of Mrs. Dyke and her brother, Hazor Wilkhurst, possessed with him, by reason of aiding him in gratifying his passion for drink, she doubted not her ability to accomplish her object.

Indeed, Hazor was determined upon carrying this grand point, and by dint of skilfull management, he succeeded in inducing the Colonel to engage Mrs. Dyke as a permanent housekeeper in his family. His judgment being continually stupefied, he acceded to all her plans for the new management of his household, and at once, in the presence of the family, vested her with the authority of their mistress, concluding with the declaration that if they disobeyed Mrs. Dyke, they might consider the offence the same as disobedience to him.

This announcement was received with surprise and grief, by the children. On that first melancholy evening, they discussed the affair by themselves for a long time, till they all wept together.

"I wonder if your mother and mine can see us now, from their home in heaven?" said Molly. But no answer being returned, she continued, "I hope not, for it would make them unhappy amidst all the singing and glory there is up there, I am sure."

"Perhaps not," said Reuben, more calm ; "if we are to suffer these things here, to fit us to dwell with them at last, they may know that it is for our best good."

"I don't know what they will fit me for," said Molly, "for I feel full of hate."

"Oh, Molly! I beg you not to talk so," said Reuben; "what would my mother say, could she hear you?"

This brought to her memory the blessed words which Mrs. Epps, in times past, had shed upon her young spirit, in its passion, like a cooling rain upon the hot parched earth, and she was softened into penitence. So true it proves, that good seed, once sown, may spring up and bear fruit, even after the sower has gone to rest from all labors for ever! Their works do follow them! ·

The next morning, the new mistress was up betimes. She bestirred herself over the house, like one who has entered upon new duties in earnest. No misgivings, no fear or trembling was manifest—only the fullest confidence in her own powers of regulation. Although, to appearance, but a few years rising of thirty, she wore a cap with strings tied in a square knot under her chin, in the mode of elderly women of her time. And on this morning, she appeared in a gown of black, stiff bombazine, with a small, palm-leaf shawl over her high, narrow shoulders, which, it afterward came to notice, she wore at least two thirds of the year.

"I'll tell ye what," said old Peter to his associates out of doors, after making covert observations, "the very sight of that ere woman stirs up the maids and gals like a long wooden spoon in a kettle of hot pudding."

Although possessing this faculty of "stirring up" affairs by her mere presence, in an eminent degree, she was slow and measured in all her movements; in nowise active or vigorous in her own personal efforts, notwithstanding it was her grand passion to make every one around her so. It soon came to light that she was as obstinate in the carrying out of all her purposes, however trifling, as a very donkey. As well might any of the family set up to run against a side of the house, as against her will, for if she was not enough potent, she brought in the Colonel to her aid, who at once settled all rebellion.

Among the first acts of this new administration, was the discharge of both the housemaids.

"There was no sense in such extravagance," she said; "the girls had been living in idleness long enough. They had now got to do the work for the family with her help and direction."

Mary had always struggled with delicate health, and this new tax upon her strength looked overwhelming. More than ever, she now thought of her dead mother, who had so tenderly shielded her from ill, and gladly would she have lain down with her in the grave, without bearing the burden of life farther over the new path, which seemed to be paved with thorns and stones, enough to mark her footprints with blood. Molly possessed the strength, but lacked the disposition for the new life allotted her. The objections of either were without weight in the scale of government, in that day of darkness.

After performing all the drudgery of the household, with the assistance, and for the most part with only the direction of Mrs. Dyke, they were made to perform their tasks at the spinning wheel until night. They were not allowed to read in the evening, as formerly, for if Mrs. Dyke had any particular aversion greater than the sight of idleness in others, it was to see people engaged in the service of books. She counted such time as even worse than wasted. A task in knitting or sewing was assigned them until a late hour, when they were sent off to bed, without a word of commendation or hope for the morrow. After this they usually talked, till they cried themselves to sleep. But while they slept, they had consolation in their dreams of the past.

Molly could not be broken into this tread-mill system so easily as Mary, and occasionally she took the opportunity to reveal certain inklings of her real spirit, or to perpetrate mischief at the expense of the new mistress. But such demonstrations invariably won her the punishment of close confinement, and the sacrifice of food for a length of time, deemed proportionate to the offence ; and, as at such times, her portion of the labor of the house devolved upon Mary, she avoided falling into such disfavor as much as possible. Whatever she might do, however, she was never in full favor, or in any favor at all equal to that in which Mary stood, for Mrs. Dyke had discovered a strong prejudice against Molly from the first.

Mrs. Dyke next succeeded in inducing the Colonel to discharge nearly all of his outdoor help, among whom was Peter, who was now too superannuated to perform much labor. It had long been understood that he was to end his days at Epps Hundred as a reward for his past faithful service. Such had been the dying request of the father of Mrs. Epps, but as he had no legal claim to the privilege, remonstrance was without avail. The Colonel, indeed, demurred somewhat about this step, but his better nature being held in thrall by intemperance, he yielded to the influence of his housekeeper more and more, as she usurped authority. So, without home, or friends to whom to go, old Peter was driven away, amid the sincere grief of all the remaining members of the family.

The object of all this retrenchment, was at first enigmatical ; but by little and little the secret came out. The property of Epps Hundred having originally been derived from the first wife's father, only the income was left to the use of the Colonel, and it was Mrs. Dyke's first effort to make this income as large as possible, so that a comfortable estate might be laid by in prospect for herself. She was determined to make the most out of her good fortune, and so began at once to impress the children, who were the only rightful owners of that property, into a service of sacrifice and slavish toil, for her individual benefit. There was no help for this, for, until the children should arrive to the age of their majority, they were under their father's control, and not a dollar of their inheritance could they attain, during the life of their father, if he chose to withhold it for himself.

It would have been no slight consolation to Mary, if the articles which had been associated personally with her lost mother, could have been given to her possession. Many of these her mother had highly valued for their rare worth;

others had been long and carefully treasured as relics of the past, and as connected with family friends ; and all of them were now sacred in the eyes of Mary. But they were all under a lock, the key to which was always in the pocket of Mrs. Dyke. Sometimes, however, Mary recognized them with a keen anguish appropriated to the private use of the housekeeper, and it was not long before several of the choicest articles of her mother's wardrobe were seen to decorate her coarse person on common occasions, as well as those considered of more importance. Once Mary ventured to mention the matter to her father, but she received only a sharp reprimand for her interference, and after this, she could not fail to see that the housekeeper used the articles with even greater freedom than before.

This was the usual result of opposition to any course which Mrs. Dyke chose to pursue. Where she could discover no opposition, as in the case of Reuben's conduct toward her, she suspected it none the less. In fact, she had soon come to dislike Reuben for the reason of his firm friendship for Molly. He had, also, some slight influence over his father, and was decidedly of consequence with the family in general, and Mrs. Dyke began to plan to get rid of him at Epps Hundred. His quiet, decided way was a greater check upon her sway than she was willing even to confess to herself. But as he ever met her with respect, and studiously avoided any conflict with her, she could not easily devise a pretext for preferring her wishes in this respect to his father.

CHAPTER VII.

A SCHEME AND ITS CONSEQUENCES.

Mrs. Dyke was a fast friend to neighborly tea-drinkings, in a common way. Consequently, she was very familiarly acquainted with the people about Epps Hundred, and, quite contrary to the habit of Mrs. Epps, exchanged visits frequently.

"There is always some good in every great evil," observed Molly, with animation, immediately after Mrs. Dyke had gone out to drink tea with a neighbor, on one Saturday afternoon, at the closing of a week of unusual irksomeness, by reason of a prolonged visit from Hazor Wilkhurst.

"Hush !" whispered Mary, half scared, "Hazor may be somewhere about and hear you."

"No," answered Molly, "I saw him start for the village a half hour ago, and your father is at the Bald Eagle. We have the house all to ourselves for once, and won't we take a little of our old comfort ? I wish Reuben would come in."

" There is our work," said Mary, sadly; " she has left us longer stints than usual."

" Dear me !" responded Molly, " I can't help but hate that woman, and her brother too."

" That is not what my dearest mother would approve," said Mary, who could never allude to her mother without tears.

" What's all this ?" now interrupted the voice of Reuben; " I expected to find you both in high good humor, having seen the black bombazine walking up the road, and so came directly to the house to have my part in the matter." Going behind their chairs, as they sat computing their tasks, he put an arm around the neck of each, and brought their heads against his own.

" Here we are, a happy trio," he continued; " and now we have got our heads together, let us agree what to do."

" *We* have got to do all this work," said Molly, impatiently.

" Then I will get my Arabian Nights, and read to you," said Reuben.

" While Mary and Molly sewed, Reuben sat between them and read aloud, frequently pausing to interlard some humorous observation of his own, which was received with a gush of merriment, such as had not been heard in that house since the introduction of the new mistress. They forgot their vexations, and began to enjoy themselves as in days past. Truly sweet was this novelty of freedom.

When Reuben had tired of reading, he brought a dish of the fairest apples, which was a signal for the girls to cease to ply their needles for a while. They had reached the cores, and had begun to count the seeds in brisk sport, when a dark shadow passed the window at which they were sitting. The next moment, the door unclosed, and Mrs. Dyke appeared before them !

A boding frown sat upon her brow, and there was a meaning in her heavy step. Advancing directly to Reuben, she took the book which he had resumed upon her appearance, and laid it upon the shelf.

"Go to your work out of doors, and not come in here to hinder others," she said.

"And you, girls," she continued, "for this, must do just as much again in your work as I told you, if you have to sit up till midnight. I will learn you not to set to playing the moment my back is turned. You have no right, either, to bring apples from the cellar unless I give you leave, and you know it is my orders that you never eat anything only what I give you at the table."

Reuben's brow flushed, and a clear, steady light shone in his eye. He rose, and taking his book from the shelf, resumed his reading, apparently unmoved. The girls went on with their sewing in silence.

"Did you hear what I said ?" asked Mrs. Dyke of Reuben, in excitement.

"I did," replied Reuben, in his usual voice.

Mrs. Dyke now hastened to the door which led to the

chamber occupied by Hazor, and summoned him below in a tone of triumph. This was wholly unexpected, for they had not the least idea of another having been in the house, while they had thus sat together. They did not know that Hazor had stealthily returned by a back way, to become a spy of their actions, and, as previously concerted with his sister, he had hung out a signal from his window that she might return and surprise them in the midst of their enjoyment !

In answer to his sister's summons, he lost no time in appearing there, wearing a smile of decided intelligence upon his sullen face, while he rubbed his hands together as if they ached for employment.

"My brother," began Mrs. Dyke, solemnly, "I came in here and found these children at play instead of their work, and they were actually eating, because they thought that no eye was upon them ! I have ordered that boy to go out of this house. I took away his book, but he has dared to take it again before my face !" Here her voice grew nervous and loud. "Colonel Epps has told me again and again to see to it that these children mind me to the letter. I shall begin as I mean to hold out, and will you be so good as to help me to bring matters straight here ?"

"We shall see what can be done," responded Hazor, walking up to Reuben, and with a single blow felling him from his chair to the floor.

Molly now screamed at the top of her voice, as was her habit when greatly angered. Hazor took her by the shoulder, and walked her directly into the parlor, locking the door without, and giving the key to Mrs. Dyke.

"She will have time to think over how she hates 'that woman and her brother, too,'" he said, with evident enjoyment of the scene.

Mary sat sobbing as if her heart would break.

"You will go out now without more trouble, I presume," said Hazor to Reuben, as he stood up before him.

Looking steadily into the green glowing eyes of Hazor, Reuben said, "I wish you to understand that I think you are a contemptible man, sir. And I shall not leave this house unless I am put out."

For a single moment, Hazor hesitated, trembling with passion.

"My brother," said Mrs. Dyke, "will you let this bad boy govern you? I am astonished!"

Reuben was now set out of doors without further demur. Again he stood up bravely, and said to Hazor:

"I made no resistance, for I wanted you to carry me out. That is all a man who can abuse a girl like Molly is fit for!"

No other words could have so much aroused the pride and anger of Hazor, and they were laid away in his heart, to rankle there amid revenge forever after. Reuben heard a muttered imprecation, and the door was shut heavily upon him. He went away by himself to reflect calmly upon this scene. The longer he thought, the less did he respect his own manliness. "For," said he to himself, "by descending to a quarrel, I have made myself even with those whom I so much dislike. If I had felt right, I should have gone out of the house at first. But it is so hard to do right when one is so provoked."

Then he thought of his sainted mother; he felt her hand upon his head; he heard the words which she used to repeat to him—"Resist not evil," and he wept as he had not before since her death. Alas! he was very miserable, although he had defended himself valiantly.

The room in which Molly had been confined was large, gloomy and cold, not being opened except on rare occasions. The windows were thickly covered with frost and snow, and the cold sand on the floor grated under her feet with a teeth-clashing emphasis. Throwing herself into a large, hard chair, which seemed lined and cushioned with ice, she thought of nothing but the scene through which she had just passed. Her heart swelled with heavy throbs, for she was fearfully angry, and her hot breath wound up through the chilly air quickly and unevenly.

It was some time before she became aware of a portrait upon the opposite wall of the room. With a sudden start at the recognition, her reflections turned into another and more soothing channel.

"Dear Mrs. Epps!" she cried, extending her hands, unconsciously, "if you could only speak one word to me now! Why did God take you away from us and bring another, who is so bad, so hateful!"

Directly under the portrait was a table, on which lay a Bible. Molly went to it for the need of something to occupy her attention.

"I remember," she thought, "that dear mother Epps used to say that sometimes when she opened the Bible, her eyes fell upon a verse which had a particular meaning. I will try now and see what I open to."

It was so nearly dark, she could not see easily at this time, but she began to be interested and looked with care. At the first trial, her eye fell upon a verse of hard names in the genealogies, and she was disappointed.

"I suppose I am not good enough to open to anything in particular," she murmured.

"But the trial of your faith worketh patience," she read next.

"That is not for me, for I was not made to be patient," she commented.

Then she opened in the Old Testament and made out these words: "I have surely seen the affliction of my people which are in Egypt, and have heard their cry by reason of their task-masters ; for I know their sorrows."

"That is good ! it is for me !" she exclaimed ; "I feel certain now that I do not suffer alone. There is One who hears my cry and knows my sorrows."

Tears came afresh, and she shut the book, with a softened heart.

She was now suffering so severely from the bitter cold,

that she was forced to walk the room rapidly, while she held her chilled aching fingers to her lips. The gloom of night increased, but yet no step came near the door for her.

"I shall freeze to death here, this night," she reflected ; "and I do not care, for I shall see my mother and good Mrs. Epps. I feel sorry to leave poor Reuben and Mary, but they will not have to cry over me any more, and they will get used to living without me after a while. The rest, I know, will be glad to get rid of me."

Crouching down in one corner of the room, she covered her face and tried to compose her thoughts. She was numb, and did not feel the cold so sensibly now. Dim visions swept through her brain, connected with the portraits which she could not see for the darkness. She began to think of how she should be found in the morning—a frozen corpse ; —of what Mrs. Dyke and Hazor Wilkhurst would say?—she wondered if the Colonel would care ? But when she thought of how Reuben would feel, she was overcome. Thus she remained till she fell asleep.

Hours after—how many she knew not, she was awakened by a sound without. She had been dreaming of the beloved dead ; Mrs. Epps had come to her and smiled till her heart was warm. But, alas ! she found that in reality, she was very cold, and a strange feeling brooded over her heart. The moon was shining brightly into the room and across the floor, so that the grains of sand here and there shone like gems. The frost on the window panes was tinged with silver and gold.

A low voice from one of the windows chained her attention :

"Come here, dear Molly ; try and help me raise this window."

Molly endeavored to move, but she felt paralyzed to her heart. She spoke, and her voice sounded fearfully odd. But with another mastering effort, she was able to reach the window.

"Is that you, Reuben ?" she asked.

"Yes ; I have been trying to pry up the window for some time ; it is hard frozen, but I shall get it quite raised soon."

"What do you try for ?"

"So that I can get you out and take you round to Mary, who is waiting in her chamber. You will freeze to death there before morning."

"What time is it ?"

"Not late. I was going to wait till father came home, so as to get him to let you out. He does not come, and I dare not let you stay longer."

A few minutes later, Molly was carefully lifted out, and the window closed again. A warm heart, full of pity, waited to receive her.

"Oh Mary !" sobbed Molly, falling into her arms, "I am almost frozen to death."

"I knew it must be so, poor, dear child," said Mary ; "and I could not rest a moment till Reuben had done something to get you out."

Mary covered her with woollen blankets and made every effort in her power for her comfort, but still she shivered with cold, and soon began to suffer a keen pain. Reuben had brought something for her supper, but she could not eat.

Long hours of pain she lay in Mary's arms, till, at last, she fell into an unquiet slumber.

In the morning, when Mrs. Dyke discovered that Molly had gone from the place of her imprisonment, she went with a step of anger to her chamber. But her step was arrested, for she found her in a high fever and delirious !

CHAPTER VIII.

NEW PROSPECTS.

To one of the unoccupied chambers of the house, containing four large windows shaded with rush curtains and a huge fireplace, which, in certain winds, emitted more smoke than heat, was poor Molly consigned, when it was discovered that she was severely ill. For some time, Mrs. Dyke refused to have a physician summoned, lest it might result a foolish extravagance, but when the old family doctor came, he gave his opinion that her life was in danger, and looked sad if questioned as to the probable result. No traveller who has missed his way at night and momently plunges farther into the dreamy obscurity, amid thorns, and pitfalls, and precipices, is more at a fault, than was Molly as she struggled through long, gloomy days of suffering, with only a partial consciousness.

She had no attendant but Mary, and at such times only as she could be spared from her domestic labors. Occasionally, indeed, the neighbors came, but they were always accompanied by Mrs. Dyke, and they talked so much and loud together, they left Molly more ill than they found her. For the most part, Molly lay in the great, high bed, neárer the ceiling than the floor, tossing feverishly, or in a state of insensibility, while the winds of March went whistling by the windows, clattering the loose window sashes, and the cold crept in through every crack and cranny, despite Mary's endeavors to preserve a cheerful and steady fire. Often she talked wildly, and would call for Reuben to come and take her away from the cold parlor, where she was freezing in the darkness.

One morning, when she had passed the immediate crisis of her illness, she awoke more natural than usual. Mary took her thin hand within both of hers, and burst into tears of gratitude.

"I have slept late," said Molly; "what will they say when they find me gone from that room?"

Mary was too much overcome to speak, and she went on—

"Oh, it was so cold there! I never shall forget it. But I hope that dear Reuben will not suffer for bringing me out."

She attempted to rise as usual, and then, for the first time, became conscious of her extreme weakness. She looked upon Mary with a bewildered curiosity.

"You have been very sick, dear Molly," said Mary, "but if you are careful and keep quiet, you will soon get well, we hope."

"And now I see that this chamber is not ours," said Molly ; " it is the one where we dried cranberries last fall. Did they shut me up here, because I got out of the parlor ?"

Mary strove to reassure her with words of love and consolation.

" If I am sick, why does not Reuben come and see me ?" inquired Molly, at length.

" He is not at home, now," answered Mary, struggling to keep back her tears.

" Reuben gone !" exclaimed Molly.

"Yes, Molly; I will tell you all when you are strong enough to hear it," said Mary, lowering her voice to a whisper and looking anxiously toward the door.

" I must know now," said Molly, with a quivering lip. " Where is he ?"

" Last week he was sent away, but I don't think he will remain long."

" Didn't he come to bid me good bye ?"

" Yes," said Mary, " and how I pitied him !" She paused to control her grief, but seeing Molly's distress, she endeavored to be cheerful. " He took the last moment and came in here unknown to all but me, to see you once more, for he had not been allowed to see you since that night. You did not know him. Then he cried, and entreated you to speak one word to him before he went.

" Didn't I ?" asked Molly, anxiously.

Mary evaded the question, but Molly would not be put away with an answer short of a direct one.

" You laughed and talked about Cave Rock," continued Mary, " and seemed to think yourself at Witch Hazel House again."

" What did Reuben say to me ? Tell me his very words, Mary."

" You will get well, and you will always love me, Molly," he said, as he put your arms about his neck. But you spoke of Mr. Rushton and his son Hollis, and then poor Reuben gave away and sobbed bitterly. But he could not stay longer, so he kissed you and hurried out with his heart almost broken."

" I shall never see dear Reuben again !" cried Molly, with a wail of grief.

" Don't speak so," said Mary; " you will get well, and he is coming home to see us at the end of three months, if not before."

" Three months !" exclaimed Molly, as if she had spoke of years; " I shall never, never see him again."

She was now so much disturbed, Mary took alarm and forbore to speak more, and Molly, like a weak and weary child, sobbed herself to sleep.

When she awoke again, perceiving Mary near, she said, with a smile :

" I have been dreaming. I thought I was down by the brook, trying to reach my lips to the cool water that I might quench my thirst, when I saw that fearful snake that was killed on Cave Rock, just ready again to spring upon me. I felt his sharp fangs in my neck, but I could not scream, though I tried again and again. All at once, Mr. Rushton stood before me, as I thought, and he killed the snake with a single blow. 'It is right,' he said to me; 'the snake has not hurt you. Come with me.' Then I followed him till we came to a beautiful meadow, filled with flowers. I next found myself on a bridge, and then we came out into a large place, such as I never saw. I was very glad, only I felt sober when I thought that Reuben was not near to enjoy so much with me. I could still see him at a distance, but there was a dark veil, like a cloud, between us."

"That was a good dream," said Mary, "and you must try and get well soon."

Long hours of the day did Molly have to lie on her bed alone, and beguile her time as best she could, for no sooner was it known that she was better, than Mary was not allowed to spend so much time in her chamber as formerly. She amused herself by tracing rude figures on the smoke-browned wall, and by watching a spider whose web was just above her bed, or by counting the squares of the patch-work quilt upon her bed. She thought, too, much of the past, and wove queer fancies for the future, often wondering where Reuben was, and if he ever thought of her. When she was able to sit up during a part of the day, Mrs. Dyke sent her knitting-work, with the direction that she must not be idle, for she had lost too much time already, besides hindering the whole house. Molly was so weak, she cried at once and made herself sick again, so that her recovery was retarded several days.

Molly now began to have an appetite, and craved certain dishes so much, she could think of nothing else. For some time she forbore to tell Mary, lest she might increase her labor, which she knew was already much too heavy for her strength. But when she could eat nothing which she brought one day, she said, with some misgivings :

"Do you know, dear Mary, what I think would make me well at once ? If I could only have some of those nice things to eat which your mother used to make. I have been thinking of them till I feel quite anxious for a taste."

"What would you like ?" asked Mary.

When Molly had told her, she promised to do the best she could for her gratification.

"Dear child," she said to herself, "if it were in my power you should have everything you wish at once; but now I think it will be difficult." The thought of Mrs. Dyke made her troubled, but she smoothed Molly's hair, and told her to wait patiently while she went to see what she could do.

"I can't be denied this once, I know," said Molly, while the tears filled her eyes.

A long time it seemed to Molly that she waited, every sound reminding her that Mary must be coming with the delicious meal. At last she heard a step upon the stairs; it was slow and heavy, but she thought that Mary was careful to prevent accident to the precious burden which she bore. Molly prepared to welcome her with smiles and words of acknowledgment.

The door opened, and, alas! she saw only Mrs. Dyke, with a bowl and a wooden spoon!

Molly had no recollection of seeing her before during her illness, and for a moment she forgot her disappointment in her confused surprise. Mrs. Dyke advanced and set her bowl beside Molly.

"There," said she, emphatically, "if you are too difficult to eat that, you must wait till you get hungry."

Molly perceived that it was bean porridge, and she was sickened at once. As well could she have eaten a stone, when she had asked for bread.

"I thought that Mary was going to get me something else," she faltered.

"She has other fish to fry," was the curt answer.

"You can carry that back, for I cannot eat it," said Molly, meekly, and just ready to cry.

"Then you shall go without till to-morrow," rejoined Mrs. Dyke.

"Well," answered Molly, very faintly. She was too weak now to feel rebellion.

"What's more, you've got to go down stairs after to-day for all you eat. I shall not allow anything more to be brought up here, to foster your idleness," delivered Mrs. Dyke, while she busied herself in going about the room, and examining the few articles which Mary had brought in for Molly's amusement or comfort. This investigation seemed in nowise to improve her humor, for, after other severe remarks, she gathered up what she could carry in her pockets, shutting the door sharply behind her.

For some time after, Molly remained like one half stupefied by a crowd of overwhelming thoughts, but every time she thought over her disappointment, it gathered poignancy and weight, till at length she found herself abandoned to a flood of tears. This, as was natural to her, occasioned drowsiness, and faint as the people who saw the honey drop from the trees, but could not eat, because Saul had cursed the man who should eat any food until evening, that he might be avenged on his enemies, she fell into a troubled sleep.

Mary was scarcely less grieved, but she was not allowed to visit Molly's chamber again that day. Many long hours of that night poor Molly lay awake, struggling with thirst and faintness. If she wearied herself to sleep, it was to dream tantalizingly of cool, running water, amid banks fringed with spearmint, or of delicious fruits, which by all her efforts she failed to reach. The next morning, she tried to go below stairs in obedience to Mrs. Dyke's commands. As she was long in coming, Mary was summoned to go for her, but found her fainted and fallen to the floor.

Not before the balmy days of May was Molly able to go out of doors and assist again in the labors of the house. The windows were opened, and the grateful perfume of lilacs came in on every breeze.

"Is it not beautiful?" said Mary, as they were sitting on the doorstep one bright hour of the morning, engaged in separating cowslip sprigs from blades of grass, which they had been gathering in one of the meadows of Epps Hundred for the dinner. "The air is soft and still, the bees are humming in the trees, and the lilacs are so sweet !"

Unconsciously, Molly tore one of the golden flowers which she held to fragments, and scattered them at her feet. A sudden thought had shadowed her heart like a cloud.

"I never see the lilac blossoms but what I think of Reuben," she said, with a slight betrayal of embarrassment.

"Why ?" asked Mary.

"It was among the lilac trees by the moss rock that he first told me "—— she paused and sighed, while a soft blush stole over her cheeks.

"I forgot to tell you, dear Molly," now spoke Mary, with unusual animation, "that I heard father say Reuben was coming home next week, and "——

"Next week !" interrupted Molly, with delight. "Oh, Mary, how could you keep it from me so long ?"

"It is scarcely an hour since I heard it myself," answered Mary, laughing. "What is more," she continued, "I am very sure that father will keep him here, for the affairs go but poorly, now that he is gone."

"That will be good !" replied Molly; "I shall count the days until he comes, for it seems a long, long time since I last saw him. This house is like a prison without him."

"Better still," whispered Mary, looking cautiously around her, as had now become her habit when she wished to speak anything which might not agree with the feelings of others,

"I hear that Hazor Wilkhurst has gone to live so far from here, he cannot often be a visitor among us. While you were sick," she continued, in answer to Molly's look of curiosity, " he beset father to get him an office under the crown. Through his influence with great men, whom he knows, Hazor has got a situation."

Molly was arrested in her exclamations of joy at this intelligence, by the sound of a horseman approaching rapidly up the yard. She turned and looking steadily for an instant, drew back with a face as pale as snow. One more look she ventured as the rider came up, then exclaimed with a hasty breath :

"It is Mr. Rushton ! He has come at last !"

Her next impulse was to run away; but she had been seen, and she heard her name pronounced in the old, kindly voice, which sent a joyous thrill through every avenue of her heart.

"Can this be you, Molly ?" he said, as he jumped to the ground, and came up with outstretched hand. " Had I seen you anywhere else, I think, I should not have known you. Wonderful ! how thin and tall you have grown ?"

Tears of gladness sprung to Molly's eyes, but she could not speak.

"I know what you would say," continued Mr. Rushton, offering a hand to each of the girls : " Tell us what has made you false to your promise which you left with us— years ago ?"

"A good reason—I assure you, which you shall hear by and by."

"We are so glad to see you, sir," said Mary, "that we forget our old disappointment."

"And all our griefs," added Molly, trying hard to keep back the tears.

"Griefs," repeated Mr. Rushton, with a serious look, "I hope these years have brought you no great sorrows. You are all alive and well, whom I last left here?"

At this juncture, Mrs. Dyke made her appearance before the group. She stopped with a chilling stare of surprise, on finding the girls conversing in so much familiarity with a stranger. Mr. Rushton met her look indifferently, and was about proceeding with his question, when he saw that both Mary and Molly were confused, and he heard the former say, with a strong effort at control :

"Our dear mother is dead."

"Is it possible !" returned Mr. Rushton ; "alas ! you have my heartfelt sympathy. Although I saw her only once, I know she was a most estimable lady."

Mary now stammered a presentation of Mrs. Dyke to Mr. Rushton.

"Mr. Rushton—Rushton," repeated Mrs. Dyke, in her hard, coarse manner, "a relative of any one here ?"

"No ma'am," answered Mary, "but he is a friend."

Mrs. Dyke now looked more stony than ever. She had no liking for "a friend" who had been welcomed in that family before her coming ; and she wished to frown him away, that no extra pains or expense might be involved in his reception.

"Finish your work, girls, at once, and not be idling there all the forenoon," she said, with a will to exhibit that she was not afraid to be mistress, even in the presence of one whom the girls received with so much deference

A glance of sorrow each cast upon Mr. Rushton, then obeyed without demur.

"Where is your father? He is well, I trust?" asked Mr. Rushton, of Mary.

"Yes, sir. He is out somewhere on the place, to-day, I believe."

"Then I will fasten my horse, and find him," said Mr. Rushton, evidently desirous to escape the presence of Mrs. Dyke as soon as possible.

"You are going to stay with us a-while?" asked Molly, anxiously, as he returned from his horse.

"Never mind ; you will see me again," said Mr. Rushton, with a smile of meaning. Taking one of the yellow blossoms from her basket, he twirled it thoughtfully in his fingers, while he went off in the direction which Mary indicated.

"Oh, dear !" exclaimed Molly, when left once more alone with Mary, " I am so glad and so frightened-like at seeing Mr. Rushton again, I feel just as though I must die."

"You don't know anything about that feeling," said Mary. " Come let us spring with all our might and do the best we can to get things trim by the time he comes back."

But here, again, they encountered their usual obstacle ; for no sooner did Mrs. Dyke discover their anxiety to make suitable preparations for the entertainment of their visitor, than she firmly declared that nothing should be changed from the ordinary course, and would not even permit Mary to bring out the best service for dinner, which her mother had always used on such occasions.

"Never mind," said Molly, "we will put on our best faces and let trouble go to the winds for once. Mr. Rushton will know what it all means, for he has been here before."

When the hour for dinner came, the Colonel appeared without Mr. Rushton, saying that he had gone to dine at the Bald Eagle, notwithstanding all his endeavors to persuade him to come to the house ; but that he would come back in the afternoon.

"His keen eye discovered how unwelcome he was to the mistress of this house," whispered Molly.

After this, the time lagged so heavily to Molly, it seemed that he never would return. Before the small looking-glass which hung in her chamber, she smoothed her hair till it was as lustrous as a fold of black satin ; and, beside the heavy mass knotted upon the crown of her head, she fixed a pendant sprig of sweetbrier, with a blossom of white and pink clover. In her simple adorning, no lady of a royal suite ever looked lovelier, even in pearls and diamonds. Molly had, indeed, become very beautiful since her illness. Her complexion was like snow, just kissed by the morning light, her cheeks were fresh and pretty as as the first red rose of summer, and nothing could vie with the witchery, or the kindling fervor of her eyes, which were

> "Quick, restless, strange, but exquisite withal,
> Like those of angels."

She was yet, however, but a bud with its folded beauty just disclosed.

At last, Mr. Rushton appeared again, and pausing only to ask Molly a few important questions, requested an interview with the Colonel. A long time did this " private interview " seem to continue to the girls, who sat by themselves sewing upon their allotted tasks, while they exchanged various conjectures as to what its business might be. Their suspense was finally relieved by the coming of Mrs. Dyke, who, in miraculous good humor, bade Molly go into the parlor and see what was wanted.

" Go with me, Mary," whispered Molly, turning very pale.

Mary obeyed with a strange foreboding in her heart, which she had secretly felt since the arrival of Mr. Rushton.

" Come here, Molly," said Mr. Rushton, motioning her to a chair beside his own, " we sent for you to talk about a new home and a new father for you."

Molly went and sat by him, while she lifted her eyes to his with a look of intense interest.

" Since that unhappy morning when I discovered that you were the instrument of saving my life, I have been desirous of repaying you. I have no daughter, only one son, and my wife has long since been dead. My other relatives are all in a distant land, and as I grow old, I shall be lonely. So I have come for you to take you to my home and educate you as my own child."

"If you wish to educate me, I don't want to go," said Molly, in one of her singular humors, which prompted her to say things quite unlike what could be expected.

"Ah ! well, I am not particular about the books," said Mr. Rushton, smiling, although he had been very serious a moment before.

"I have been taught," continued Molly, looking mischievously in the direction of Mrs. Dyke, "that whatever belongs to educating is sheer nonsense. So I shall beg you to let me stay here."

"Don't 'talk in that way," said Mrs. Dyke, impatiently, while she quickened the click of her knitting needles, "your wishes are of no sort of consequence in such a matter as this. Indeed you should not have been consulted at all, if I had carried my point."

"I should have come for you long before this," Mr. Rushton resumed, noting the flush on Molly's cheek and the fire lighting her eye ; "but I had no sooner arrived home in New York than I was summoned to England, my native land, on business of importance. Before embarking, I directed one of my clerks to write to Col. Epps a letter of explanation, but as no such letter was received, I infer that my order was forgotten. I returned a few months since, and as soon as possible started to seek you out."

Molly heard a heavy sigh; she looked up, and saw that Mary was struggling to suppress her strong agitation.

"I shall do well by you, Molly," continued Mr. Rushton; "you will have nice rooms of your own, and fine clothes to wear, with nothing to do but study or play, whichever you choose."

"I am grateful to you," said Molly, keeping her eyes upon Mary; "but this place seems so much like home, and then it would be so hard to leave dear Mary and Reu "——

"Don't be silly," interrupted Mrs. Dyke.

"You will go, dear Molly, for all us," now spoke Mary, in tremulous tones; "for just think what a benefit it will be to you !"

"Then you will be glad to get rid of me ?" said Molly, pouting her lips.

"Oh, no indeed, darling," replied Mary, bursting into tears, despite all her efforts.

"You had better go with Mr. Rushton, certainly, for he has the means of doing by you, very different from what I have," remarked the Colonel.

"Since you all wish me to go, I suppose I must; but it is very hard," faltered Molly.

"Hard !" repeated Mrs. Dyke, derisively; "everything is hard to you. It's hard to work, hard to eat what we have here, hard to mind what you are ordered to do, and now it's hard to go away, is it ?"

"It will not be hard to leave you," retorted Molly, the thought of her new freedom dawning upon her spirit.

"Leave this room," said Mrs. Dyke, reddening high with vexation; "I rejoice that I shall soon see the last of you."

"You will be ready, Molly, so as to set out with me early to-morrow morning," said Mr. Rushton, as he rose to go out.

"Yes, sir," she replied, with animation.

No sooner was Molly alone in her chamber with Mary, than she gave out and fell to grieving not less than Mary.

"Now, I know that I shall not see Reuben more," she sobbed; "what will he say when he comes and finds that I am gone?"

"He will feel very sorry not to see you, but he will be glad you are where you are better off," said Mary.

"Then, dear Mary," continued Molly, "who will comfort you when I am gone, and who will help you in this round of work?"

With an expression of almost hopeless agony, Mary looked upward from the window to the sky, as if thus expressing what hope remained to her of consolation.

"Alas!" she cried, covering her face and groaning heavily in the desolation of her spirit, "first, my blessed mother was taken, then Reuben, and now you must go!"

"I will not go!" exclaimed Molly, passionately, while she threw her arms about Mary's neck; "I will stay with you, and they cannot force me away."

"Oh, no!" said Mary, after a silence, "it is best that you should not remain here; every month will make your lot harder to bear, while in your new home you will grow happier day after day."

"I am not so selfish," said Molly, "as to wish to enjoy life, while those I love are miserable."

"I shall not be unhappy," observed Mary, "especially if Reuben remains at home. You must learn to write as soon as you can, and then I shall live in hope of getting letters from you. How pleasant it will be."

Mary now began to assist Molly in her preparations to leave, lest a gloomier thought thould come, and leave them both too sad and undecided to make any progress in what must be done.

That night the two girls sat up late, and talked together by the light of the moon, picturing brightly-tinted fancies for the future, as young hearts will, before they have learned that there is nothing truly beautiful or enduring but Heaven. Very sadly Molly fell asleep, while Mary kept vigils beside her with a heavy heart. In the morning, Molly arose long before the dawn, so as to gain time to take a parting look at the old cherished places about the home she was to leave.

When Mr. Rushton came again, and the hour of parting was announced, poor Molly was quite overcome. Embracing Mary again and again, she whispered her not to forget to bid good bye to Reuben for her, and tell him how bad she felt that she could not see him again. The Colonel offered her his hand in silence, which Molly took reverently and said :

"Ever since I first came here, you have been good to me, sir. I hope that you will get your reward."

"Don't talk about that, child," said he, passing his hand

across his eyes, " be a good girl hereafter, and I shall be satisfied."

" What a fuss !" said Mrs. Dyke, half aloud, not approving of so much attention being given to Molly. She went out, and standing near Mr. Rushton, said :

" Now, I know more about this girl than you do, and I warn you to begin as you mean to hold out; if you don't you will rue this day."

" No, no," said Molly, who had heard her words; " it will not be so much *rue* as *wormwood* to him."

" Whatever bitter herb I find it," said Mr. Rushton, shaking his head at her, " I shall certainly es*chew* it."

The Colonel now lifted Molly upon the pillion behind Mr. Rushton.

" Mary, darling !" she said, " remember and tell Reuben to write me a good long letter, just as soon as he comes home."

Mary could say nothing more, for her grief. The horse now began to move off; Mr. Rushton bowed to the Colonel, and Molly looked back and smiled upon Mary, while the tears fell fast.

" Good bye, all of you; good bye, dear Mary," she exclaimed; then casting one more look over the scenes she had left, she turned and covered her face with her hand.

CHAPTER IX.

TO ARMS !

We pass over the tedious details of a long journey in the times of which we write, and introduce the reader to the home of Mr. Rushton.   It was a large, handsome residence, in the English style of country seats, superior to most of the homes even of the wealthier classes, and situated on the Hudson river.   After the emigration of Mr. Rushton to America, until the death of his wife, his home had been in the metropolis of New York.   Upon that event, he had resigned a portion of his business to a junior partner, and sought retirement in this wild and secluded spot, which he had adorned and designed for continued improvements from the models of his finely cultivated taste.   The adjacent forests he had transformed into parks, through which he had opened winding drives and avenues.   In the midst of this leafy solitude, upon a commanding eminence, stood the mansion, built of stone, with various wings and porticoes, which were thickly laced with woodbine and running roses. From this spot was an extensive and delightful prospect of the surrounding country, embracing hoary mountains, with their shagged forests, the beautiful cascades of the Catskill, jagged precipices overhanging dark ravines in gloomy grandeur, the winding river, with its wooded islands and occasional white sails, and nearer, the smoke ascending from the low houses of a sparse settlement, with a few other seats of neighboring gentlemen along the river.

"There is Rushton Hall," said Mr. Rushton, as they neared their destination, at the hour of sunset, on their way from the city. "God be praised that I live to see those blessed walls once more."

Molly held her breath with admiration. It was to her a picture of olden dreams of Paradise.

"Do you think you will live contented here ?" asked Mr. Rushton, "if you are taken occasionally to New York with me ?"

"It all looks very beautiful," said Molly; but she thought of Mary and Reuben, and she did not venture to promise contentment without their society.

As they halted before the door, a tall youth came out to welcome Mr. Rushton, followed by several servants, who manifested various signs of joy at the return of their master. One of them was about to assist Molly to alight, when the young man, whom Mr. Rushton had introduced as " my son, Hollis," assumed to perform the office himself, offering to take her in his arms. But with her usual temerity, she darted aside and touched the ground like a bird, refusing any assistance.

" I think you will have courage to mount my Black Princess, one of these days," said the youth, with a look of admiration. But he blushed with real diffidence as he met the keen, merry glance of her eye.

Molly tossed her head carelessly and entered the hall. But here, unmindful of those who were waiting to receive her, she paused on tiptoe, with lips parted in surprise, and her eyes opened wide with curiosity. On one side of the lofty, oaken-panelled wall, were groups of sculpture, which, being wholly a novelty to her unpractised eye, impressed her with astonishment and awe. On the opposite side, in niches of the wall and upon marble shelves, were ranged collections of minerals, fossils, and other curious relics, for which the son of Mr. Rushton had an insatiable passion. There were also, at various angles, stuffed animals, inhabitants of the sea, and grim skeletons of mammoth proportions, so that the whole apartment seemed little less endowed than a museum.

Molly would have gazed on in total forgetfulness of all but the wonders about her, had she not been aroused by a sweet voice, which was so nearly like that of the dead Mrs. Epps, she was half overcome with fear, dimly associated with the spectral objects about her. She turned and saw a young lady, apparently a few years her senior, with a pale, interesting face, and large, melancholy eyes, which were in harmony with the mournful music of her voice.

" I am glad you are here to welcome us," Mr. Rushton said, taking her hand and motioning Molly to his side; " you will assist in making this new child of mine learn to love her home."

The young lady answered pleasantly, and smiled upon Molly as she advanced.

"This young lady we call Miss Jane, in honor of her distinction in society, as the daughter of a late most estimable man," continued Mr. Rushton to Molly; "she is at present residing with her brother, who is our nearest neighbor, and she will be in here often to see you, I presume, if you get to liking each other."

"Nothing could give me more pleasure," replied Miss Jane, taking Molly's hand in both her own, "if I can in any way add to your happiness."

"David would not approve of your saying that," commented Mr. Rushton, in a lower tone; "you must make some reservation in his favor."

Miss Jane now dropped her long eye-lashes till they fringed the delicate blushes of her cheeks, and murmuring a word of expostulation, led Molly into the adjoining room.

"He is well, I hope to hear, after my long absence?" continued Mr. Rushton, following closely.

"Quite so, I believe," replied Miss Jane, betraying her effort to appear unconcerned.

"You don't know, certainly, then!" said Mr. Rushton, laughing, as he caught her eye. "Affairs go on prosperously at the school-room?" he continued.

"Very," answered Miss Jane.

"Yes, sir," said Hollis, who had entered in time to hear his father's last question, "since Miss Jane came back from home, Mr. Brown has been unusually good-humored. He recommends me to begin to study the French treatise on Geology, which I found among your books."

"That is all you have really studied since I have been gone, I dare say," remarked Mr. Rushton, smiling upon his son, affectionately.

"No sir ; I have been in the inside of a whale, to find how many bones they have, for a long time."

"As long as three days and three nights?" asked Molly, with an arch look.

Hollis ventured an answering glance of curiosity, and perceiving that a laugh was circulating at his expense, went out, for he was no match for anybody in word tilting.

Molly was next welcomed by the housekeeper, an elderly woman, who wore pockets on the outside of her dress, which were made of patchwork and were used for storage of a great variety of domestic stuff. From her apron belt was suspended a pair of scissors by a steel chain, and a pincushion was affixed to the centre of her rotund bust. Her pleasant matronly face and manner won Molly's heart at once. Mrs. Rogers, for such was her name, had been sewing in company with Miss Jane, but now arose and received Mr. Rushton's orders for tea, and his request that a messenger might be dispatched for Mr. David Jones, which sent the blushes anew to the cheeks of one of his listeners. At the request of Mr. Rushton, Miss Jane conducted Molly to the rooms which had been prepared and assigned for her especial use. In her sleeping chamber, the south windows opened to a fine view of a garden sloping toward the bluff which bounded the river. They were richly curtained with green damask, as was also the bed, with the addition of lace draperies. Upon the centre of the floor was a small carpet of sombre color, in the draught board pattern. Two or three high, cumbrous chairs, with cushions of wrought leather, and a toilet service which Mr. Rushton had purchased abroad, completed the furniture. About the fire-place were white and red tiles, descriptive of impressive scenes in sacred history, and upon the hearth was a large jar filled with boughs of pine and cedar, the tops of which aspired quite out of sight up the chimney. From this chamber, a narrow door communicated into an apartment, which Miss Jane informed Molly was to be her library and general study room ; the only evidence of which design was a book-case containing a few books. Upon the table, Hollis had previously placed an offering which he had regarded the most acceptable—a fossil frog, lacking only one leg, and the stuffed skins of a weasel and a snake, which were so nearly like life, Molly drew back with fear, until reassured by Miss Jane. She was much better pleased with a few casts which she found ranged about the room ; and when Miss Jane called her attention to a harpsichord, the gift of Mr. Rushton, by playing a prelude to a song, her delight knew no bounds.

"That thing," she exclaimed, rapturously, "is worth more than all I have seen yet since I left Epps Hundred—without I except these noble woods about here."

" If you would like to learn to play on this," said Miss Jane, admiring her enthusiasm, "I will gladly teach you what I know—at least while I remain near you.

" It would be beautiful! glorious!" continued Molly, as she attempted a few sounds, then added, musingly :   " I wonder what Reuben and Mary would say to hear this harpsichord !"

That evening, Molly felt quite at home amid the pleasant group which were reunited in Mr. Rushton's parlor. Mr. David Jones, who had come in to tea, remained to talk with Mr. Rushton upon the contemplated war of the colonies with Great Britian.   Though a native of the mother country, Mr. Rushton was a staunch republican and warmly advocated the independent measures, which seemed rapidly culminating towards adoption. But Mr. Jones betrayed his sympathies with the royalists and averred that in the event of war being declared against the only proper government of the country, he should go immediately to Canada and enter Burgoyne's army.

Miss Jane turned pale, as she listened with intense interest, which Mr. Rushton observing, he remarked, with a smile, to Jones :

" You would not leave your sweetheart, certainly, to take arms against your country ! I had thought better of you than that."

" She will say to me like the lovely Ruth of old—' wherever thou goest, I will go, thy people shall be my people, " answered Mr. Jones, looking upon Miss Jane with inexpressible fondness.

"I hope that she will not call her people the oppressors of her land, even if they are yours," said Mr. Rushton, looking upon Miss Jane inquiringly.

There was no look of disapproval in her sad eyes, only of trust and affection, as she replied :

"I trust that David will not form any resolutions for a future course of action, without careful deliberation."

"Who is this Mr. David Jones?" inquired Molly of Hollis, in a low tone, "he should be as good as a prophet to love Miss Jane, who seems to me like an angel."

"He is a teacher, at present," answered Hollis, very much embarrassed at being obliged to speak to Molly.

"Then I don't like him," said Molly.

"Why not?" inquired Hollis, venturing to look towards her.

"Because I have known enough of one worshipful teacher, whose name is Hazor Wilkhurst."

"You will like Mr. Jones," observed Hollis, still tremulous in voice, "he is always pleasant in the schoolroom."

"How can he teach, if he is pleasant?"

"He has consented to instruct a few of us about here, in a room of Miss Jane's brother's house, because we have no other school."

"What makes Miss Jane look so sad?" inquired Molly. "Is it because she has to go to school?"

"No," answered Hollis, with a smile, "she has looked so since I first knew her. But her father, who was a minister in New Jersey, died last year, which makes her sadder even than ever. We have a house and farm in the neighborhood where they lived, and I have been there occasionally, for many years ; she is always good and lovely, but inclined to melancholy."

"How can she be melancholy and in love ?" asked Molly, "I should think she would be merry, especially when. Mr. Jones was near."

Hollis did not reply. These familiar words sent the blood tingling to his hair and then to his fingers' tips. He could not have opened his lips, if the house had been on fire, for that moment.

"She has a shadow over her face which bodes no good fortune," continued Molly, with a mysterious air ; "old Goody Wythe would say she is born for black luck."

"What woman may that be ?" stammered Hollis.

"A fortuneteller, who lives not far from Epps Hundred."

"I had my fortune told once," said Hollis, "but I don't believe anything in it."

"Tell me all about it," said Molly, drawing nearer to him, with a lively interest.

Hollis shook his head, and fastened his eyes upon a stuffed sturgeon, which lay in one corner of the room, as though he could not dare to trust them away at freedom.

"Oh! I don't like you," said Molly; "Reuben Epps would always tell me whatever I wanted to know. Neither do I like all these horrid animals which you have stuck up so thick around here ;" she continued, watching the direction of his eyes, " they will stalk through my dreams."

" You can't help liking them, if you once become interested as I am," answered Hollis, with an animation, which he had not shown before. He then went for some of his boxes, to display his choicest specimens of fish, insects, and other things which he seemed to regard with a passionate reverence, fairly cringing when Molly took them carelessly and made mirth over their peculiarities..

" If you haven't got a spider !" she exclaimed, at length, "horrid creature ! I confess I am less indifferent to a real live snake, only one of the sort which has rattles."

" Nonsense !" remarked Hollis, glad to feel his superiority in a single point.

" Nonsense, indeed !" repeated Molly, " the first large spider I find I will make you take in your hand. See then, if you will be so easy."

" Certainly ;" said Hollis, " I will kill all the spiders for you with pleasure. There are a plenty about this house."

Molly soon became domesticated in her new home, and for a few days was fully engrossed in making discoveries over Rushton Hall and about the premises with Miss Jane and Hollis, who ventured to accompany them, though for the most part in silence. One morning, when the novelty had somewhat worn off, Miss Jane persuaded Molly to enter the school-room with her. The first day she sat a spectator, but on her return home she solicited Mr. Rushton to permit her to become one of Mr. Brown's pupils.

"So, then, you think you will conclude to take kindly to books, Molly ?" he said.

" Not that," answered Molly, " but I wish very much to learn to write."

" What for ?   That when I go from home, you can send me word how you do ?"

" I had not thought of that," said Molly ; " but I want to be able to write letters to my friends at Epps Hundred."

"They will not care to hear from you," said Mr. Rushton, jocosely.

" O ! yes," said Molly feeling saddened, " Mary and Reuben were going to write a long letter to me just as soon as Reuben found out that I was gone.   How shall I get any letters, sir ?"

" The post comes to the next settlement, once every week," answered Mr. Rushton, " but I don't believe they will write to you, Molly."

" As surely as yonder sun shines in the sky, they will," said Molly, " and I shall watch the post every week, till the letter comes."

" In sober earnest, I do not doubt it myself ; I only wished to know how you felt about your old friends," said Mr. Rushton, soothingly, as he saw the tears gathering in her eyes.

"Is it too far for me to walk to the post-office ?" asked Molly.

· " Yes, it is four miles, but I will send one of my servants, as I usually do."

"If you are quite willing," rejoined Molly, with hesitation, "I will go myself. I should not mind walking that distance."

"What a prodigy for an American girl!" exclaimed Mr. Rushton, "to talk of walking all those miles and back, merely to see if there is a letter for you! Had you been reared in England I should not have wondered. Alice—poor child! used often to walk farther than that for the sake of meeting a friend or getting a letter."

Mr. Rushton ended these words with a deep sigh, and a shadow of pain crossed his noble face.

"I very much prefer to go myself," urged Molly.

"Why?"

"Because if there should be a letter, I could read it at once. And then, if any one else should get it, it might possibly be lost, which would almost break my heart."

"If you feel so much anxiety," concluded Mr. Rushton, "you shall have one of my horses. Hollis rides that way frequently after minerals, which he is collecting, and he will go with you."

Molly expressed her gratitude for this compliance, less by words than by her expressive eyes, for her heart was full when she thought of soon receiving a letter into her own hand which had been penned by the dear friends whom she had left, as it seemed to her so far away.

When the day came for the arrival of the post which Molly had awaited with secret impatience, Hollis brought up to the door the Black Princess, a fine young horse which he had late broken to the rein, and Lucifer, the noble grey which Molly had first seen with Mr. Rushton. Announcing the animals, Hollis offered Molly her choice to ride. She declared her preference for the Black Princess at once, for the fiery turn of the horse, with its beauty set off by a rich caparison of scarlet, pleased her fancy. But Mr. Rushton appearing at this juncture, objected to such an arrangement upon the score of its being decidedly unsafe.

"I am used to horses," answered Molly, confidently, "and they soon know that I love, not fear them."

Upon the flowing mane and the face of the horse, she passed her hand caressingly, speaking softly in her own witching tones ; then dropping the rein and going forward, she called the animal after her with a perfect carelessness of danger. Mr. Rushton was about to remonstrate in alarm for her safety, when to the surprise of all, the Princess lowered her head and followed Molly about the yard, submissively.

"Bravely done !" cried Hollis, forgetting his usual embarrassment in his admiration ; "you will pass muster now, for Princess has not a drop of sheep's blood in her veins, but is as unmanageable as a tigress, on occasion."

Mr. Rushton offered no farther objections, only adding another caution to be careful, as she sprang to the saddle with a single effort and rode off in high spirit.

"How much she reminds me of Alice !" exclaimed Mr. Rushton, as he gazed after them and saw Molly's erect, lithe figure, with the long plumes of her beaver hat waving in the breeze, and heard her gay laugh echoing far out into

the surrounding forest.   " She, too, was beautiful, and made
all things love her by a strong indescribable charm.   Alas'l
God grant that Molly may be spared her fate !" he concluded, as he turned sorrowfully into the house.

An hour or two later, Mr. Rushton saw them returning,
and went out to meet them.

" What luck ?" he inquired, " Did Princess go steadily ?"

Hollis answered in the affirmative, for Molly seemed too
sad for words.

" Not bad news, I hope ?" continued Mr. Rushton.

" There was no letter," faltered Molly.

" Oh, well, no news is good news, always.   It is hardly
time yet for you to hear, so my dear child, you must exercise
patience," said Mr. Rushton.

" I shall have to wait another whole week !" exclaimed
Molly, forcing down a rising grief, that struggled hard for
expression.

" I have been so situated, that I could not hear from
friends for a year," said Mr. Rushton.

" But that does not help 'me," said Molly. " If I should lose
my forefinger, it would not supply it, if you had lost your
whole arm."

" Or, if you had lost your heart, it would not mend the matter, if I should lose my life," observed Hollis, with a laugh.

These words, unimportant as they were, and scarcely noted
by Molly then, were recalled, years afterward, with a startling signification !

As Hollis emptied his pockets of the new mineralogical

specimens which he had collected, he said, with a sly look at Molly :

" What a valuable addition to my cabinet ! I regret that one should give so much heart to an event so trifling, as the failure to receive a letter."

" How foolish to set such a value to a parcel of rough, common stones and all sorts of rubbish, no better !" retorted Molly ; " I am certain that I am a vast deal more sensible, am I not ?" she appealed to Mr. Rushton.

" Both of you, my children, are sensible in your own way, but neither is sufficiently so. . If you were, you would cheerfully concede to each other the freedom of action and feeling which is your right. However, you are only an epitome of the world, to which you belong," replied Mr. Rushton.

Molly scarcely understood these words, but was too much out of humor to ask more questions.

After this, Molly interested herself actively learning to write, and began to take lessons of Miss Jane upon the harpsichord, in which she made rapid and brilliant progress. Although becoming daily more engaged in her new pursuits and friends, she did not forget the return of the day which brought the arrival of the post. Her visit to the post-office was repeated as before, but again she returned dispirited, without a letter. When she had progressed sufficiently to be able to write a letter, she wrote to Mary and Reuben a long account of her present life, often interspersing doleful complaints of their silence. Again and again she wrote, but her efforts were all and equally unavailing.   No letter from the loved ones came !

Then, Mr. Rushton wrote to Col. Epps, and after waiting till the weeks numbered months, bringing no response to poor Molly's yearning heart, he was forced to abandon every hope of hearing from Epps Hundred.   Amid so many warm-hearted friends, and, more than all, in the daily and intimate companionship of Miss Jane, who shed about her love and sweetness, like light, Molly could not be unhappy.   She was of a temperament too active to fall back upon herself a prey to melancholy regrets and hope deferred, but gradually launched her full, passionate interest in her various pursuits, and, more than all, in the spirit stirring, all absorbing topic of the time, which she heard discussed by Mr. Rushton and his guests, with the vigor of brave hearts, kindling to bold heroic deeds.

One afternoon, when Mr. Rushton was away on one of his visits to New York, and Hollis had gone out on a hunting fossil expedition, she sat alone in her room and watched the westering sunbeams, with thoughts of Reuben and Mary, till the warm tears fell fast.

"If I could only know that they were not dead, it would be such a consolation !" she exclaimed.

At this moment, she heard a strain of melody awake upon the harpsichord which stood in the next room, so sweet, low, and spiritually beautiful, she started in affright, half believ-ing that it could not thus be moved by mortal fingers.   It soon died away to silence, and a light step approached her side.   She turned quickly and saw Miss Jane, with a sadder face than usual ; but seeing Molly's tears, she inquired in a cheerful voice what caused her grief.

"I was thinking of the friends at Epps Hundred," said Molly, "and fearing that death was the reason of their silence to me.   When I was aroused by the harpsichord, I thought, for a moment, it was a mysterious warning from the other world."

"Forgive me if I startled you," said Miss Jane, "but I wished thus to inform you that I was coming, for Mrs. Rogers told me that I should find you in your room."

"I am so glad that you have come !" exclaimed Molly, offering her a seat by her side, "for I am very, very sad to-day ; quite unlike my usual self."

"I shall be but a poor comforter, I fear," remarked Miss Jane, looking anxious and distressed.

"What is it ?   Tell me, dear friend, has anything happened ?" now inquired Molly, in alarm at discovering a marked change in one habitually so serene.

"Mr. Rushton has just returned from New York, and is now at my brother's.   I ran over only a few minutes in advance."

"So soon ! we did not expect him till to-morrow, at the earliest," replied Molly.

"He is the bearer of important news, and therefore lost no time," continued Miss Jane, turning paler and trembling, despite her efforts to preserve self-control.

"What news ?" demanded Molly, breathlessly.

" Our country has openly declared war against the English."

" I am glad !" now exclaimed Molly, with keen enthusiasm,
for she had so closely listened to Mr. Rushton's expression of
republican sentiments, as to fully catch their spirit ; " I am
glad with all my soul, for they have no right to oppress us
with taxes and stamp acts, and "——

" Hush !" interrupted Miss Jane, " such words make you
a rebel, Molly."

" I care not. I am a rebel, then. I would go out and
fight to-morrow, if I could do anything for my country.
How can you, who are so good, feel so coolly in such a
glorious cause ?"

" Have you thought," answered Miss Jane, " that this war
will make Mr. Rushton join the army ; our school will be
broken up ; Mr. Brown will go away, and we shall be left
almost desolate ?"

Miss Jane clasped her hands tightly, and the tears trembled upon her cheeks.

" We must not think of anything, care for anything, but
to gain our freedom," said Molly ; " when the war is over
and our independence declared, then how gloriously happy
we shall all be again ! That is," she added, after a pause,
" if none whom we love, prove to be among the slain."

" I have a dreadful presentiment of impending calamity !"
said Miss Jane, with an icy shudder.

" I have a glorious presentiment that we Americans will
yet be free," responded Molly. Then throwing her arms

about Miss Jane's neck, she continued in a winning tone :
" Do try and persuade your dear David to take up on the
right side.   It is so strange that he can't see as we all
do !"

Miss Jane bowed her head to hide her emotion ; her hair,
which was long and abundant, fell from its confinement and
rested over her fair shoulders like a veil.   Molly took one of
the tresses and twined it on her fingers till she had formed a
perfect ringlet.

" What beautiful hair !" she exclaimed, involuntarily.

" These words remind me of a fearful dream, I had last
night," observed Miss Jane, in low, anxious tones ; " I
thought I saw my hair weaving in the loom, into a shroud,
black as night !   After it was finished, I was about to put
it on, when I felt a heavy weight fall upon my heart, and
with a cry of anguish, I awoke."

" That was only the nightmare," answered Molly ;   " but
there comes Mr. Rushton, he will expect me to welcome him.
Let us go with cheerful faces."

Molly ran down with breathless interest, but Miss Jane
went out sorrowfully, and chose to return by a retired way
which led from Rushton Hall to her brother's house.   The
sun was setting at this hour, and, between the interstices of
the trees, she could see the river, which looked like a sea of
blood.   She started and paused, for the picture was the
expression of her reflections.

" Beautiful, is it not, dear ?" said a voice, near where she
stood.

She turned, and saw Mrs. Rogers approaching among the trees, with a basket of roots in her hand, which she had been gathering in the wood.

"I will go through the park and come out nearer the water," said Miss Jane, "for it is pleasant to walk at this hour. If I am inquired for, you will know where I am—down by the moss-bank."

"Mr. David has gone to the valley-settlement to-day, so you will not be disturbed, I dare say," answered Mrs. Rogers, with a smile, as she passed on.

Miss Jane pursued her way, thoughtfully, till she reached the bank, where she sat down, and with awe contemplated the grand and gorgeous picture before her.

"The river is but an emblem of what our own fair land will soon become!" she exclaimed.

"Bathed in blood? O, if the blood of one of the dear ones around me must flow to mingle with the mighty death-current—if *he* who is dearer than all should be slain, how wretched! how desolate!"

At this moment, a sound of martial music broke upon her ear—so spirit-thrilling, so clear, and yet so preternaturally modulated, as if springing from no definite location, she started in pure affright. To all directions she threw a hurried glance, but nothing unusual was visible. Still the music went on, making the blood leap wildly in her veins, as such strains ever quicken the soul :—

"A flourish proud,
Where mingled trump and clarion loud,

> And fife, and kettle-drum,
> And war-pipe with exultant cry,
> Making wild music, bold and high,
> Did on the breezes come!"

Soon the sounds gathered more distinctness, and following their direction, she looked upward and afar _over the river. In an instant her glance was fixed to the sky, for there, on a dark and boding cloud, was painted a picture of men in the array of war, moving onward in solid column to meet the invisible foe. Ever and anon, they brandished their glittering swords aloft, in time with their footsteps, and thus they left on the cloud a fissure, which sent forth white lightning flashes and scintillations of blood! It was directly over the water, flooded with the red light of the dying day.

Involuntarily she knelt to the ground, and gazed in breathless terror, till the picture grew fainter and gradually disappeared, leaving the sky as before. Then she covered her eyes and wept, with a solemn prescience in her heart. Thus she remained until she was aroused by the sound of an approaching tread and a familiar voice spoke her name. She raised her head quickly.

"Oh, David!" she exclaimed, "have you been looking at that fearful scene? Did you hear the music?"

"What sight! what music, dear Jane?" said the young man, throwing himself by her side.

"The army in the sky. There it was, just over the river," said she, pointing with tremulous earnestness.

Perceiving that he smiled incredulously, she continued, in excited tones :

" As sure as I believe that there is a God in Heaven, I saw men marching on the clouds. They were soldiers, for I heard their martial music and saw them flourish their arms."

" You have been dreaming, dearest."

" No ; I was just as awake as at this moment. But a short time since, I left Rushton Hall and came here, thinking the while of the war that has begun in our land."

" If you have really seen anything like what you believe, Jane, it was doubtless a reflection of a detachment of soldiers somewhere in the vicinity," said her lover.

" The music ! There was nothing from which it might come, to be seen anywhere."

" Nevertheless, it must have proceeded from the same source. You are getting superstitious, my love."

" The comet which has appeared of late, is another evil omen," pursued Miss Jane.

" You think, then, it is really shaking from its horrid hair pestilence and war ?"

" Before, and in time of war, I've always heard that there are signs and wonders in the land," she said, solemnly.

" No other wonders than what may be accounted for. I heard persons at the valley-settlement, to-day telling of seeing a cannon going alone over a bridge near which they were trouting, and, after watching it a moment, they said it went off into the water, discharging a sound like thunder."

"How can you explain that?"

"Probably their empty bottles in their pockets were the best solution of the mysterious phenomenon. But, dear Jane," he continued, drawing her nearer to himself, "I came to talk over matters of more importance than these."

"Oh, David! what will you do, now that this war is coming on? Since I heard the dreadful news, I have been distressed to think what might happen."

"My resolution is deliberately taken. I shall go from here and enlist under Burgoyne without delay, for I will have no part nor lot in a rebellion."

"You will not join the enemy, dear David? you cannot fight against the country which gave you birth!" said Miss Jane in a voice of sorrowful emphasis.

"I will be loyal and true, to the only lawful sovereign over my country. Have you no confidence in me, dearest? Do you think I am governed by unworthy motives?"

"No; Heaven forbid! but it will break my heart to have you go where I cannot see you, nor hear from you," answered Miss Jane, with many tears.

"I must leave you for awhile, but I shall return with glory, for the right will sooner or later win the victory. But I will not wait for the issue; I will send for you to join me at Canada, when the most favorable opportunity presents. Will you go?"

She hesitatetd and looked upon her lover with a silent entreaty, which he could scarcely resist. The tears came also to his eyes, as he continued:

"Think that I shall be far removed from all I love. There will be no sweet voice to sustain and soothe me in the hour of trial ; and, should I perchance be mortally wounded, who would come to me—hear my last words, hold my head, and finally, see that I was decently buried ?"

"Talk not thus David," cried Miss Jane, sobbing convulsively; "such word will kill me. I only hesitated, because I thought of my brother and his family. Since the death of our parents we have been much to each other. It was painful to think of leaving other friends—dear Molly, for instance, who has become to me like a sister, with her wild, impulsive sweetness. It is no light thing, either, to leave the land of my birth, especially in such a season of peril."

"You shall be free to decide, dearest. Choose between me and all other considerations, for I must leave you now."

"Now ! Oh, David, you cannot mean that you are going to leave me directly ?"

"Yes ; no time must be lost. The crisis has come, though suddenly."

"What shall I do ?" exclaimed Miss Jane, in a tone of anguish.

"Trust in Heaven, and wait in this settlement till I can send for you. Will you agree to this ?"

For a moment they sat in silence—her head, with its long, beautiful hair, still unconfined, resting against his breast—his arm about her slight and trembling figure. He was brave and handsome, and in his dark, thoughtful eyes, there was almost a womanly tenderness—an affection strong and deathless for the fair girl he pressed closer to his heart, which she could not fail to see as she lifted her eyes to his once more.

"I will wait, for I can make any sacrifice for you, my dear David," she murmured, in a voice of exquisite sweetness, like the gentle fall of water among the flowers of summer.

"My own! my best beloved!" responded the lover, pressing her lips with passionate kisses; "Heaven bless you for this devotion; now I can go forward with a strong arm and a brave heart. Now, I can live on through gloom and perils it may be, with the hope of meeting you again!"

She lifted her eyes to the heavens above, and whispered, "There!"

"No; on earth, God grant that we be reunited, to part no more in life," he said.

"I will remember you in every prayer, and if I die before we meet again, I will be your guardian angel in heaven," she added, in a more cheerful voice.

"I must go," he said, rising to his feet, "for my time has already expired. You have always refused to kiss me, but you cannot hesitate now?"

For a moment she dropped her eyes, and the roses suddenly bloomed upon her cheeks. But he had bowed his lips to hers, and she could not longer withhold the seal of her love. He then severed a long tress of her hair with his sword, and a curl from his own head, which Miss Jane received as an invaluable talisman for the future.

They spoke not more, for their hearts were full. With a last, agonizing clasp of the hand, they parted. Miss Jane watched his retreating figure till he had disappeared, then she knelt and prayed silently to Heaven.

CHAPTER X.

A YEAR of the sanguinary conflict between the British and Americans had transpired, since the manifesto had been issued from public authority to the army, and from the pulpit to the people, containing these memorable words :

"Our cause is just ! our union perfect ! our internal resources are great ! and if necessary, foreign assistance is doubtless attainable. * * * With hearts fortified with these animating reflections, we most solemnly before God and the world declare, that exerting the utmost energy of those powers our beneficent Creator hath graciously bestowed on us, the arms we have been compelled by our enemies to assume, we will, in defiance of every hazard, with unabating firmness and perseverance, employ for the preservation of our liberties ; being with one mind resolved to die freemen rather than to live slaves."

In several of the most important engagements, Mr. Rushton had been present, and acquitted himself with glory.

The battle of Trenton had just been fought, and the inmates of Rushton Hall awaited the intelligence of the issue with the utmost anxiety, for no tidings had arrived from Mr. Rushton since he had written a few days before that active hostilities had commenced. Then, his words were animated with high hope, and he sketched, briefly, the plan of their preparations to meet the enemy in the liveliest colors.

"I have just finished," he wrote, "the superintendence of a fort, or redoubt, covered with heavy artillery. In the channel under these batteries, we have sunk several ranges of frames, or machines, which we have technically named *chevaux-de-frise.* These must prove fatal to every ship which strikes against them. It is the opinion of General Washington, that if our plans can be carried out to their utmost extent, we have a fair opportunity to ruin the army of Sir William Howe, and possibly decide the issue of the war. Keep up brave courage, my good children, and, in your prayers speed on our glorious cause. As soon as the engagement is over I shall, if alive, join you for a short furlough, to make some necessary arrangements in my affairs."

The cool weather of autumn had commenced, and late one afternoon Hollis, Miss Jane, and Molly, sat before a smouldering fire, conversing of the exciting topic now uppermost in their hearts. From the windows they looked forth upon the surrounding forest gorgeous with the hues of gold, russet, and crimson, over the variegated groundwork of deepening green, and heard the ripened nuts from the old trees about the house shower to the ground in every rustling breeze, while the apples fell from the few native wildings, with an unfrequent and mournful sound.

"How sad!" exclaimed Miss Jane, who seemed to grow more melancholy daily, for no tidings came from her absent lover; "the leaves of the wilderness about us are like ourselves. Hope tinges our hearts with various brilliant hues, only to leave them more sombre and sere than before. Soon they fall to be covered with the snow of death, and at last smoulder in the earth!"

"How beautiful are the gay trees!" exclaimed Molly, now springing to her feet, and beginning to dance lightly over the floor, with her own inimitable grace of movement; "the hearts I find are not like leaves of the wilderness, but rather like so many sugar bowls filled to the brim!"

"Into which you thrust your fingers, and take great lumps for your own cup," added Hollis, with a smile

"Yes, I gather sweetness from every flower like the busy bee. We may more easily do that, than draw vinegar from every homely cask."

"You know very little of life yet, my dear Molly," said Miss Jane, irresistibly relaxing her countenance to more cheerfulness.

She next sat down before her harpsichord, and began to play a lively air with a spirit which made the blood dance in her veins. Her favorite kitten, a handsome tortoise-shell of three months, directly arose from her cushion in the chimney corner, stretched herself into the picture of a minature camel with tail erect, yawned, and then skipped forward to the window-sill, near which Molly sat. Here, the playful pet began to amuse herself with some curious pebbles, which had been spread there to dry in the sun, by Hollis, till, unseen, she had softly pushed off the greater part of them into Mrs. Rogers's workbasket underneath.

"Now Tamar," said Molly, taking her in her lap, "you sing, while I play."

With her almost wonderful power over all dumb creatures which she loved, Molly had succeeded in training the kitten, so that when a certain tune was played, she would essay a kind of sound between a purr and a mew.

As usual, this feat possessed Molly with such playful sympathy, she could continue only a few minutes without yielding to a fit of uncontrollable mirth. Hollis turned his eyes upon her with a decided blending of admiration and affection, betraying more than many words.

Fortunately, he thought, Miss Jane now went out to see Mrs. Rogers a moment, and he said :

"I believe you worship that cat."

"I love Tamar, blessed creature, better than anything else in the world !" replied Molly, pressing the kitten to her mouth with a rapturous caress.

"Luckiest of animals !" responded Hollis, in a low voice.

At this moment, his eye fell upon his scattered pebbles, and he arose with some impatience to gather them up, changing his epithet of the kitten to one much less flattering.

"You shall not get up until you have made a solemn recantation to Tamar, and asked my pardon," said Molly, seizing the opportunity, as he bent down in search of his pebbles, to hold his head.   No sooner was this done, than Hollis arose to his feet, and clasping Molly about the waist, held her powerless in his strong arms. It was the first time he had ever attempted such familiarity, for he was not only afraid of all girls naturally, but he regarded Molly with a feeling akin to reverence, notwithstanding her waywardness and ease of manner in his presence. There was a something about her, which from the first meeting, oppressed him with a sense of inferiority, and he accorded to her a secret, but most passionate love, which made him, in her presence, either silent or dissatisfied with whatever words and actions he ventured upon.

Molly did not pout her rosy lips now to hide her love, as she used to do when caressed by Reuben, but she kept her face averted, and said, coldly—

"Leave me alone, will you, Hollis?"

"Not till you give me your kitten."

"Take it, then."

"What! will you give *me* that which you just said you loved better than anything else?" exclaimed Hollis, in a tone of gratification.

"You entirely misunderstand me," replied Molly; "I offer Tamar to you, that I may be free.   You surely will not harm her?"

"Harm her ! do you think I could harm anything that ever belonged to you ?"

" I do not mean to give her to you to keep always," said Molly.

" Then I shall not take the cat. I shall sit here by you till you give me something to keep, forever."

" If you are determined, you may have Tamar, provided you will let me be free."

" No, I prefer that you be bound. I am in no haste to go from you."

"You shall take her !" said Molly, with flashing eyes, "for on that condition you have said that you would go."

And she gave the kitten into his hands.

" I will accept the gift," replied Hollis, with a seriousness which caused Molly to study his face with curiosity ; " Tamar shall henceforth be mine, cherished carefully as a reminder of this moment. Whenever I caress her, which shall be often, you will know there is meaning in my caresses."

" If you attach such importance to this trifling affair," said Molly ; " you shall see how I regard it. Give me the kitten a moment."

She took and held it to her lips with a gush of kisses, which Hollis interpreted in his favor with a new and blissful emotion. Then walking directly to the window, she threw up the sash with a quick strong impulse, and before Hollis could comprehend her purpose, she struck the kitten against the stone work of the house, till it fell lifeless to the ground.

" There !" exclaimed Molly, with white, quivering lips, but in a steady tone, " I have destroyed the pledge of that which had no existence, dear as the creature was to me !"

No tears came to her eyes, though they flowed through her heart like an impetuous torrent over jagged and well-grounded stones. She could not weep when most strongly excited. But she sat like a queen, who has just signed the death-warrant of a subject, under the tyranny of a will directed by motives of policy, when her heart is dying within her. Her natural born passion had once more triumphed. Alas ! it had been better, if like Hercules, she had strangled the serpent in her cradle !

Hollis shrank within himself in actual affright, brave as he was—for he could face a panther, or a hostile Indian, steadily and unflinchingly, but her eyes scathed his heart, till it beat high and almost audibly.

When Molly saw that he looked upon her in sorrow and compassionate surprise, mingled with fear, her hot temper fell suddenly to cooled lead. Had there been scorn in his eye, had he uttered a word of reproof, she would not so suddenly have repented her rashness. Now, as she saw him leave her presence like one stricken to the inmost heart, she shuddered at the thought of what she had done, and burst into tears.

Molly sat alone, struggling with her unhappy reflections, until her attention was diverted by the sound of wheels coming up the yard. This being unusual, as visitors usually came upon horseback, the prevailing mode of travel at the

time, she went to the window to ascertain the nature of
the arrival. A stranger, with two horses, in a rude hay-
wagon, stopped before the door. She saw Hollis go out, and
after a few words between him and the stranger, he hastened to the wagon with a face that had suddenly taken the
look of death, so great, it was evident, was his new emotion.
Molly's first impulse was to rush out and make inquiries, but
the recollection of the scene which had just transpired restrained her. She lost no time in summoning Miss Jane and
Mrs. Rogers, who took alarm at her representation and hurried out.

The stranger and Hollis, at this moment, were bearing
with great care, a body of some person into the house.

" Mr. Rushton is brought home dead !" exclaimed Molly,
with a frantic scream.

" Not dead, lady," answered the stranger, " but he was
wounded in the late battle, and although when he began the
journey, he was considered comfortable, the route has so
much taxed his strength, he is at present insensible."

" He will die !" murmured Miss Jane, now fainting at the
terrible sight of the blood-stained garments which covered his
body. She would have fallen, had she not been supported
in the arms of Mrs. Rogers.

" All depends upon proper care," said the stranger ; " his
wounds have been skillfully dressed, but he suffers again as
at first, on account of this effort. He would start for home,
though warned of the peril. Dispatch a messenger for the
nearest surgeon without delay."

A few hours later, partial tranquillity was restored in the household.   The surgeon had arrived and newly dressed the wounds of the sufferer, discovering that a ball had been extracted from his right shoulder, and another from his side. He gave out that there was a hope of Mr. Rushton's recovery, but that he was in a critical situation.   The courage and energy which were perfectly natural to Molly now proved of decided advantage, for Hollis was so nearly overcome with the ever-present thought of his father's danger, he could do little more than watch by his bedside.   She proved herself, seemingly without effort, a most efficient manager, nurse and counsellor in this crisis.   Even the surgeon tacitly deferred to her capability of clear judgment in his own province, and Hollis listened to all her suggestions with implicit faith.   In her unfailing, excellent care for his father, he seemed to have forgiven the past, when she had been more than

> " Uncertain, coy, and hard to please,
> And variable as the shade
> By the light quivering aspen made."

For some days after his immediate danger was past, Mr. Rushton was unable to speak to those about him, although apparently in recovered consciousness.   Often he made efforts to converse with Hollis, for a matter of importance evidently lay upon his heart, impatient for communication, but he was yet too weak to only express his simplest wants.

But when he had so far recovered as to be able to converse without injury, he informed the family that they were threatened with danger, and that therefore he had lost no time in coming home even though severely wounded.

"The British army are marching nearer," he said, "and compelling our American forces to evacuate their quarters. The Indians, also, under the direction of Burgoyne, are making stealthy scouts over the country, massacring defenceless women and children. Safety must be sought without more delay than is actually necessary, for if it were known that this was the home of an officer in the American army, the most disastrous consequences would speedily ensue."

Miss Jane, who was present, began to weep, and inquired what would become of her brother's family.

"Your brother is less in danger," replied Mr. Rushton; "for as yet, I believe, he stands uncommitted to the defence of either side. You need not entertain fears of safety ; at least, I see no cause for you to do so at present."

"If they come come here," now broke out Molly, with sparkling eyes, "I will take up the first thing I can find— be it chair, shovel, or broomstick, and knock their brains out quicker than they can wink."

"Ah ! my dear child," said Mr. Rushton, "you feel bravely now, but you must remember how powerless is a woman in the hands of hostile savages."

"True, true," murmured Miss Jane, with a shudder.

"I'm not afraid of losing my scalp yet awhile," commented Molly.

"Neither am I," said Miss Jane ; "but Mr. Rushton is wise to take precautions."

" What do you propose to do ?" now inquired Hollis of his father.

Mr. Rushton then requested to be left alone with Hollis, for he said he had plans of great importance to talk over, and they were not suitable for the ears of others.

Miss Jane and Molly received this invitation to leave with an exchange of smiles.

" I suppose it is thought," said Molly to Mr. Rushton, " that women are not wise enough to hear secrets."

" Hardly wise enough to keep them," answered Mr. Rushton, with a laugh.

" Thank you," retorted Molly

" Oh, you need not put on airs," continued Mr. Rushton ; " you know just as well as I do, that I think highly enough of both you and Miss Jane.   There's no danger of my forgetting your worth."

" Yet, we are useless to keep secrets," said Molly, as she closed the door after her.

This interview continued as long as Mr. Rushton was able to speak.   That a subject of incalculable importance had been discussed was evident from the pale face and absent manner of Hollis afterward.   Mr. Rushton's recovery was retarded by the excitement of this conversation, so that he was unable to see the family again for several days.   By degrees he found strength to relate minute details of the engagement to Molly, who never wearied of listening to accounts of battle scenes.   She would lead him on with glowing cheek, and with her large eyes opened wide with interest, often exclaiming in passionate outbursts of admiration.

"Yes," concluded Mr. Rushton, on one such occasion, "I thought this time to return covered with glory ; but our calculations frequently miss.   The enemy is victorious at present, and I came home much in the plight of that valiant knight, Don Quixote, who, it is recorded, returned from his second sally, covered with wounds and stretched upon a truss of straw in the bottom of a wagon, drawn by oxen."

"How can you talk so lightly of your misfortune," returned Molly ; "when we first saw you, we thought you were dead, and our lives were almost sacrificed with grief on the spot."

"Are you really so much attached to me ?" asked Mr. Rushton.

"Yes indeed ; you seem to me just like what I should suppose a father would be to a child," answered Molly, somewhat moved.

"Then," continued Mr. Rushton, in a changed tone, "will you let me advise you about a matter of the highest importance to you and to us ?   Are you prepared, my dear Molly, to give me the obedience of a child ?"

"Certainly ; why should I hesitate to do your slightest bidding ?" replied Molly.

"Listen to me patiently, Molly, while I tell you more clearly what I have upon my mind," Mr. Rushton went on. "You are aware of the danger that threatens us every moment.   For your greater safety, I wish to take measures, so that when I am able to join the army again, you will be in greater security ; otherwise my heart would be so burdened, I could not fight on to help win the victory, which, sooner or later, must be ours.   You must leave this place."

" Leave this place !" exclaimed Molly ; " you will not send me away from your home now ?"

" No ; not alone, not unprovided for.   I have a small and pleasant estate in New Jersey, in a more thickly settled spot. Thither you and Hollis, with Mrs. Rogers and one man servant, must go as soon as I recover.   But, Molly," continued Mr. Rushton, with a steady and troubled glance upon her, " I have yet another arrangement to propose, which at this crisis, I regard as equally indispensable to your happiness and mine.   When perils thicken, we cannot pause to observe the delays which attend security.   Therefore, I wish you to be married before leaving this place."

Molly turned pale instantly, while she fastened upon Mr. Rushton a look of excited inquiry.

" From the time you first came here, my dear child," he pursued, " Hollis has loved you.   Every day has exalted you in his devotion ; but such is his embarrassment, he would rather die than open his lips to you on the subject.   Indeed, when I mentioned my wishes to him a day or two since, he plead as I never heard him before, to extort a promise from me that I would never speak to you in relation to this matter.   He misunderstands you, does he not, Molly, when he thinks you are indifferent to him ?   You will consent to the proposal ?"

"Oh, Mr. Rushton!" cried Molly, with the tears starting to her eyes, "this can never be!"

"Why not?"

"Because, it would be wrong for me to marry Hollis, when I love another better than him."

"In the right of being your best friend, I ask who is that other?"

Molly hesitated. There was a look in her eye which betrayed that she regarded such a secret as inviolable. But when she looked once more upon Mr. Rushton, and saw that fatherly affection rather than cold self-interest had dictated the question, she yielded as she would have done to no other, and replied in a very low voice:

"It is one who is far from here—whom I have loved ever since I can remember."

"I understand now," said Mr. Rushton. "I knew that you loved Reuben Epps, but I thought it was as a brother. You have heard nothing from him since you left Epps Hundred?"

"No; but he cannot have forgotten me," sobbed Molly.

Mr. Rushton was silent for some time. At length he said:

"My dear child, Heaven forbid that I should unduly urge you in such a matter as this. I am not the man to take advantage of trust and helplessness for the accomplishment of even my most cherished plans. I leave you free to act henceforth; only informing you that your answer is a disappointment, the extent of which you can never know."

"I wish I could die before the day is done," cried Molly,

at this juncture, "rather than live to be the cause of the least pain to one so dear to me as you are.   But how can I help my heart going which way it will ?"

"The heart, it is said, is deceitful above all things," replied Mr. Rushton.

"But I am not deceitful, when I say that I love Hollis as a brother, and only that way," said Molly.

"That is the best kind of love in the world," said Mr. Rushton, " on which to found domestic happiness. However," he added, " I repeat that I leave you free. I cannot speak longer now, only to advise you what to do. Write once more to Reuben Epps. If he replies, and in the spirit which you believe he feels toward you, I will never attempt to thwart your wishes. But if you still hear nothing, or an unfavorable answer, I entreat you, Molly, to give my proposal a serious consideration."

She went out of his presence, with a new sorrow and anxiety in her heart.

On that day, she wrote another long and earnest letter to Reuben, withholding all allusion to Mr. Rushton's proposal, but entreating to let her hear from him at the earliest possible date. After the letter was sent away, she went about like a shadow of grief, so fearful was she, lest it should fail of reaching its destination, which she never doubted, of late, had been the fate of her previous letters. During the long and weary days in which she waited for a answer, she remained alone for hours, a prey to the most overwhelming emotions. That Reuben was still devoted in heart, and faith-

ful to his old promises of love, she most implicitly believed ;
but she greatly dreaded the consequences of not hearing from
him.   Until now, she had never realized how well she had
loved him, how dear was every association with his memory,
and the thought of living on without receiving another word
of affection from him, seemed a sorrow almost too great to
be borne.   She would then have no plea to urge against the
wishes of Mr. Rushton, and to persist in the course which
she had marked out for herself, she feared would bring upon
her a suspicion of ingratitude—perhaps dislike.

Meantime Hollis avoided her as much as possible, and
what time he could be released from attendance on his father,
he devoted to preparations for removal, not forgetting to
take from their pedestals and shelves his valued collections
of curiosities.

Two weeks passed away, and one day, when Molly was
sitting in Mr. Rushton's room reading aloud for his entertainment while Miss Jane also sat and listened, Hollis entered
with a letter in his hand.   Molly saw it and believed it was
for her, but she was powerless to utter a word.   He advanced and gave it to his father.   Molly's heart fell and she
closed her book.

On opening the first enclosure, Mr. Rushton found it contained another.

" Here Molly," he said, " is a letter for you, with a post-
mark, written Emps Hundred."

" My stars in Heaven !" she cried, springing to his side,
" it's from Reuben I know !"

At this moment, she met a piercing glance from Hollis, and was so suddenly struck with the look of pain he wore, she blushed deeply and said no more. Once alone in her chamber, she tore open the precious missive with trembling fingers, and read the beloved name at the close ; a great and swift tide of joy rushed through her heart, making it beat almost audibly. She next began to read what he had written.

At first, came an account of occurrences at Epp's Hundred, since her departure. His father had joined the army ; he had taken his place at home, and Mary was teaching school in a neighboring district, with some other minor matters. Next, in glowing terms, he alluded to an interesting family, in her absence removed into the neighborhood, with whom he was on terms of intimacy. Their oldest daughter, a few years younger than himself, reminded him especially of his Molly in past time. She was a charming girl and most bewitchingly beautiful. Mary already loved her like a sister, and, for his part, he would say in confidence, that she was even dearer than any sister in the world. He should have written before and told her all his heart, as he always used to, only failing to receive a letter from her since she went away, he was at a loss to know where to direct. He then made some allusions to their old love, which, he called " children's play," and concluded with:

If you do not hear from me again, remember that you continue to have my sincere wishes for your happiness in the society of the friends of later life, as, I hope, I have yours. Give my regards to Mr. Rushton, and, especially to his son Hollis, who I presume, by this time, is dearer to you than was ever,   Yours truly,

                                        REUBEN EPPS.

When Molly had read this, a sharp, scathing pain shot through her heart like a heated arrow. For a moment, she sat in motionless silence, her lips parted, her eyes distorted, and her bosom heaving with great throbs. Then, tearing the letter into fragments, she lighted a taper and burned them all, one after another, till nothing but ashes remained. She had thus burned her fingers several times, and now they ached severely, but such suffering she heeded not. She only sat and watched the relics scattered around her, writing them over anew, with the excited thoughts which coursed rapidly through her brain, till hours passed unnoted.

At length, when Miss Jane, in compliance with Mr. Rushton's suggestion, went to ascertain what had detained Molly so long, she found the lighted taper in her room, although it was yet in the open day. But Molly was not there.

CHAPTER XI.

THE SEPARATION.

To the recesses of one of the old forests, bordering upon the grounds of Rushton Hall, Molly had gone to seek the consolation, which no other scene could vouchsafe her. Striking into a familiar path which wound through to a neighboring settlement, she came to a dim and silent spot, where, throwing herself upon a moss-covered stone, she abandoned herself to her emotions. The luxuriant gloom and the stillness, only interrupted occasionally by the whirring of a wood-bird, or the light agitation of the insuperable branches of the quaint trees overhead, unconsciously soothed her spirit to a degree of tranquillity. But she had no thought for the wild beauty and the whispering mystery around her. The dark brown shadows crept near and afar, like stealthy dragons, and great spiders traversed swiftly the aisles of the acorns and leaves about her feet, unheeded. She was crushing down the broken and sullied memories of the once beautiful past—mastering the rebellion which welled up in

"

her heart like a hot spring, and, as she thought on and on, her labor was not in vain.

"I will be free from this foolish misery," she cried, at length, starting to her feet, "no more—no more, henceforth, will I think of the bitter, maddening name of Reuben Epps ! Thanks to Heaven, that no human eye has seen how much one person has power over me. I will have glorious revenge —in perfect indifference. I am no love-lorn maid to hold myself moonstruck at his beck. As for love, I despise the word now, and will ever from this hour ; but those who are friends to me, I will accept to be my friends for life."

Selecting a tree which was suitable for her purpose, she climbed among its branches with the agility which character- ized all her movements, and seated herself in a recess of strong limbs. Here, conscious of safety, she composed her- self to greater peace, and, as usual, after mental excitement, soon fell asleep.

She slept soundly and long, so that when she awoke, it was moonlight. Not recalling where she was at first, she started, and came near falling, but she soon discovered it was far into the night. It being rather late in the season of autumn, she was benumbed with the chill, frosty air, and, in the heart of that solitary wood, distant from her snug bed- chamber at home, her situation failed to inspire her with the heroic fervor which had sustained her on going to sleep.

" Ugh !" she shuddered, peering far into the dark shadows around her, "I am rewarded now for my rashness. What would dear, dead Mrs. Epps say to me, if she could know where I am! But why did I think of *that* name?" she reproved herself, impatiently.

She was beginning to descend the tree, resolved to dare her way home, fearing that alarm would result from her absence, when she stopped, attracted by the sound of heavy steps approaching. A thought of wild beasts which had been reported to infest those woods, made her hold her breath and listen sharply. But next, she distinguished human voices, and she soon descried the figures of two men coming nearer, on the path which led directly past the foot of the tree where she was. Drawing within the covert of the leaves as much as possible, she held herself motionless, prepared for observation.

"Yes," said one of the men, "this is the way that leads out in plain sight of the house. We'll soon be there, now."

"We'll get our money's worth in plunder, arter settin' it a-blaze," responded the other, in a voice which was so well known to Molly's ears, she started quickly, with lips half parted in exclamation.

"I tell ye what, Vanhorn," continued the first voice, "we must look out and get the old feller for our prisoner. Sir William Howe will give us enough to make it pay well."

Let me on for that sort o'business ; I'm used to capterin' folks alive," was the reply.

"Dead, too, eh ?" sneered the other.

"I never do nothin' only what's lawful, as sartin as my name is Pinkle Vanhorn."

" Pinkle Vanhorn !" repeated Molly to herself, "I never knew any one of that name, but if that voice doesn't belong to Button Husley, I am dreaming."

Carefully she looked out between the leaves, to get a view of the man's face as they came nearer. She could not see distinctly, but the round, twinkling eyes were not to be mistaken, neither was the short figure, with its odd rolling gait.

They passed on, and their voices fell into indistinctness. A sudden thought struck Molly that she had thus overheard a plot of some of that famous band, known in those parts as the Cow-boys. These refugees, belonging to the British side, lived upon plunder, and destruction of the property of those who espoused the American cause ; and that Button and his companions were now on their way to Rushton Hall, she did not doubt.

To prevent this depredation, and more than all the capture of Mr. Rushton, she at once determined. No time was to be lost, and hastening down the tree, she started off rapidly, so that she might reach home in advance of the marauders. She soon gained upon them so that they were in sight again ; but, too much pre-occupied with themselves, the slight sound of her footsteps did not attract their notice.

A new difficulty arose. There was no other path from the woods, save the one which the men were pursuing, and Molly knew that it would be impossible to trace her way out through the trees, without any guide. She could therefore do no more than to follow them as closely as she dared, prepared to make an effort to get before them, when they emerged into the open land.

They had reached the edge of the woods, and come in full view of Rushton Hall, when one of the men halted and said :

" Wait here a bit, Vanhorn, while I go forward and reconnoitre. If they are all asleep and the lights out, and I conclude it's the right time to go at it, I'll give my sort of whistle, which you'll know quick enough, and then you come on."

" So be it," answered Button, throwing himself down upon the ground, with his musket beside him. Before Molly had thought to slip behind the trunk of a tree, his eye had fallen upon her figure, which was now but a few yards distant.

Starting to his feet again in an instant, he called ont huskily :

" What's that ?"

He was about to take aim upon her with his gun, when, with her usual coolness in times of extreme danger, Molly hit upon an expedient which saved her life.

" Beware ! I am a ghost !" she said in a hollow voice, which went off in a long unearthly groan.

" A ghost !" cried Button, " Oh, Lord ha' mercy !"

" Button Husley !" began Molly, in a tone of awful abjuration.

" Yes, yes," responded Button, breathlessly.

" Where is the spirit of that murdered man that you hid in the closet at Witch Hazel House ! Where ?"

Molly groaned again.

"Down on your knees and confess, if you would have a whole head on your shoulders."

"Heavens and 'arth !" gasped Button, sinking to the ground, "have ye come to take me off to hell ?"

"Blood calls for vengeance. Repent. Go not on with your work to-night," continued Molly. "If you do, your old sins shall all stand up before you and strike you to the heart."

"Lord ha' mercy ! You've mistook, I'm Pinkle Vanhorn." entreated Button.

"Button Husley !" answered Molly, in a half shriek, "I know your name and your crimes. Where's that gold case ? It belongs to me."

"Then you're the spirit of that 'ere woman who died at Colonel Epps'! Have mercy, and I'll be your servant forever ; I've got the case, but it's down at New York."

At this juncture, a shrill, peculiar whistle fell upon the ears of Button. Springing to his feet, he darted off, without stopping to take his gun. Molly seized it, and flew after him with her utmost swiftness, for she was nerved with a purpose which admitted of no delay. At every few steps, Button turned to see if she were pursuing him, and finding that she came nearer and nearer, for the way being perfectly familiar to her, she lost no time, he renewed his pace, with a cry of terror.

Molly now discharged the gun in the air and throwing it aside with a shout, struck off into another way which led more directly to the house.

A few minutes later, she reached home, nearly overcome with mingled mirth and terror. She found that the household were aroused at the late report of the gun, and met her overwhelmed with anxiety. But when she had briefly related what had happened, efficient measures for protection were put in train at once. No Cow-boys, however, appeared there that night. Molly had entirely succeeded in her stratagem.

"Ghost for ghost," said Molly ; on the following morning, when discussing the events of the preceding night ; "I remember hearing how Button Husley used to don the character of spectre to frighten people into his snares."

"But were you not afraid, when you were carrying out this perilous scheme, there by the lonely woods and in the dead of night ?" inquired Mr. Rushton.

"I had no time for fear," answered Molly ; "beside, if Button had stirred toward me, an inch, I would have called up spirits out of the ground, like the Witch of Endor."

"You are so valiant, Molly, you make me think of Pompey, who, when asked by Cicero how he thought to oppose Cæsar, replied, 'I have only to stamp with my foot and an army will rise out of the ground.'"

"Ah well," said Molly, "you know that I dislike art of all things. If I had been a man, I would have chosen to have met Button, face to face."

"More victories are gained by stratagem than by hard fighting," said Mr. Rushton.

"Such make-believe parts don't agree well with me,"

remarked Molly ; "I came near bursting out with laughter several times, in the very cream of my ghost business, especially when Button fell on his knees and began to sue for mercy."

"If ever a man deserved to lose his head, it's that one," said Mr. Rushton, shuddering at the memory of his own peril at Witch Hazel House. "Of late, I have often heard of Pinkle Vanhorn among the Cow-boys, but I little thought it was my old would-be-murderer."

"If I am not mistaken, he led a band of Skinners at first," said Hollis, who had listened to Molly, with secret admiration.

"The Cow-boys, he found, went further in villainy, and gave better pay, I presume," replied Mr. Rushton.

"Else he would not have been in their ranks," remarked Molly.

"Until we leave, we must keep up a strict watch," said Mr. Rushton, "for ' to be forewarned and forearmed is half the day.' In the meantime, we will remove and dispose of all our valuable property, so that there will be little object in burning the inner walls of a stone house like this."

"I hope it will be long before I shall have to part with Miss Jane," said Molly.

The loss of one who had long been dearer to her than all other friends, influenced her to turn with renewed love to those whom she could still trust.

"She is very dear to me, as I have no mother or sister," continued Molly, the tears coming to her eyes.

" Is she ? Then, she is **glad**," interrupted a low sweet voice, at this juncture.

Molly turned quickly, and saw the object of her remark entering through the open door Miss Jane came forward and embraced her affectionately, saying :

" I couldn't wait a moment after I heard your adventure of last night. . Heaven be praised that I meet you again in safety !"

" You remember the old proverb about somebody being always near when you are talking about him ?" remarked Molly, suddenly changing her mood to her characteristic perversity.

" *Ride si sapis*," said Hollis.

" Don't have over any tedious lingo out of your books," said Molly, " I suppose you mean that you deride, with a sigh, my sappiness ?"

" I only said to Miss Jane—Laugh, if you are wise."

" I am inclined to laugh for other reasons," said Miss Jane, producing a letter.

" Ah ! from your David," said Mr. Rushton. " What's the news ?"

" He will send for me in the spring, he thinks ; though possibly, later."

" How does he get along in his army ?"

" Well, I should infer, from the fact of his being commissioned a captain," answered Miss Jane, blushing deeply.

" Captain Jones !" repeated Molly ; . " he should fight on our side, then he might be a colonel, or something higher."

" Yes, it is a pity, commented Mr. Rushton, with a frown. " I am glad, however, for your sake, that he is well," he added, when he saw Miss Jane's look of sorrow.

" Now, were it not for this man," remarked Molly, " you might go with us when we leave here."

" Yes," said Mr. Rushton, " it would seem like home to you, having lived so many years in the vicinity of our future home. I don't know how Molly can get along without you."

" It would be very pleasant to go, but I have agreed to remain here," replied Miss Jane.

" No man, not even a captain, should have such power over me," rejoined Molly.

With the shadows upon his face which he now usually wore, Hollis turned suddenly and looked out of the window.

" I have been so much occupied in your exploits with the Cow-boys, I omitted to inquire about the letter which you received yesterday, Molly," now spoke Mr. Rushton, looking upon her with interest.

These words took Molly by surprise, and though quick in expedients, her tact failed her this time, and before she could command herself, her face was tell-tale with blushes.

" It was from an old acquaintance—no news of importence," she faltered out.

" Was it not from Reuben Epps ?" pursued Mr. Rushton.

Molly now almost gasped for breath. The last few hours, she had been so much excited and overtasked, she was weak and nervous, and notwithstanding every effort to preserve self-control, she burst into tears.

Hollis turned upon her a look of heartfelt sympathy, and when Miss Jane abruptly changed the conversation, his face was expressive of gratitude.

Molly escaped to her room, where she abandoned herself to the flood of grief, that had so fearfully struggled in her heart since her unhappy letter was read. For some time after this, Molly was ill, though not sufficiently to awaken apprehensions. She suffered from a severe cold, resulting from being out in the chill night, which with her great mental anxieties, proved too much to overcome with her usual spirit and resolution. Miss Jane was her constant and most affectionate attendant, beguiling the weary hours which Molly was obliged to spend in her room, by reading or pleasant conversation. Hollis manifested his solicitude by frequent messages of inquiry, and by sending some of his most cherished collections for her amusement.

Mr. Rushton had now regained his health, and having completed the preparations for the removal of his family, only awaited Molly's recovery. But he was not wholly inactive, at this time, in the great service to which he was devoted. The American army which had been formed for only one year, now formally dissolved, and during the winter, the most efficient measures were being carried out for the gaining of recruits. In the Middle States, General Washington was still carrying on a determined conflict, while at the North, various events of importance were transpiring. Sir Guy Carleton had retreated from Crown Point and retired to Canada, where he distributed his army for winter quar-

ters. General Schuyler was indefatigable in his preparations for the approaching spring campaign. Mr. Rushton,
who had late received the commission of Colonel, kept up a
correspondence with Schuyler and Gates, who, since the departure of Carleton, had joined General Washington, and,
also with Wayne, who commanded the troops remaining in
garrison. He was urged to make every effort to gather
reinforcements for the ensuing conflict, and, as such efforts
were little practicable in his present location, he was desirous to take his departure. As soon as Molly became aware
of this fact, she entreated to be left for the present with
Miss Jane, who warmly seconded the proposal.

"If you will consent to reside with Mrs. McNeil, who lives
upon a small estate of mine, and to whom I should be glad
to give further pecuniary favors, I will agree to your wishes,"
said Mr. Rushton.

Mrs. McNeil was a widow lady, without children, save one
son in the British army, and was, Molly knew, a most worthy person. She could there be sure of excellent nursing,
and of the society of Miss Jane as before, therefore gladly
assented to the arrangement. A few days later, all the preparations for the separation were completed and the last
adieux remained only to be spoken. Molly went through the
silent and deserted rooms with a sadness which she had
never felt before, and when she came to the family parlor,
where she had spent so many happy hours, the tears rushed
to her eyes.

"Oh dear ! what a place this world is, after all !" she

exclaimed to herself, aloud. A sigh so heavy tnat it sounded through the hollow walls like a groan, responded to her words. She turned quickly, and perceived Hollis standing in one of the alcoves before a window. The tenderness of her heart was awakened at once ; and going to his side, she said in a low voice :

"Are you so very sorry to leave here, Hollis ?"

He looked upon her inquiringly for a moment, and reading that she was for once in earnest with him, he replied, "Yes ; but it is a weakness as unmanly as uncontrollable."

"Why ?"

"Because, I regret to leave one who is glad to have me go !" he said, with bitterness.

"Do you mean me ?" asked Molly, soothingly.

"You know how it is—how it will always be."

"No, I don't ; for I really feel very bad to part with you, dear Hollis. You have always been kind to me—kinder than I have deserved."

He looked upon her, doubtingly.

"I shall miss you more than I can tell," Molly added, in corroboration of what she had said.

As you would any piece of furniture that was in the house, to which you have become reconciled, by long habit," he replied.

"Don't I How can you say that, when something dreadful may happen before we meet again ?" expostulated Molly, earnestly.

"Molly !" said Hollis, in an excited though resolute voice,

"until now my tongue has been palsied in your presence. I have been, to appearance, most like a cold dumb statue. But from the first moment my eyes fell upon you I was strangely influenced. Every day since has increased your power over me, for I have a heart as capable of passionate emotions as any other. Now, when we are about to part—*forever*—do not interrupt me," he said, as Molly tried to remonstrate, "when I know that you love another, and that you can never love me, I must speak. I will tell you all. You know that I love—nay, worship you, madly—that you have power to will me after you, as you have over a dumb beast, with this difference : I do not require to be coaxed or caressed. I can't help loving you, though I get only indifference, perhaps scorn, in return. To live on, week after week and year after year in this way is torture, and I have made up my mind. No one, not even my father, knows my intentions. But I shall join the army in the spring."

"I thought it was arranged that you should come for me to go to Monmouth then," said Molly.

"It is so arranged, but I shall never come. That we shall be married then, is concluded. But I would voluntarily give myself to be hung as a spy, before I will make one move towards bringing you into such an irksome bondage. I am going to the battle-field, wherever I can find it, till I get killed—shot through the heart, I hope."

"Oh Hollis !" cried Molly, "have you gone mad, to speak thus ?"

"No ; I have only come to my senses. Hitherto, I allow

that I have been about half crazed. Now I have strength to mark out my course. Life is worth nothing more to me only to devote to my country. It is blasted, withered, blackened, cursed forever."

He paused, shut his lips firmly, while his eyes looked far out on to the landscape before him, which was one vast picture of snow and ice, and his words echoed through the deserted room startlingly. The scene accorded with his mood.

"These words are not right," said Molly, much moved.

"I know they are wrong," answered Hollis, "but I believe God will forgive me for being almost desperate, now. He is merciful, which is my only consolation for the future."

"If it would be any consolation to you to know," now began Molly, strangely embarrassed—but she stopped and blushed, while a look of deep pain flitted over her face.

"Know what?" demanded Hollis, eyeing her intently.

"That you are mistaken about my—loving another. That is all past—past forever," she said, with a strong effort.

"Impossible!" responded Hollis.

"No ; I speak the truth," she added, while she struggled anew to keep back the tears.

"Thank Heaven!" exclaimed Hollis in a tone of relief. "It will be a consolation greater than you can imagine to know, henceforth, that your heart is not all devoted to another, though you can never love me."

There was a pause now. At last Molly broke the silence.

"You will not try very hard to kill yourself, Hollis?" she said, looking up into his face with an arch smile.

Hollis started quickly, and the hope that had lighted his eye for a moment, now went out.

"How can you speak so lightly of my misery? Oh, Molly!" he almost groaned, "you are so changeful, I can never know what to believe.   Your words are all a mockery."

He turned to leave her abrubtly; Molly exclaimed in a changed tone :

"Will you go from me, Hollis, without one word of forgiveness for all my errors ?   We may never meet on earth again, as you have more than intimated."

"I know that I am wild and capricious," she went on, as he paused before her, with folded arms, like a doomed man ; "but you must not expect of me more than I have power to be. Your friend I have been from the first ; indeed, I should never deserve the respect of any again could I be otherwise than friendly to one who has been so generous and good to me. As for love, I have now no faith in it—not enough to outweigh a mustard seed. It is a word, a mere fancy, that goes into the air like a thistle bloom with the first puff of wind, and falls quickly to the ground to be trampled under foot. The firm friendliness of one true heart I value as much higher than the passion of so-called lovers, as I do a brave, noble mountain, like our Catskill above an ant heap. There, I have said my say—up in shape, haven't I ? Good bye, and God bless you from this time henceforth and forevermore."

Ah ! why could not Molly be like other people ?   Why could she not wear the same face through, at least one sitting, as artists would say ?   It seemed impossible for her to get over a serious remark, without edging it off by something sarcastic or trifling.   Her variety of humor, her quickly succeeding smiles and frowns, were enough to drive one of the shy, distrustful, yet secretly passionate nature of Hollis, half distracted.   He believed in love.   How could he believe in anything else for a substitute, when his whole heart was enthralled by it ; and now, even more than ever, as he looked upon her once again for the last ?   He could not fail to see how beautiful was Molly in that moment.   Her ill health had reduced her figure to delicate outlines, and she looked taller than formerly, almost queenly, with her erect decided carriage and the high bearing of her young head, which held more wisdom than she discovered on every day occasions.   Her face was very pale, but excitement had brought out upon her cheek a bloom as of the fairest blossoms.   Her eyes were dark and lustrous, and so very bewitching, yet powerful were they, under their long, brown lashes, Hollis, as of old, dropped his before them in secret acknowledgment of his inferiority.   Her raven hair fell to her waist in long luxuriant curls, and her sweet, pouting lips, "threaded with scarlet," were tremulous with feeling, yet half smiling carelessly at every breath.

Hollis durst not trust himself to remain, for his heart was dying within him.

"Farewell, Molly," he said, unsteadily, and before she

could move, he had gone.   No sooner was Molly alone, than she drew up the large shawl she wore, over her entire person, and covering her face, burst into tears.   It was more lonely now to feel that one, who had so long dwelt with her a brother and friend, was gone, than she had before imagined.   She could not remain in that silent room, which had suddenly become as a tomb, so she went out of the house, where she met Mr. Rushton, who had been seeking her.

"Molly, let me put you upon your horse, to take you to your new home," he said.· "I shall leave Black Princess with you, for as soon as you are able, you must ride every day ; but have a care not to go into unsafe places, in these perilous times."

Molly could not speak for her grief.

"There, my child," concluded Mr. Rushton, "Heaven keep you till we meet again, which I hope will be on this .earth. Remember to get well by the warm season, when you will be expected at Monmouth.   Confide in Miss Jane, who is good as an angel.   I left her this morning, quite overcome at the idea of the separation from us, and she promised to meet you at Mrs. McNiel's."

These words he said hurriedly, and with an effort to preserve his usual calmness.   He now hesitated, with his hand upon Molly's.

"Oh dear ! this is awful !" exclaimed Molly, finding voice.

"What is ?"

"This parting.   After all, I am glad you are going to

fight our enemies. If I could only go to battle, I would send more than one dozen of the red-coats into—Heaven."

"That's brave ; keep up a brave heart always, Molly, and don't forget to pray for the triumph of our cause. I must begone now, for they have started before me, and Lucifer is impatient. I don't hold to long, heart-rending parting scenes, so good bye, darling, you can never know how dear you are to me."

Molly could not restrain a fresh gush of grief, but in her old spirit struck Black Princess smartly with her riding stick ; so that the horse started off with a gallop. Once more, Molly turned, and said :

"Hurrah ! for our country !"

"Victory or Heaven !" responded Mr. Rushton.

"I shall be out of sight first !" shouted Molly.

"But never out of my heart," concluded Mr. Rushton, sadly, to himself, as he gazed after her retreating figure.

CHAPTER XII.

THE THUNDER STORM.

The house of Mrs. McNiel presented a contrast to Rushton Hall.   It was small, unpainted, gabled and without shutters to the windows.   But the rude simplicity combined with
a certain inartificial beauty, with which, as a whole picture,
it was stamped, impressed Molly with pleasure.   Its old,
brown exterior, was yet so home-like, and all its precincts
were so scrupulously well ordered, it seemed the right spot
for her to regain health, and, if possible, repose of spirit.

On entering her small, half-upright chamber, she glanced
about her upon the neat white floor, the small, puffed bed,
with its tester of muslin, the window looking towards the
river, curtained simply, the light-stand, on which shining surface lay a Bible and a prayer-book, the little mirror with
paper cut adornings, the cumbrous arm-chair with its patch-
work cushion, and smiled in perfect contentment, although
conscious of the prim homeliness of the arrangements.

"Here," said Molly, with something like a sigh, " I will

try and forget those who do not love me, and pray for those who do. It is just the place to be good."

She was interrupted in her reflections by Mrs. McNiel, who was too thoughtful to leave her alone in this first, trying hour.

' "Miss Jane has got everything ready for you, below stairs," she said. "How do you like your chamber ?"

"It's a perfect band-box, lined and wadded with white comfort," she replied gaily.

"I am glad you are pleased, for I was afraid you would feel homesick here, after the good things you have been used to," said Mrs. McNiel.

" Oh, no !" answered Molly, "I shall be as snugly comfortable as a keepsake in cotton."

" You're a kind of a keepsake, yourself," continued Mrs. McNiel ; Mr. Rushton would have us keep you awhile to remember him by, and Hollis, too, for the same reason, I dare say. Poor fellow !" she continued, "he looked sad enough to move one to pity, the last time I saw him. I never knew a young man grow gloomy so fast as he has, of late. Singular, Molly, that with all your light-heartedness, you couldn't keep up his spirits."

"How in the world did you have patience to make such patchwork as this ?" now spoke Molly, affecting to be engrossed in the quilt which covered her bed. Her head was dropped so low, that her hostess did not notice the color that had suddenly heightened upon her face.

" The fingers which put those squares together are now

turned to dust ; they were the work of my children," answered Mrs. McNiel, in a saddened tone.

Molly said no more, but hastened to join Miss Jane, who
met her, as usual, with the tenderness of a sister. Had it
not been for her society at this time, Molly would have
grown strangely sad, when the first excitement attending her
change of residence had subsided. As it was, many an
hour she spent in her white chamber, alone with the memories of her heart—memories which brought not peace or sunshine. Now that Hollis was gone, where she could see him
no more, she missed him at every hour with unavailing regrets. She knew not before how much and faithfully he had
contributed to her happiness. Often, indeed, of our best
blessings are we unaware, until they are gone from us !

"He loved me to the last," she would sigh, "while one,
whom I love, even yet, despite all my resolves to the contrary, was faithless to me !"

Spring soon came with its wealth of beauty, and Molly escaped from her reflections to the open air, where she became
more like herself again. Especially was the simple home of
Mrs. McNiel a charming spot, in the warm season. There
were old trees shading the smooth, green lawn, which sloped
to the river ; running vines covered the rude porch over the
door, and aspired even to the moss thatch of the low roof,
from which they wandered off like delicate streamers, strung
with wild blooms, whose fragrance in the bland winds stole
in through the open casements, filling all the rooms.
There were lilac bushes, which ever made Molly think of the

sweet dell at Epps Hundred, where, years ago, she had sat
with Reuben and trifled with his passionate love. Now, she
did not love the lilacs ; a thistle was more pleasing in her
thought. On one side was a small garden patch, where Mrs.
McNiel cultivated her vegetables and herbs. Upon another
was a row of hives, from which wandered forth the bees
amid the fragrance of the few blossoming wildings making
such music, on soft, hazy days, as to lull the soul of the lis-
tener to a luxurious calm.

This place was situated near the foot of a hill, which
memorable spot is thus described by a writer of American
Biography : " The side of the hill was covered with a
growth of bushes, and on its top, a quarter of a mile from
the house, stood a large pine tree, near the root of which
gushed out a perennial spring of water."

Upon this hill, Molly often wandered with Miss Jane, and
under the pine tree, which, to this day, is standing as a venerable monument of the past, they sat together, and talked
of those things, which now were uppermost in their hearts.
The departure from this vicinity of both Miss Jane and Molly,
had been delayed by new circumstances, longer than they
had anticipated. Their separation was not now expected
until the summer, and neither regretted this, save when they
thought of the absent who were dear to them. Molly had
received intelligence from Mr. Rushton, that he was engaged
in the defence of Ticonderoga, and, subsequently, of the Star
Fort at Crown Point to repel the attacks of Burgoyne and
Carleton. The northern army would encamp at Fort Ed-

ward, on the Hudson some weeks later, and then, in their immediate neighborhood, he should be prepared to arrange her departure.   Of Hollis, he wrote nothing, except that he had joined the army.   "Keep up good heart, my dear child," he concluded this brief letter, "and ever be brave in the cause of truth and justice.   Before we meet again, I know not what may happen, but in the words of the immortal poet :

"Death is the worst, a fate which all must try ;
And for our country, 'tis a bliss to die.' "

Miss Jane, on the other hand, was newly interested by a message from her lover, stating in words of passionate love that they would be re-united, as soon as General Fraser's division, to which he belonged, should encamp at Fort Anne.

As the progress of each army was regulated by the movements of the other, the two girls looked forward to leave their present location at nearly the same period.

In the meantime, they occupied themselves by various means.   Although Miss Jane continued her home with her brother's family, she was with Molly daily, and they had thus become so much attached to each other, as to be inseparable for a longer time.   Sometimes, they assisted Mrs. McNiel in her garden, for, in the absence of men in battle, women were compelled to such labors ; and thus, Molly's health improved rapidly, so that the bloom came back to her cheek in deeper richness than ever, and her dark eyes kindled anew their wonted fires.   She often rode Black Princess

about the immediate neighborhood, and trained her to accomplish many surprising feats of docility and daring. She
never hesitated to go to the pasture for her horse, when
wanted. On such occasions, Black Princess would raise her
head in reply to Molly's winning call, and with an answering
neigh, start toward her at a gentle trot, while she fearlessly
awaited her coming. After caressing the long, shining
mane of the horse, Molly would say, "Stoop now, while I
mount." The trained creature would lower her body easily,
till Molly had sprung upon her back, when she would start
directly for the house. There, under a particular tree
she would await Molly's pleasure, without bridle or
chain.

Wherever Molly wished to go, Black Princess was faithful, making her way over uncertain places with an Indian
caution, passing danger with speed, and always obeying the
sound of her mistress' voice.

On one oppressively sultry afternoon, she had slowly
rode her horse to the top of the hill, which we have mentioned, while Miss Jane walked by her side; when dismounting,
Molly bade Black Princess go free, leaving the bridle upon
her neck. The two girls seated themselves under the pine
tree by the gushing spring, sighing for a breath of air, but
they had scarcely done so, before Miss Jane exclaimed :

"Look, Molly, toward the west. That black cloud is
bringing up a thunder shower."

"Never mind," replied Molly, when she had glanced in
the direction indicated, "a rain will be delightful in this

dead heat. How the parched earth, with its withered herbage, will rejoice in renewed freshness!"

"But we must hasten back," said Miss Jane, with a troubled brow, "for, although we have been too engaged to notice it before, the clouds are gathering rapidly."

While she yet spoke, they saw a zig-zag line of fire cut the distant black horizon, and Miss Jane shuddered with fear. She was one, whom a thunder storm strongly moved, for an electric sympathy thrilled through all her delicate organization. In the words of the great German poet, she could say : "When the most ancient, holy father, with quiet hand, sows lightning over the earth from rolling clouds, I kiss the lowest hem of his robe, my faithful heart deeply impressed with filial awe." Molly, on the contrary, was seldom so much at home with her nerves and spirit, as in the height of a terrific thunder storm. The solemn majesty and sound of the striving clouds, the fall of many waters from the upper deep, and the whole picture of empurpled gloom, inspired her with exultation and delight. Had she ever read the grand scenes of gods and men, engraved with immortal pen by "the blind, old man of Chios," she would have recalled them, at such moments, as a glorious illumination of the battle of the elements.

"I have often thought it would be a grand thing to watch a real thunder shower, out of doors upon some eminence commanding a wide prospect of heaven and earth," said Molly ; "and as all appearances promise one at this time, I shall remain here, while you may go to the house."

"Remain here, Molly!" exclaimed Miss Jane, turning pale at the suggestion; "you cannot be in earnest."

"Never more so," answered Molly, with a merry smile.

"But what will you do? Your health is scarcely established, and you will get drenched with rain. Should the lightning strike this tall tree"——

"Not more likely to strike it to-day, than through all the summers it has stood here; besides I am going to stay under there," Molly said, indicating a rude shed near the tree, which had been put up for temporary use by woodmen in the previous winter.

"This is madness!" said Miss Jane; "Mr. Rushton would greatly disapprove of such an act."

"Fortunately he is not here."

"Dear Molly, how can you be so determined?" said Miss Jane, the tears filling her sad eyes; "is not my love to you of the least influence?"

Molly threw her arms around her friend's neck, and kissed her impulsively.

"Now dearest, be good, and let me have my own sweet will for once," she said, in her fascinating manner, which no one could resist, could they see her face in all its beauty. "Do go home, and leave me to myself and the lightning. If it is ordered that I shall die here, it will be magnificent to have my spirit go out of life on a shaft of fire!"

"Don't speak thus," expostulated Miss Jane.

"Why not? I am unshackled by love. No Captain Jones would mourn for me."

The magic name, as usual, brought a slight color to the pale cheek of Miss Jane, and she said :

" But there are those who would mourn for you. Oh, Molly, is it possible you have never suspected how dear you are to Hollis ?"

" See !" now broke out Molly, with pretended indifference to the last words, " between yonder hills the rain falls in sheets ! if you don't hasten, you will be overtaken."

" Then I must leave you here alone !"

" Not alone. I will get Black Princess here, for my company," said Molly, spying her horse, grazing quietly in the vale below.

" I only hope you will not regret this freak, dear Molly," said Miss Jane, as she walked sadly away.

" One would think I had chosen to be left in a desert, to hear her talk," said Molly to herself ; " she speaks in all kindness, but I am glad I am not so soft-hearted."

Before Miss Jane had reached the house, Black Princess had been called to the pine tree, and bidden to stand there till the rain was over, while Molly stationed herself beneath the shed, where she could note the progress of the shower.

The threatening clouds came on, shedding darkness over all the earth beneath. Next, there was a perfect stillness— an ominous pause, as if the contending forces of the heavens were silently contemplating their path for the approaching combat. This feature of the scene inspired Molly with sublime awe. An incident which Mr. Rushton had once told her came to her mind—of Alexander, her prince of heroes ; when he had crossed the river Granicus with his troops, to attack the Persians, both armies halted on the brink of the river, and surveyed each other for a few moments in deep silence.

. This boding stillness was broken by a loud, heavy and long peal of thunder, which made the very pillars of the earth tremble, succeeded quickly by another shot of lurid light from the fissures of the mountain clouds. Great drops of rain began to fall. The trees of the neighboring wood swayed violently in the strong wind which had sprung up, bringing the shower nearer every moment.

The scene was now fairly opened, and Molly was content. With folded arms and steady gaze, she sat, looking near and afar, drinking in the inspiration of each changing aspect around her.

Soon the rain fell in torrents, and the thunder roars followed fast upon each other, like the the chariot wheels in the Olympian courses, or like the linked thunder-bolts, with which the hundred-armed giants warred against the Titans, while the lightnings played almost incessantly. Molly was drenched with the rain, for the rude hut in which she sat was but a poor shelter ; but she cared not. She thought this glorious spectacle was a recompense for all personal inconvenience ; so she only rang out her long, flowing hair, threw it back from her neck and brow, gathered up her dress from the pool of water which had opened its course near her feet, and marked the progress of events with not a whit less enthusiasm than at first.

Sometimes she saw a chain of lightning fall so near the house in the vale, which now seemed strangely insignificant, that she involuntarily stretched forth her hand to avert what seemed its certain doom. But the sharp light died out, and the old house remained unharmed.

"How much they are to be pitied down there!" she exclaimed, involuntarily ; "they lack the will and the courage to dare peril for the gratification of the sublimest exaltation of the soul !"

She had scarcely finished speaking, when she was attracted to look toward the neighboring wood by the sound of a crushing of the underbrush, under what seemed the rapid leaps of some animal. She strained her vision in a moment of doubt and fear. A bright flash of lightning now distinctly revealed a panther, issuing from the wood toward the spot where she sat. In an instant of terrible certainty, she comprehended her danger ! the panther had chosen this hour for the capture of the horse, as no domestic animal was left out over the night in this quarter. As yet, he could not have discovered her, for she was nearly concealed by the shed, but she knew that to hide herself with ultimate safety would be impossible. To attempt to escape by out-running the panther would be folly. She saw no hope.

"God have mercy !" she cried, with a low wail of agony, already, in fearful imaginings, seeing that last, fatal spring, which would bring her body under the teeth and claws of the monster.

Black Princess now discovered the approaching animal,

and with a wild neigh of terror trembled in every limb ; she had started to run, when a new thought struck Molly. There was not a moment to be lost, for the animal was coming on, gaining ferocity at every stride, as the distance lessened getween his prey. Molly cried aloud to Black Princess to stop. The horse obeyed, crouching low, till Molly had sprung upon her back.

"Now fly to the house," screamed Molly, seizing the mane, "Fast ! Faster ! Faster !"

Clinging convulsively to her neck, Molly held her seat firm-ly, while the horse shot forward with an almost supernatural speed. Suddenly, a chain of lightning fell athwart the air, and seemed to strike into the ground directly before them— so near that Molly felt its heat to the very core of her heart. A rattling, crashing, roaring peal of thunder immediately succeeded.

Black Princess stopped short. For an instant she reared, plunged violently, and betrayed a fear to go on over the path of fire ; but, seeing again the panther in unabated pursuit, she wheeled about and sat off in another direction, which Molly, saw with a new sense of desolation, took them farther away from human habitation, and, consequently, from the chance of escape. She urged her horse forward, however, with new cries, for the instant of delay had brought the pan-ther nearer than before, so that she could now distinguish his fierce tread, and the sharp growl of his exultation. Black Princess heard the sounds also, and with distended nostrils and panting breath flew over the ground so that her feet scarcely touched the surface. She was now gaining.

They had proceeded thus for some time, when the sounds of the pursuer seemed to have died away, or ceased altogether. The horse was ascending a slight hill, and naturally slackening a little, Molly ventured to turn and look behind her. The panther was not there!

"Oh, joy! we are safe at last; we have escaped!' cried Molly, to her horse. She breathed a long, free breath, and praised God. Gaining the top of the hill, Black Princess made a full stop and looked wildly about her.

"There he comes! Now we are gone!" gasped Molly, as she discovered the panther coming on in such a way as to face them directly. He had left the air-line of pursuit, and gone round the hill, doubtless planning by this stratagem to secure his victim without fail.

For one breath of time the horse stood eyeing the foe, undecided, then turning in a new direction, leaped off again, keenly, evenly, mightily. Molly beheld with amaze. Before them, now, was the river. She lost all hope once more, for her horse, goaded to madness with terror, was making directly for the steep bank! Now her fate was certain. No word of hers could restrain her horse, and, even if it could, she had not power to move her lips, they were blanched and parched with more than human suffering. Her face was pale and cold as marble, but strongly marked with veins, which had swelled to cords! There was ice in her heart, in every nerve; it needed little more to change it to the ice of death!

They reached the brow of the cliff. But a few yards lay between them and the panther, who was foaming with rage.

Dashing down the bank—over brushwood, and avoiding impending rocks, with a strong, yet sure step, Black Princess sprung into the water.

Molly closed her eyes. The fangs of the panther had reached her horse she believed, and they were sinking in the struggle.

A loud noise was now heard in their rear. The panther, intent upon his object, had thrown himself over the cliff, without noting his path, and fallen upon the rough rocks. With a horrible yawl of agony, he rolled off into the water, from which he never rose. The horse moved on, slowly but safely, for she was a fine swimmer, having been trained by her master.

"When they had gained the opposite shore and struggled up the cliff, to clear and safe footing, Molly stopped Black Princess, and looking toward the river, shouted :

"There ! Thanks to Heaven ! we have got over as much awful danger as the people who went over the Red Sea ! We have come off victorious at last ! Panther ! you may do your best now, for only Tophet is before you ! Black Princess !" she continued, in a soft, low voice, "noble creature ! you deserve Heaven for this. You shall be my own beloved horse, for evermore !"

It still rained, though the weight of the shower had passed over, and the lightnings played at some distance. Molly and her horse distreamed with water, presented but a sad spectacle now, of which she, with her ever-present sense of the ludicrous, was fully conscious.

"So much for my passion for the sublime !" she muttered. "The bounds from that to the ridiculous have been leaped."

Molly allowed her horse to take its own way, and, stricking into an easy trot, in half an hour she arrived at a dwelling-house, before which she stopped. The people, who were known to Molly, rushed out, and divining that some unusual event must have happened, overwhelmed her with inquiries. The reaction was too great for Molly's endurance. The sense of security, the change of motion, the relaxation of her nerves, which had been strung to the last tension, all conspired to gain the mastery. Without speaking a word, she fainted, and fell into their arms.

CHAPTER XIII.

The Revolutionary War, it is well known, was a period of most important action to the Indians, as well as to the Americans. This struggle brought into notice powerful chiefs, who led their tribes upon the side which policy or predilection dictated. No efforts were spared by the British on the northern frontier, and by individual refugees who had espoused their cause, to prejudice these chiefs against the Americans, and consolidate a belligerent union with themselves. Ambition, jealousy of encroachment upon long established rights, avarice, the memory of old wrongs, were all artfully appealed to, that their already heated spirits might be kindled to the height of revenge against those, who were termed "the disobedient children of the common Father, over the big water." In the spring of 1777, on the western banks of Lake Champlain, Burgoyne and Carleton met the Indians in a grand council, after which they gave them a war-feast.

To retain them in the British interests, Burgoyne promised a tempting reward for all prisoners from among the rebels, although it was alleged that he endeavored to impress them with the difference between enemies in the field of battle, and helpless, unarmed inhabitants. Subsequent events proved that the Indians were too savage or avaricious to stand upon what they looked upon as nice distinctions. Notwithstanding this must have been foreseen by the British, they made no scruple in engaging them in the work of blood among those whom they had regarded as kinspeople. Lord Suffolk, secretary of state, advocated the employment of the Indians in the war against the rebellious colonists in the memorable words which take high rank upon the page of inhuman sophistry.

" Beside its policy and necessity," his lordship said, " that the measure was also allowable on principle, for it was perfectly justifiable to use all the means which God and nature had put into our hands !" A measure, justly compared by Lord Chatham to that which armed Spain with blood-hounds to extirpate the natives of Mexico.

From these vindictive foes, great peril impended over those Americans who were known to be in favor of the cause of independence, but those who were neutral, or favorable to the British, felt comparatively secure. The present location of Molly was regarded by Mr. Rushton as among the safest, for many of her immediate neighbors, among whom was the brother of Miss Jane, were in favor of the British interests.

Under these circumstances, Molly sometimes ventured in

At the first touch of the bridle, the horse sprang backward, and rearing almost perpendicularly, she came down and struck the Indian with her hoof so sharply upon his breast that he fell to the ground instantly.—PAGE 211.

the public road which led to the next settlement, alone upon Black Princess, for the purpose of ascertaining if letters came to her from Mr. Rushton. Her adventure with the panther had not destroyed her courage, for in that time, all lived in expectation of peril and remarkable experience on every hand. But her resolution to gratify her love for the sublime, against the advice of friends, was certainly lessened for the present.

One day, she was returning home somewhat thoughtfully, having received no tidings from Mr. Rushton—a disappointment which she had repeated of late—when coming to a lonely spot at some distance from a human habitation, she saw a young Indian in full war-dress, suddenly spring out and confront her with an eye which boded no good. Black Princess stopped and breathed furiously, as was her habit when alarmed.

"Go on, like a dart," said Molly to her horse, in hurried accents.

Before Black Princess could move, the Indian seized the bridle firmly with one hand, while with the other, he aimed his tomahawk at Molly's head.

At the first touch of the bridle, the horse sprang backward, and rearing almost perpendicularly, to the eminent risk of Molly's losing her seat, she came down and struck the Indian with her hoof so sharply upon his breast that he fell to the ground instantly.

The horse then passed over the body with a fierce tread, leaving the Indian either dead, or perfectly insensible.

"Well done, my noble Princess !" cried Molly, when fully conscious of her almost miraculous escape ; "a second time have you bravely saved my life !"

She then gave the rein to her horse, and sped forward as rapidly as possible, till she had come to a small building by the way—the residence of an old man and his wife, who had often received the charities of Mr. Rushton, and Molly was well known to them. Meeting them before the door, she recounted what had happened with great animation.

"Ah ! child, you've got the real spirit of bravery in you, no mistake ; and that are horse o' yourn is worth her weight in gold," commented the old man.

"Are you sartain, Molly," said his wife, " that the savage is clean killed ? May be he'll take it into his head to come to life again, and so will be here to scalp us."

"Don't be a coward, mother," expostulated the old man.

"I can't help feelin' amazin' different sence my boys have gone to the wars," she continued ; "it makes me shake in every jint now, ef I hear of an Injun within ten mile."

"He may not be wholly dead," replied Molly, thoughtfully ; "Perhaps Black Princess only knocked the breath out of him."

"Ef he does come to life, he'll take to his heels most likely," remarked the old man.

"To leave him there half dead, were more cruel than to dispatch him outright," said Molly ; "I cannot go home till I know certain."

"Sposin' I take my gun, and get on ter your horse, and

go back to where the dog lies, while you stay here," said the old man.

"What ef he should be live 'nuff to kill you?" suggested his wife with terror.

"Don't mind me," returned the old man, "I can level a bear or red nigger jest as slick as ever I could in my young days. Ef he crawl an inch, I'll make sure on him afore he can wink.',

"But I must go, too," said Molly, "for you don't know the spot so exactly as I do. So, just put Black Princess to your old cart, there, and we'll jog along together."

"Well, if you must go—go, though I should'nt think you'd want ter, for you may lose that fine head of yourn, Molly, after all."

"I'll risk it," answered Molly, springing to the ground.

The arrangements were completed in a few minutes, and Molly, with the old man, started off, while the old woman shouted after them "to be careful, and come back soon with whole heads on their shoulders."

They were, indeed, a comical picture of two brave scouts. Molly unconsciously acted upon the maxim of one of the Grecian sages, "Know your opportunity."; She would never let slip an opportunity for adventure.

Approaching the spot where the Indian was left, they perceived that he had revived sufficiently to raise himself upon his hands. Molly next comprehended that he was young and remarkably handsome for one of his race, having fine intelligent eyes and regular, though sternly chiselled features,

and clothed in a war dress, strikingly becoming and
picturesque. The small portion of his hair which had been
suffered to remain upon his head, hung low, and was ornamented with silver brooches and feathers of various brilliant
colors. Silver drops hung from his ears. His blanket was
fastened with a clasp on which was a large plate with a
picture of a wild animal. A belt of scarlet, from which was
suspended his scalping knife, circled his waist. The red
buskins, and moccasins ornamented with various colored
beads, graced his limbs and feet. All this, Molly, with her
woman's eye, saw at a glance. But her companion only
understood the necessity for immediate action.

Springing down from the cart, the old man took up his
gun, while he said, in a low determined voice :

" I'll put the dog savage down again, quick, so he'll stay
quiet for one long spell, I reckon."

A wild emotion sent the blood from Molly's heart. There
lay the young warrior with his dark, liquid eyes fastened
upon hers with a look of admiration—half supplication, perhaps, though he scorned to open his lips to sue for mercy.

" Stay !" she cried with a loud voice to the old man, just
as he had taken aim, " stay, for the love of Heaven !"

" What now !" he responded.

" You must not kill him. I cannot see him die here."

" Turned into a coward, so soon, gal ? But a few minutes
ago, I set ye down for the right smartest gal I ever see in my
life. Turn your head one side, if ye don't want to see him
shot."

"No, no," said Molly, hurriedly; "let him live now, if he will."

"Live ! this ere critter that would have killed ye, ef it hadn't been for your luck. Nonsense ! The more on 'em that's cut down the safer."

Again the old man raised his gun.

"Stop !" cried Molly, with a voice of authority, not to be mistaken. "He belongs to me. He shall be my prisoner. If I wish to spare his life, I have a full right to do so. By the memory of all which Mr. Rushton has ever done for you, I ask you this one favor. Can you refuse me ?"

"You don't know nothing what you're talkin' about," said the old man, impatiently. "The sight of this ere Injun has charmed you just like the eye of a snake. Sposin' I save him, what can you do with him ?"

"We'll help him into the cart and take him home."

"He'll kill us jest as soon as he gits back his strength."

"No," said Molly, looking the Indian in the eye, "he cannot harm one who spares his life."

The young brave returned her glance with interest, which made Molly blush roses. But recalling her humane purpose, she immediately settled into calmness, and with decision went forward in its execution. When the old man had bound the Indian's hands with his neckerchief for greater security, by dint of various efforts, he was laid in the cart.

"Now," said he, "you drive away smart, Molly, while I hold this ere dog down by the feet, for I couldn't trust myself on the seat there with you under sich circumstances as these, for what my neck is worth."

Molly could not refrain from smiling as she turned and saw the picture behind her : then giving her horse intimations to lose no time, they went on, jolting up and down over the uneven road in a fashion which must have operated upon the Indian's prostrate body like continued shocks of galvanism.   When they had come to his house, the old man informed his wife that all was well, as yet, only Molly had taken it in her head to do a mighty strange thing, the account of which, he promised to give her in good time.   Molly drove on to Mrs. McNiel's, well knowing that there would be no quarter for her prisoner in the home of the old people. When she had arrived home, she was met by Mrs. McNiel and Miss Jane, who had awaited her return with unusual anxiety, on account of her protracted abscence.

"What can have happened, now ?" they demanded, seeing her in such a singular plight.   Molly pointed mysteriously to the Indian, and was silent.

"I'll tell ye, what's happened," broke out the old man, "this ere gal, that I've allers thought one of the most knowingest in all these parts, has, all of a sudden turned fool!"

Molly laughed lightly, and briefly narrated her adventure, concluding with a whisper that perhaps the Indian was in the service of General Fraser, and might be able to communicate something in regard to Captain Jones.   This supposition operated entirely to her expectations, and the Indian was assisted into the house without remonstrance.

Molly strove at once to effect the recovery of her captive by such means as were recommended by Mrs. McNiel, who was well skilled in the art of healing, and a few wounds which had been made upon his head, she dressed carefully with her own hands. When this was done, and the Indian was able to sit up, he broke the grave silence for the first time.

"The great Spirit smile on white squaw. She save Iroquo from the Long Knife. White squaw's face like the sun ; shine on Iroquo's heart when he go to the battle of the braves."

"You would have taken my life," replied Molly, fearlessly, "had it not been for the Great Spirit, who permitted my horse to save me One moment more, and I should have been stiff in death, and my scalp would now hang from your hunting-belt."

"Me no tell white squaw so brave. Me see white squaw on horse ; me say—another scalp for Iroquo. Then lift tomahawk," returned the young warrior.

"The great Spirit never made you to kill people in this way," pursued Molly.

"Iroquo kill no more Long-Knives if all like white squaw," he said, with profound admiration lighting all his stern face.

"Remember that I have saved your life, and spare the white squaws, as you call them, hereafter," said Molly, earnestly.

"None so beautiful as this one," said the Indian ; "none so much like the roses in the moon of strawberries."

Molly blushed again, and moved away. Miss Jane then

asked him if he knew aught of General Fraser's division of the British army.　　But the warrior was wily, and cautious, so that he evaded her question.

"You will tell us something about Captain Jones," said Molly, coaxingly, "you have seen him, I presume?"

The young warrior nodded, but remained silent.

"Was he well?" continued Molly.

Another nod.

"Do not hesitate to speak," said Molly, " this young wo- man here, is to be his bride.　　She would be glad to hear from him, if you can tell where and how he is."

The Indian then made them understand that Captain Jones was well, and that the division to which he belonged would encamp near Fort Anne, on the Hudson, in a few weeks.

Miss Jane then inquired if he would take a letter for her to him, and being answered in the affirmative, she sat about writing a few lines, hastily to her lover.

" Don't put in a word about my adventure to-day," said Molly in an aside, " for should he know that our lives were thus perilled, he would not rest a moment."

" I have already thought of that," said Miss Jane.

The Indian recovered his strength rapidly, for with the hardy firmness of his race, he refused to submit to pain.　　He was, by and by, able to stand upon his feet, and he walked to the door, impatient to be gone.　　Still he would occasion- ally cast a look upon Molly, which betrayed that his heart, at least, was content in her presence, however much his brain

might counsel other movements. Once more erect and clothed with the grave majesty of his natural mold of form and
feature, he was a picture, not a whit inferior to that of a
Grecian athlete. His figure, straight as an arrow, and lithe
with blended grace and strength, was certainly a model of
manly beauty.

Molly could not refrain from questioning him as to his history, to which he replied with evident pride :

" Iroquo is the first born of the great chief Elskawora, the
Iron Heel. His tribe is powerful as the mighty river ; in
battle, hot as the sun and victorious as the strong wind
which sweeps down all in its path ; in death, brave as the
rock, which bends not, nor groans. Iroquo is known, among
the braves, as the *medicine man.*"

" You fight with the British, against us," said Molly, sorrowfully, " will you not promise me to kill no more of my
people ?"

" The young warrior shook his head and frowned.

" The Long-Knives drive our fathers from the big lake to
the mountains. Next, drive red man farther, till no ground
of their own is left. They kill our squaws and pappoose.
They cheat us with smooth words ; give bad pay for our
peltry. Me no promise not to lift the tomahawk—not to
flourish their scalps from my belt. Iroquo hath spoken."

" But you will promise to spare our women and children—
for my sake ?" pursued Molly, drawing nearer to him, and
looking up in his stern face, entreatingly.

" Iroquo promise to save this white squaw, and all loved

by her," he said, with a tender glance.   " Come to our wig-
wams, and me make her a queen."

"Oh ! no," returned Molly, with a merry shake of her
head.   " I should be frightened out of my wits to be among
your people for a moment.   You forget how near I came
losing my own precious life, but a few hours ago."

Miss Jane had now completed her brief letter, and gave
it to Iroquo, who promised to see it safely delivered.   He
was preparing to go, when he paused and waited irresolute,
as if desirous to say something more.

" What would you speak ?" asked Molly.

" Let Iroquo have one lock of white squaw's hair—then
he will bound away like an elk ?"

" What for ?" asked Molly, with a smile.

" Me wear it in this belt, instead of scalp.   Me proud of
it.   Me keep it till go to the Great Spirit's hunting grounds,
for a charm ?"

" And whenever you look at it, you will remember the
promise which you have made me ?"

" Iroquo hath spoken."

Molly, laughingly, severed a long tress of her dark hair and
gave it to Iroquo, saying :

" My name is Molly, and by this hair, remember evermore
the words you have spoken to me this day."

" Iroquo may meet Molly again," he replied.

" If not, you may meet those whom I would wish you to
spare," said Molly.

The young warrior thrust the hair into his bosom, and

with one more look of passionate admiration upon Molly, bounded away with fleet strides.

"You have made quite a conquest," said Mrs. McNiel to Molly, as she stood in the door and watched the retreating figure of Iroquo.

"Thanks to a merciful Heaven! I have been able to save my own life and that of another," she returned.

At this moment, the Indian stopped once more, for an instant, looked back on Molly, then turned and vanished from her sight.

"Ah! me!" said Molly, gaily, "how handsome and lover-like these young savages are!"

"Hollis would not like to hear such words fall from your lips," commented Miss Jane.

"Hollis has no power over me," returned Molly.

"Not when he would lay down his life for yours, if need be, so greatly and truly does he love you!"

"There is no such love as that," said Molly, forcing a serious look. "Once, I was foolish enough to have faith in the idea—the chimera,—as you do now. But I am too wise henceforth to trust in any man."

Miss Jane shook her head, incredulously.

"I fear you do not understand or appreciate true love—such as, for instance, I think Hollis hides in his heart," she said.

"You may say rather Captain Jones, if you like," returned Molly, "Hollis lacks the stuff which makes a hero. A cabinet of curiosities, made up of odd rocks, dead bipeds, quadrupeds, and the like, inspires him infinitely above a field of brave men in deadly combat, or any other scene which requires sublime courage and god-like fortitude. He is not enough like the brave conqueror—the great Alexander—for me to admire.

"Would you have him a slave to various vices, among which cruelty was conspicuous through life, and die vanquished by brutish interference and excess, before he had lived half his days, as did this same lauded hero of yours?" asked Miss Jane.

"I would have Hollis what he is *not*," replied Molly, with impatience.

"My dear Molly," said Miss Jane, "would that you could estimate your friends by the standard of true goodness, rather than by a greatness which has no solid foundation—which cannot stand the test of righteous judgement."

"Ah! but there is something so noble, so glorious," continued Molly, her dark eyes flashing with the light of passionate enthusiasm, "in one whose valor fears nothing—not even death! Whose right arm, is invincible, while its strength endures! Who will, as you say, offer his life to save the life or the honor of the one he loves, as did the chivalric knights of old. Such an one, I could more than love—for love is but a flickering fancy. I could—were it not sinful—worship!"

"I begin to think that you will never find your hero, so high do you rate the requisites of the ideal," remarked Miss Jane, with a smile.

A thought of Reuben Epps now smote Molly to the heart. He *had been* her hero, she could not but confess to herself, although no warrior, nor wonderful personage. She said no more, but escaped to her little white chamber, to think and weep alone.

CHAPTER XIV.

"HARK! THEY WHISPER."

THE British troops were rapidly advancing upon the northern army of the Americans. St. Leger had joined Burgoyne at Ticonderoga, upon the evacuation of that post, and they were now moving down the Hudson. To arrange their plans for an attack, the enemy halted some miles above Fort Edward, near which were encamped the two divisions of the American army, commanded by general Schuyler and Arnold. At this point, Captain Jones, of General Fraser's detachment, had promised to come in person for Miss Jane, and their marriage was to be solemnized immediately after. In the home of Mrs. McNiel, she was awaiting her lover, for this place had been selected by the British officer, as affording greater security than her brother's residence, which was below the American camp. Mrs. McNeil was to accompany them to the British camp, in the expectation of meeting her son, and it was arranged that Molly was to remain with a neighbor's family until the return of Mrs. McNiel, or the arrival of Mr. Rushton, which was now daily expected.

The day appointed for the departure of Miss Jane, had come. Notwithstanding the anticipated bliss of a union with him from whom she had been so long separated, she was sad when she remembered that she must now be parted from Molly, who, with her odd, winning ways, had become endeared to her heart with an imperishable affection.

Molly was like herself, not less on this occasion than all others,—now the embodiment of a sunbeam aslant a flower, and again a dew drop under the shadow. It was a very warm day in midsummer, and she proposed that they should choose seats in the open air, beneath the old trees which whispered softly over the door ; thus they could catch the first glimpse of Captain Jones, and with the neighbors and children who had come to see Miss Jane go away, they would form a picturesque group to await his coming. On that morning and the day previous, Molly had gathered wild flowers plentifully, and she now busied herself, with the assistance of the children, in arranging pretty knots and wreaths for Miss Jane, who looked etherially lovely in her dress of snow white muslin, without other adorning than a delicate blue sash, beautiful as the girdle of Venus, and her long hair falling in curls over her bosom.

" There !" exclaimed Molly, poising Miss Jane's straw hat upon her fingers, when she had completed its decoration with flowers, " is not that beautiful enough for a royal bride —or," she added with an arch look, " for the bride of a royalist ?"

"Too gay for me," replied Miss Jane, faintly smiling ; "It would better adorn your own face, Molly."

In answer to this, Molly persisted in trying it over Miss Jane's curls, to witness the triumph of her skill, which at once elicited various expressions of admiration from the assembled group.

"Pray don't look so sad, my blessing," said Molly, kissing her friend under the hat, "one would think you were preparing for a funeral instead of a wedding."

Sounds as of approaching persons now being heard from a distance, all turned their eyes in the expectation of seeing Captain Jones. After waiting anxiously for some time, nothing unusual being visible, the noise was attributed to proceed from the picket of soldiers which were stationed on guard upon the hill, just beyond the pine tree, and out of view from their position. Once more Miss Jane was disappointed, for the hour appointed for the coming of her lover had passed.

"Every hour of this delay is one more for me," said Molly.

"Only yesterday," said Mrs. McNiel, "when Miss Jane reminded you of the danger of going so far out alone after flowers you said that you should be glad when she was gone."

"Oh, that was only talk," replied Molly, "but what I now say is serious confab.

"'How blessings brighten as they take their flight.'

"After you are gone," continued Molly, throwing her arms

about Miss Jane, "I shall truly be almost in despair—perhaps quite. I am alone in the world. Every body I ever loved has left me, and "——

Her voice failed; tears of real sorrow trembled upon her long lashes.

"Dearest Molly!" said Miss Jane, returning the caress, and drawing Molly's lips to her own, "I will not leave you, but remain here till Mr. Rushton comes. It is no more than right that I should do so."

"No!" replied Molly, rallying immediately, "I could not consent to your making such a sacrifice for me. Mr. Rushton will be here in a day or two, and until then, I will try and keep heart. I am no sniveler or coward."

"But do not venture beyond protection, I beseech you, Molly," said her friend, with a troubled look.

"When you are fairly out of the way," continued Molly, with a toss of her head, "I intend to go down to the American encampment, present myself before the General, and say—here is a new recruit for you. Give me a picked body of dragoons, the very flower of the army, to lead in the face of the enemy, and I, with Black Princess, will win glory or death; ever repeating Alexander's favorite maxim, 'no place is impregnable to the brave!' "

Molly's auditors now laughed, and various were the comments elicited in response.

"General Arnold will, probably, commission you without a moment's delay," remarked Mrs. McNiel.

"I shall not offer myself to Benedict Arnold!" returned Molly, with spirit.

"He commands the division stationed nearest to us."

"Yes, but I do not like him."

"He is a brave man, Molly," said Miss Jane, "have you forgotten his gallant action at the capture of Ticonderoga, the storming of Quebec, and the battle on Lake Champlain?"

"Or at Danbury," continued Mrs. McNiel, "when his horse was killed under him, and in the next moment, without stirring from his saddle, he coolly shot an enemy who was rushing towards him with a fixed bayonet!"

"He may be brave in a certain sense," said Molly, "but there is something in his eye which is uncertain. I saw him, once, at New York, when with Mr. Rushton, and I disliked him."

"How did he look?" inquired one.

"His eye was like a piece of burnt glass set in flint, and there was an ugly frown on his brow. His face was all over a bad one."

"I should have supposed that Arnold, whose bravery has won such distinction, would have taken high rank upon your list of heroes," said Miss Jane.

"Hark!" exclaimed Molly, "I heard those sounds again. What can they mean?"

After again listening in vain, and perceiving that Miss Jane looked more troubled and anxious, Molly began to plan for something new to consume the time.

"Let us sing before we part," she suggested at length, "I feel just sad enough to hear once more your sweet, melancholy voice, dearest Jane."

Accordingly, all joined in singing a favorite and familiar hymn. Being near the water and in the open air, the melody was particularly beautiful and impressive, and under the present circumstances, it was even affecting, so that as the strain went on tears came to every eye.

After they had ended, at Molly's request, Miss Jane commenced singing alone the immortal ode of " The dying Christian to his soul." When she came to the lines—

"Hark! they whisper: angels say,
Sister spirit, come away,"

an indescribable presence of awe fell upon each heart, and the overarching trees seemed tremulous with the sublime mystery of that hour. Miss Jane ever sung this with surpassing sweetness, but now, her tones were more than usually pathetic and expressive.

Like one of the gods, of whom it is said the daughter of Aristacus annointed his lips with honey, sweet as the juice of flowers, were the solemn words upon her lips. In a vanishing breath of music, like the wind-harp, her voice ceased, leaving a profound silence broken at last, by Molly.

"As I listened, I could almost imagine myself in heaven," she said ; " dear Jane, you seem now as though you only needed wings to be an angel of the first water."

" I always think of· my dead father when I sing those words, for they were upon his lips in the dying hour," observed Miss Jane, in that low, softened modulation of voice, into which relapse sensitive souls after exquisite melody, as though but late communing with spirits of the upper realm. " I saw him last night in my dream," she continued, " and I was never so happy. My soul seemed triumphant over earth, and crowned with that glory which eye hath not seen nor ear heard. I thought he cut from my head a lock of hair, and just then I awoke thinking of a passage in Virgil which I used to read with Mr. Jones, in school."

" What was it ?" inquired Molly.

" One which speaks of Juno sending Iris from Olympus, to relieve Dido in the struggles of death, by cutting a lock of her hair."

" That was equal to my clipping off a tress of my hair for Iroquo," returned Molly.

But she had scarcely spoken these words, before Mrs. McNiel sprang up, and pointing toward the hill, cried in a voice of affright—

" See the Indians !"

Now, the alarm was not a vain one, for all could plainly discover a small party of Indians rapidly descending the hill, towards that very spot. So much had they been pre-occupied, that they had not perceived the savages until their near approach. With blanched faces, they cried at once :—

" We must fly for our lives !"

" Oh ! where is David !" exclaimed Miss Jane, in tremulous tones, " shall I never see him again !"

They were attempting to escape, when the Indians shouted to attract their attention and made signs that they were come upon an errand of peace.

"They hold up a letter?" exclaimed Molly. "Perhaps it is from Captain Jones."

Somewhat reassured, all now awaited the coming of the Indians, but the spectacle was not one to inspire the defence-less group with courage.

The red warriors came up and intimated that the letter was to be opened. Miss Jane received it with great agi-tation and read as follows :

"Dearest Jane :—I find it is impossible for me to keep my promise to go for you to-day. General Fraser has just ordered us to prepare to march forward, and an imperative duty is assigned me. But these Indians are friendly to us, and I have promised them a handsome reward for conducting you to me : so, accept their escort, till I can fold you in my arms and end our long and painful separation. Until then, every moment will be an age of suspense, to your devoted,

"DAVID JONES."

Miss Jane briefly communicated the purport of the letter, and the Indians signed to her to follow them.

"The way is not long," said Mrs. McNiel "and we will go."

"Then I will walk with you as far as the pine tree," said Molly.

"Molly, darling," said Miss Jane in a low, tremulous voice, as they went forward, "should we never meet again, let me intreat you to fix your trust in Heaven. Do not for-get Hollis, for his great love for you should not be unre-warded.'

"I shall never see him more ;" returned Molly, "all my

friends are taken from me. You, my best friend must go now!"

She burst into tears, and Miss Jane tried to console her with words of love and hope.

They now met other Indians, who had evidently awaited their coming, to join them. Molly was reminded of Iroquo and sought to discover his face among them; but he was not there. No sooner had the parties of Indians met, than a quarrel arose between the two chiefs, and all halted upon the spot. With a face like marble, and speechless with terror, Miss Jane looked despairingly upon her friends, while the savage warriors exchanged angry words and looks of menance. At length they sprang upon each other with violent blows, when one of them suddenly drew backward a pace and leveled his musket at Miss Jane.

With a wild shriek, Molly sprang forward to rescue her friend; but it was too late. She fell, shot to the heart, and instantly expired. So died Jane MacCrea, whose tragical story is imperishably written in the annals of the American Revolution, and, in the words of a distinguished historian, " will be perpetuated as a memento of the melancholy fate of suffering innocence, and an affecting record of the horrors of savage warfare !"

The murderous chief completed his deed by striking the body of the dead till he had gloated his fury; then, exchanging his tomahawk for the scalping knife, he grasped the long curls and quickly took off the scalp, which he flourished before his warriors with a yell of triumph, echoed

It missed the object of her aim, but struck another Indian, who stood a few steps behind, fatally cleaving his skull.—PAGE 233.

by every savage present. This was too much for Molly's
endurance. Seizing the tomahawk which lay upon the
ground, she threw it with all the violence in her power
at the head of the chief who held the scalp. It missed the
object of her aim, but struck another Indian, who stood a
few steps behind, fatally cleaving his skull. At this, the
Indians set up a furious war-cry, and bidding a few of their
warriors to go on with the other white prisoners, they seized
Molly, bound her hands and fastened her to the pine tree.
They then made her understand, if she screamed, they would
also shoot her upon the spot, for their position being not
far from the American camp, was by no means secure.
Molly looked earnestly about her to discover the picket of
soldiers, commanded by Lieutenant Van Vechten, whose
station had been near the pine tree, but all were dispersed,
and a narrow inspection disclosed to her sight, the dead
bodies of several of the soldiers lying among the surrounding bushes. She now comprehended the cause of the singular disturbance which they had indistinctly heard, prior to
the appearance of the Indians, and with terrible forebodings
she could not resist the fear that she was destined for a
similar fate. If strength had remained, she would have
yielded to grief at the contemplation of the spectacle before
her, including most conspicuously the corpse of her beloved
friend ; but the thought of her own situation overwhelmed
every other. Her attention was soon attracted to the
Indians who were now hastily collecting sticks and bushes,
which they heaped about her feet, as she stood confined to

the tree. Not imagining their design, she beheld their motions in amazement, till one of them attempted to strike fire with his flint.

A new, terrible suspicion rushed into her thought.

"Oh ! Great God !" she exclaimed huskily, "I am not to be burned alive ?"

"The pale squaw will soon roast in the fire of the red braves," returned one of the savages, with a look of stern exultation.

"White squaw must burn," assented several voices : "Our dead brave calls to us, as he goes to the Great Spirit's hunting grounds."

In a similar spirit which prompted Achilles to sacrifice twelve Trojans to the manes of Patroclus, and Evander numerous captives at the funeral of his son Pallas, they determined upon the death of their captive ; and, to entirely and suitably destroy her life, she must be burned alive, like Triptolemus. Therefore, let it be remembered that the remorseless brutality of the North American savage is not without a parallel, even in the most distinguished annals of classic antiquity !

"Have mercy !" cried Molly, grasping her hands till her fingers were torn with wounds. "Will none of you release me ?"

The Indians pointed to the body of their warrior and were silent, while they continued the preparations for their fiendish work. In that moment, a memory of her past-life darted through her brain upon the swift current of her agony, and with uplifted eyes she commended her soul to God. The Indian approached with the kindled torch. Unconsciously, Molly struggled to free herself from the awful doom ; but in vain. Nothing was clearer than that she was wholly in the power of the remorseless savages. In frantic despair, she cried out :

" Shoot me dead at once, I implore, and let me not perish in the fire. Is there none to save me from this horrid fate ?"

As if her prayer had been heard in that moment, a soldier emerged from the neighboring thicket with rapid strides, and, before the Indians could rally, he stood before the tree.

" Hollis !" screamed Molly, her eyeballs dilating with astonishment, "save me ! save me ! See, they are going to burn me to death !"

Two Indians quickly grasped Hollis, for it was he, and bound his hands behind him.

" Let her free," spoke Hollis, in a tone of mastering energy, "and you shall have *gold*—more gold than a British hand has ever given you."

The chief who had killed Miss Jane, shook his head and answered :

" The pale face has killed our brave Openochorekough, the long-haired warrior of the Lakes. She must die. The great chief Wolf-teeth hath spoken."

The other Indians responded to this with a low growl of approbation.

" You. can spare her for a prisoner, and get a large reward," urged Hollis. "It is money from the white men that you most want."

"Blood! blood!" howled the chief, whose looks warranted his appellation, as he ground his teeth with fury and cast ravenous glances upon poor Molly—the trembling, half-dead victim. "We will drink the blood of white squaw's heart."

"Then," said Hollis, with a solemn fortitude worthy of a martyr, "shed my blood.' I will die in her stead. Unbind her, and you shall have gold, while my blood shall be sacrificed for the loss of your warrior."

"No, no!" remonstrated Molly, "I will not be saved at the expense of your life, Hollis. I will burn up all to ashes first."

"It must be so, dearest Molly," answered Hollis, in a tone of measureless affection.

"Oh! never," groaned Molly; "I could not live another moment after No, unsay those words. I will die."

The Indians, perceiving at once with their keen penetration that Molly was unwilling that Hollis should suffer, fell upon a new expedient, after holding a brief war-council together. To heighten the misery of their captive, Hollis should die first, by slow tortures, before her eyes! Accordingly, Molly was unbound, and, notwithstanding her wild entreaties, Hollis was placed at the tree. Then, taking several instruments of cruelty which they invariably carried in their hunting-belt, they began their operations.

First, they drew the nails from his fingers, while Molly

was compelled to look on, in sympathizing agony. But Hollis, though pale as one of the dead bodies around him, did not yield to a murmur.

Meantime, the Indians sent up a harsh, wild-cat yell, like the cry of exultant fiends, gaining strength and ferocity at every repetition.

They next proceeded to cut off the crown of the skin of his head, with a dull scalping-knife. Now he groaned aloud with the unendurable pain, at which sound, Molly faintly moaned in complete exhaustion of nerve, and fell down in a deathly swoon.

As Molly was too insensible to be longer tormented by the sight of Hollis's agony, the Indians prepared to burn him, without further delay, lest they should be interrupted before the completion of their work. The torch was thrown on to the dry bushes of the pile ; the flames quickly arose, crackling and sparkling in the air, when, suddenly, the savages gave a loud and peculiar yell—the war-cry when surprised by an enemy. A band of soldiers from the American camp was approaching rapidly upon them !

Hollis was now quickly released from the tree, and, waiting only to secure him their prisoner, they all fled in an opposite direction, and were soon beyond the reach of their pursuers.

CHAPTER XV.

As Hollis came near the British encampment, a prisoner among the Indians, he perceived an officer rush out to meet them, and after hastily surveying them, pause, as though seized by some new emotion. He recognized him to be Captain Jones, and, notwithstanding his unhappy situation, the familiar face was a sudden pleasure.

Hollis was about to run the peril of addressing him, to make known his presence, when he was prevented by the officer demanding of one of the Chiefs, wherefore they had not conducted to him, her, whom he anxiously awaited?

"Was Miss McCrea not to be found where I directed? Or, was she unwilling to come with you?" he continued, in great excitement.

Wolf-teeth then produced the scalp of Miss Jane, and threw it down before him, with an exclamation of keen satisfaction.

Captain Jones stood motionless, as if stricken to the heart;

the color fled from his face ; and the words which trembled
upon his tongue, he could not utter.

"Wolf-teeth go with Walk-In-The-Water," spoke the
chief who had been sent for Miss Jane ; "he quarrel about
money get for white squaw. Then he shoot gun at squaw ;
she fall like a deer ; make no sound, die. Wolf-teeth take
off scalp, bring it to white chief.

"Wretches !" cried Captain Jones, in a voice of frantic
despair, "I would have given every drop of blood in my
veins to have spared her life. She was more precious to me
than all else on earth. Murderous wretches !" he continued,
with deeper emphasis, "how shall I punish you for this foul
work ?"

"Me think white chief want squaw for prisoner, bring
scalp to please him," answered Wolf-teeth, greatly astonished at the unexpected aspect of the affair.

"Take live prisoner, too," continued Walk-In-The-Water,
"kill Long Knives with guns, bring more scalps. For all
this fight, big chiefs in war-council call *glorious*, we think to
get much money."

The bereaved man comprehended the fatal mistake and
spoke not another word, lest his heart's blood should rush
from between his lips. Lifting the long hair of the idolized
dead from the ground, with a motion of the profoundest
grief, he disappeared into the camp.

The chiefs then sought audience with General Fraser and
delivered Hollis as a prisoner, for which service they received the ordinary reward. He was immediately put in irons

and consigned to a retired part of the camp. The situation in which Hollis now found himself, though infinitely preferable to the one from which he had escaped, was far from agreeable. In extreme pain from the wounds occasioned by the tortures of the Indians, with no future prospect save imprisonment, perhaps death ; and entirely uncertain of Molly's ultimate fate, his spirit, which by reason of a recent great misfortune, had been desponding, at first utterly fled. But it was an inexpressibly sweet reflection that he, who had ever deemed himself insignificant, had been instrumental in saving the life of Molly, in that most perilous hour of doom. When he thought of her, his distress was for the moment assuaged, if not forgotten ; his misery lightened of half its gloom. To his imagination, her bewitching face arose with a wonderful potency. It was cinctured with radiant beauty, and through tears, beamed on his soul with smiles of hope. Thus, he derived partial consolation, from what Aristo called "things sweet to see and sweet deceptions," till he remembered another heart in that same camp, which now bled at every pore in an anguish, exceeding his own. The picture of the scalp in the tremulous hand of the lover, brought the tears to his eyes for the first time, on that day.

Hours dragged on heavily to the suffering captive, bringing in the night. Amid the bustle of the camp, which was about breaking up, preparatory to the forward march, he was a solitary, for whom none bestowed an office of mercy, or, as he believed, a thought ; but in this he was mistaken. Suddenly, the light of a lantern shone within his small tent-prison ; and a face, dimly lighted by the flickering rays, looked upon him. It was so haggard, Hollis started, making his chains clank loudly.

"Move not," spoke a low voice, in a tone broken and utterly forlorn, "speak low, lest I be discovered."

The figure then entered, setting down the lantern before Hollis.

"Captain Jones !" he spoke, in a whisper of surprise.

"Is it possible that you, Hollis, are the prisoner that those infernal Indians brought in with "——

Jones could not command himself to speak the remainder.

"Yes," returned Hollis ; "well may you call those hell-hounds, infernal. Look at my hands and my head !"

"Heavens ! you have been tortured ! Tell me the circumstances," said Jones.

Hollis then briefly related the scene in which he had been an actor, adding that he knew nothing of the death of Miss Jane, except that he saw her dead body, near the pine tree.

Jones shuddered at the recital, familiar as he had become with bloodshed and cruelty.

"Oh ! my God !" he groaned, "would that I had never lived to see this day. This morning I was elate with happiness, in anticipation of meeting her whom I have long worshiped as the light of my existence. I counted the hours, the moments which intervened, with impatience. In obedience to the orders of my superior, I unwisely trusted treacherous fiends. To-night I am the most miserable of men ; my heart is broken !"

"I compassionate you from the depths of my soul," said Hollis.

"I will never struggle more," continued the stricken man, in a tone so low as to be scarcely audible; "my military career is over from this day. Since uniting my fortunes with the British troops, I have been continually disgusted. As soon as possible, I shall get my discharge from the service—that I may die."

"Well may you hate men," said Hollis, "who seek to trample upon justice—who, to effect their purpose, will league even with blood-thirsty savages against brethren who sprung from the same land as themselves, and whose only crime is the resolution to throw off the yoke of their oppression."

"True," responded Jones; "now that all hope is gone, I confess that I espoused the wrong cause. I was deluded—not false at heart. But I see my error when it is too late; its punishment will abide with me, evermore."

"With such feelings, you will not hesitate to effect my escape from here !" pursued Hollis, with emotion, "I cannot remain in such agony."

Captain Jones shook his head, while he said :

"You know the penalty of such an act. Indifferent as I now am to death, I would not be hung as a traitor. But I will serve you in another way. I have just learned that Mrs. McNiel and others arrived here to-day with Indians who belonged to the party which made you prisoner. I have not strength yet to go to them and hear all the particulars, lest my feelings would master me, and 1 should betray myself; for Mrs. McNiel's son is in my own company. I will send you medical aid at once. In the meantime, keep up heart if you can, for *you* have others to live for"——

"Alas!" interrupted Hollis, "I, too, dare not speak of another woe which I hide in my bosom, lest I should cry aloud, ' Curses on the British !' Another time, come to me, and you shall hear all."

" An opportunity may soon occur for your release, by an exchange of prisoners, which is talked of, at present, by General Washington and General Howe," said Jones. "In any way that I can aid your interests, I shall not be inactive, it is certain ; after which, there will be no more work for me."

He took up his lantern to go. Hollis brushed the tears from his eyes with his chained and bleeding hands.

" I must leave you, or I shall be missed. God bless you, my dear fellow," concluded Jones, not less affected himself.

A few minutes later, the surgeon of the army came to Hollis. He was a clumsy, stolid Englishman, who, at this late hour, and under circumstances when he had not calculated upon the requisition of his services, was evidently past clear judgment, from the effect of an unusual drinking bout. After fumbling about his person for instruments, and talking foolishly of operations, rebels, etc., for a few minutes, he said, as if aroused slightly by a new thought—

" There's a red dog about 'ere who 'as more knowledge o'

the practice than 'alf the surgeons in Lunnun. I'll send 'im along to ye, as I'm goin' to turn into my 'ammock for the night. Aw! I 'ave too much 'o skill to waste hammunition on these d—— rebels."

"An Indian, even, is preferable to a British animal, like that man," said Hollis to himself, after his disappearance. "At all events, I shall not be scrupulous, if anything can be done to relieve my terrible distress."

The surgeon's visit was tardily followed by the appearance of a young savage, who was generally acknowledged to possess remarkable skill in the art of surgery. His mother had been the most famous "medicine squaw" of all her tribe. With a grave look, the Indian announced himself.

"I am Iroquo, the son of the brave chief, Elskawora. The Great Spirit has given me power to heal."

"And I," returned Hollis, laughing unnaturally, "am a scalp, and in it is a mill-wheel. Hark! how it turns and throbs! turns and throbs! Never stops. Molly, hold my hands against your heart. Heavens! how that wheel keeps a turning! The water is changed to fire, and it burns around my feet."

He was now delirious. The Indian shook his head, and examined the wounds, while Hollis talked of Molly incessantly.

"Molly," repeated Iroquo; "they called the white squaw that saved my life, Molly. If this Long Knife came from her, he shall not go to the Great Spirit in this moon. Iroquo's Manito will come."

He then opened his medicine-bag and selected his choicest concoctions, which he applied with numerous incantations and repetitions of charms. After he had concluded his efforts, he lighted his scalp-adorned pipe, and, reclining on the ground, remained to watch his patient. Presently, Hollis became calm, then fell into a quiet slumber.

When he awoke fully, which was about the dawn of day, he was sane. Looking about with curiosity, he demanded of his physician what he had done that he was so much relieved.

"Iroquo heal white prisoner from his medicine-bag," he answered. "Tell me why he say *Molly* so much?"

"Have I talked of Molly?" said Hollis, faintly smiling. "I saw her in my dreams."

"White squaw Molly save my life."

"Where was it!" inquired Hollis.

"Down river, by Fort Edward, where is big stone house; farther up a little house made of tree. White squaw young; her face like the brightest star of the ice-moon."

"It is Molly!" exclaimed Hollis, with great interest, "she is like a sister to me."

"Then," said the Indian, "ask of Iroquo what white prisoner most want. It shall be his, or Iroquo will drink the blood of him who dare say *No.*"

So fiercely were these words spoken, Hollis started involuntarily, still suffering from the haunting impression of his late fearful encounter with Indians.

"Give me freedom," said Hollis, in reply. "Help me to

leave this camp in safety, thát I may return to the settlement at the Fort."

"Wait," said Iroquo. "This morning, the red-coats go on down river. When they march off, Iroquo let white prisoner free."

"Such a service shall be rewarded," replied Hollis; "but I cannot understand how you can accomplish it."

Iroquo said no more ; but there was an added lustre in his keen, dark eyes. Concluding the dressing of Hollis' wounds, he quickly disappeared. But it was not long before he came again, and from under his blanket produced an entire Indian dress. With an art which was learned of his British employers, he took off Hollis' irons, and covered his clothes with the suit, in great rapidity. He next painted his face, and nearly concealed his head with various fantastic feathers.

"White man be red brave !" announced Iroquo, with stern satisfaction. "Go out slow, like Indian ; say to sentry, 'Kill Long-Knives in battle'—what all Indians say— then sentry let you by. Dart off for the forest. Tell white squaw, Molly, Iroquo set her brother free."

"She shall know all," returned Hollis.

Iroquo concluded by fastening under the blanket which he had thrown over Hollis, a preparation of a plant of great virtue, which he directed him to apply to his wounds till they healed. In return, Hollis bade him take a piece of gold from a secret pocket, which had escaped the cupidity of his captors, on the day previous. He then left his place of confinement, with a prayer in his heart for success. With the keenest apprehension of momentary discovery, he found himself among the British soldiery ; experiencing not less emotion than the last of the *Horatii* when he marched with covered head under a beam, before the Roman populace.

The ordeal was soon and safely passed. He was beyond the camp ! He was free ! When he had gained the seclusion of the wood, he would have realized rare happiness from the freedom which he had so dearly learned to prize, had he not still remembered Molly with painful uncertainty as to her fate. To her, it was his first purpose to hasten with all possible dispatch. His course was directed to the house of Mrs. McNiel, not pausing to consider the possibility of Molly having sought another home. His way was perfectly secluded, and he saw no person of whom to inquire, until he reached the house. There all was silent and deserted. The door and windows were closed and fastened.— Looking between a partially drawn curtain, he saw upon the table and floor, knots of faded flowers, and a time-worn hat, hanging upon a nail, which he recognized with delight. It was the same which he had seen many times flying about the grounds of his old home, upon a head now dearer in his thought than that of patron saint to the devotee. The beloved name, he called aloud, half hoping to hear a reply from some nook of the house, but a solemn, hollow echo was the only response.

With a sigh, he turned away and hastened on. He would have next gone to the encampment of the American army,

which he knew was in his vicinity, for he had important intelligence, gleaned from the British camp, to communicate,
but the impulse to first see Molly was too powerful to resist.
unwilling to lose a moment, he took the most direct course
to the house of Mr. McCrea, the brother of Miss Jane, where
he hoped to terminate his doubts. But even in this hour, he
was true to his old habit. His eye fell upon a fine goldsmith beetle, which was resting upon a leaf of a tree. Securing it with difficulty by his bandaged hands, he wound it
in its leaf, to preserve as a trophy of his adventures. When
he at last approached his destination, with high heart-throbs
he perceived a person at the window, who his heart whispered, was Molly! She was leaning forward upon her
hands, seemingly overcome with grief. To surprise her
with his sudden presence, was his intent. He, therefore,
stole softly forward, under the shadows of the trees which
skirted the garden patch, till he had come up near the very
spot. His footfall attracted her attention. She looked up.
But instead of the joyful reception which he anticipated, he
heard a cry as of mortal fear. In an instant Molly had disappeared, arousing all the house with words of some terrible
import which he could not understand.

Hollis paused, as if struck with an invisible blow. But
he had scarcely time for revolving this singular circumstance
in his mind, before Mr. McCrea rushed out with his gun and
fired directly upon him! Fortunately, the ball just missed
his head, grazing his forehead and taking off the top of his
ear. He saw no alternative than to fly for his life, for every

word of expostulation he uttered, was wholly lost in the confusion of the household, who now shrieked as if distracted with some terrible emotion. Before he had retreated a rod, another ball whizzed by his arm. It was certain that they intended to murder him upon the spot. The swift thought, that his old friends—that she, for whose life he had offered his own above all others, should meet him thus, after such an absence, well nigh overwhelmed him beyond the power of attempting his escape.

Mr. McCrea now seized the first object in his reach and sprang after him, while Molly looked from the door and shouted at the top of her voice : " Quick ! kill him ! kill him !"

Weak and nearly exhausted from his late perils and sufferings, Hollis only made a feint of escape, keeping as near the houses as possible. Unawares he had come upon a small pond which was used for fowl, and in the distraction of the moment, he ran off the bank which concealed the water and fell headlong into its depths. Instantly rising again to the surface, after a hard struggle, he gained the opposite side. His pursuer was now joined by other men, who had been attracted to the spot by the loud alarm, and he saw that only one more effort remained for him. If die he must, it should be at Molly's feet. He rushed toward the house, Molly turned toward him with a drawn sword ; the fearful cries were redoubled, and Mr. McCrea was just upon him.

" Molly ! For Heaven's sake, stop ! What have I done that you"——

He had not concluded, before a new sound fell on his ears
—an exclamation of surprise, joy, grief, commingled in one
inspiration of hope for him.

"What is this!" cried Molly, as she looked upon Hollis,
struck with a new emotion, "it cannot be you!"

At the same moment, seeing Mr. McCrea, aiming to shoot
once more, she sprang forward and encircled Hollis in her
arms.

"Stand off!" shouted Mr. McCrea. "Are you crazed?
Or, has the savage murdered you?"

"It is not an Indian. We have been deceived!" exclaimed Molly. "See!" turning Hollis' face fully upon
him.

"Merciful Heavens!" ejaculated Mr. McCrea. "This is
Hollis Rushton! As God is my witness, but a moment ago,
not only your dress, but your face was that of an Indian!"

These words recalled to Hollis the fact of his disguise, for
the first time. The clue to a mystery as wonderful as the
Cretan Labyrinth, was now furnished, without the aid of an
Ariadne, save Molly. He had been taken for an Indian ;
his fall into the water had washed the savage paint from
his face, and established the certainty of his identity.

"How did you come here, Hollis?" continued Molly,
greatly excited, "I have been crying, for I thought you
must be killed. God be praised that I see you again, alive.
Oh! I shall never forget that awful scene of yesterday!"

"In there," said Mr. McCrea, pointing to an inner room,

"lies the dead body of my beautiful, beloved sister. She was slain at the hands of the Indians. Can you blame me, that mistaking you for one of that accursed race, I was determined upon your death?"

Hollis was too much moved to speak. He offered a wet and bound hand to each in token of peace and sympathy. Molly received the one, with kisses, Mr. McCrea, the other, with tears.

Others, among whom were the women of the family who had been frightened away, by the intelligence of the approach of an Indian, now come around and overwhelmed Hollis with inquiries. When he was sufficiently composed, he gave a brief account of what had transpired since his capture of the day previous. His relation of Captain Jones moved all to passionate grief. And when he detailed the singular circumstance of his escape, Molly blessed Iroquo with fervent gratitude. The first overwhelming excitement of the meeting having passed, Molly found opportunity to inquire of Hollis for his father. He started at the sudden mention of the name, and with an ill concealed effort, replied that he had not seen him for a few days. This emotion did not escape Molly's quick searching eye.

"Is he ill, or wounded again?" She pursued, anxiously.

"No, he is not," Hollis replied. Then, as if suddenly reminded of something which he had forgotten, but in reality, to imperceptibly withdraw Molly's attention from the subject, he produced the hoarded golden beetle from his pocket, and offered it for her inspection.

"I found it by the way, as I came," he said, "and is it not beautiful, with its shining head, its lemon-colored body, on the under side covered with whitish wool, and its brazen feet, shaded with green ?"

She would have smiled at his curious enthusiasm, had she not been too much saddened.

"I know that it is nothing but a beetle," continued Hollis, as if answering her thought, "but even beetles are distinguished. Eusebius says that they were held by the ancient Egyptians as the animated image of the sun, and were generally embalmed with their mummies."

A woman at this moment entered, and made some inquiry of Molly, respecting the robing of the corpse. Both started, and Molly sighed heavily.

"I shall get flowers for ———, before the burial," she replied amid tears. She then related to Hollis in low, sad tones, the circumstance of their wreathing flowers for Miss Jane's bridal, and the coincidence of the words of the impressive hymn which she had sung, before being summoned away.

"It was so remarkable," she continued, "that you, Hollis, should come there, to that awful spot, just as the Indians were about to kill me, and then "———

Her voice failed. Hollis drew nearer, and told how his father had sent him to her, being prevented from coming himself. "Although I had determined," he added, "to see you no more, I could not refuse him." He seemed to have fallen upon ill chosen words, and he went on with an effort:

"I could not do otherwise under the circumstances. I hastened here without pausing for food or rest, for I feared that something might have occurred to you in the protracted absence of my father's protection. I halted first at the house of Mrs. McNiel, but found there only a neighbor's young child, from whose words I gathered that you had gone to the Pine tree, with Miss Jane and others. By the shortest way, through the trees, I went forward in search, and came upon you and those horrible savages, most fortunately."

" Oh, Hollis !" returned Molly, " not fortunately for you. Remember your tortures ! But for me—you saved my life ! How can I ever repay you for such a sacrifice ? How can I ever say what I feel ?"

Hollis drew her to his heart with an irresistible impulse of affection. She sobbed there like a child, while she held his hands, with loving tenderness. Then, throwing her arms about his neck, made him bend down, that she might press her lips to his aching head.

This caress was far more gratifying to Hollis than was ever the garland of oak bestowed by the Romans, in all honor, on him who saved the life of a citizen. The bliss of that moment he would not have exchanged for all the happiness he had known before, not even for life itself, without the hope of its continuation. But wherefore did Molly start so suddenly, and turn even paler than before ! Why did she shrink from Hollis with an air *distrait*, as if haunted by some newly recruiting pain ? Hollis readily attributed the cause to the fact of two neighbors riding into the yard and speaking in low, solemn voices, of the fearful death of Miss Jane. He did not dream that a single spoken word of one of those neighbors to the other—the mere address of *Reuben*—had effected this change. So much was he absorbed in his own heart, he had not even noted the sound of the name, which thrilled Molly through and through with emotion. Thoughts of Reuben, the once beloved ; the long cherished, but shattered idol, who had put away that first, absorbing, beautiful child love, for another ; thrust her from his heart for evermore, rushed over her memory like a flood.

It was well for Hollis that he knew not this—could never know it. His brimming cup of bliss would have been dashed to the earth, as " water spilled on the ground, which *cannot be gathered up.*" Molly went away, where she might weep alone, for, unused as she was, to yield to such mastering sensibility, the events of yesterday had unsealed the inner fountains of her life, and divested her of the old strength to put sorrow away lightly. She was changed. The breeze-dallying, delicately beautiful flowers of her heart, had been swept away like blossoms upon the trees in a May storm. But there was yet an embryo upon the branches, which, under the genial influence of light and warmth from Heaven, might gradually be perfected to golden fruit, such as grows in the paradise of God !

On the close of the following day, the remains of the dead were committed to the earth. This hour was chosen by reason of greater security from disturbance, and also for

being more consonant with the preferences of the mourners.
A time most befitting of all others for a burial, emblematical
of the close of life and the consignment of the weary body
to the repose of the grave. It was a calm and beautiful
summer evening ; the western sky was still faintly tinted
with the set of the sun ; every object was visible, though
sobered to gloom by the sombre shadows of night. The
few neighbors came in, and after a prayer for the occasion
was read by one of the number, the procession of mourners
followed the body to the grave. No clergyman was acces-
sible to conduct the services, but the scene was a sufficiently
impressive teacher.

By the melancholy way, the song of woodbirds of night
fell upon the ear, and running waterfalls from the distance.
Low sobs occasionally gushed from overflowing hearts.—
When they reached the grave, which was in a lonely spot,
the body was set down that all might look once more and
the last upon the face of the beloved. It was sweet and
beautiful, as in life. White flowers were wreathed about
it, and were grouped upon the pulseless bosom. The
pale lips seemed to have just smilingly. closed over the
words :—

> "Heaven opens on my eyes ! my ears
> With sounds seraphic ring."

Many tears and kisses, invisible jewels of love, were left
on the perishable clay ; but they were also imprinted in
Heaven. The service of the English church was read by

the light of a torch. Then as many as could command their voices, joined in singing the same words which had been sung by the dead so solemnly. None who listened could ever forget the touching impressiveness of that strain. The coffin was lowered into the grave.

There was a pause, succeeded by the sound of falling clods upon the coffin, the most mournful of all sounds of earth.

Molly yielded to a passionate outburst of grief ; she could restrain herself no longer. Hollis, who supported her upon his arm, said in low tones of sympathy :— "Let us not mourn as those who have no hope. 'Blessed are the dead who die in the Lord.' Angels have whispered to our dear friend, to come up hither, and she has passed through the 'gate of pearl' into the glories of immortality."

With such words he essayed to comfort and soothe one who would now have been desolate indeed had it not been for his presence. They turned to leave the lonely grave when a whippoorwill alighted upon a rock near the spot and began to pour forth its sonorous complaint.

When all was over, Hollis spoke to Molly, with much of his old constraint, of her departure for Monmouth.

"I will rejoin the army, which is now in this vicinity," he said, "but I have learned that an old friend of my father will start from Fort Edward, for New York to-morrow. With him, I can safely intrust you ; and he will engage to secure you a safe conveyance to your future home. Our house-keeper will be overjoyed to see you."

The tears started anew to Molly's eyes.

"I thought you would go with me," she said, "you surely will not leave me now?"

"I supposed you would prefer the arrangement I have
proposed, or it would not have been made," replied Hollis,
also much moved.

"Oh! Hollis!" cried Molly, "whom have I to care
for me now, but you? If you desert me, I am alone!"

"Gladly will I go with you, dearest Molly," interrupted
Hollis—"more gladly than I can express, provided you will
frankly tell me when you would prefer to have me leave you.
Then I can rejoin the army."

Molly could not say more.

CHAPTER XVI.

In her new home at Monmouth, Molly missed Mr. Rushton more than ever since he had joined the army. Familiar household objects recalled his memory, at every turn. The manner of Hollis when questioned respecting his father troubled her ; she, therefore took the earliest opportunity to ask Mrs. Rogers, the old housekeeper, for an explanation.

"I am certain that something must have gone wrong," she said, " else Mr. Rushton would have written to me long before this. And there is no time mentioned when we may expect his return."

·" Ask Hollis," replied Mrs. Rogers, looking very much distressed. " He knows more about it than I do."

" It is not possible that he is taken prisoner by the enemy ?" pursued Molly.

Here Mrs. Rogers gave out, and covered her face. Molly hastened to Hollis, who was busy in rearranging his cabinet.

She repeated her new suspicion, adjuring him to tell her the facts, even the worst, if such there were.

He paused from his labors, as if suddenly struck with a pang of pain. Perceiving that Molly was now determined in her purpose, he replied with the deepest sadness—

" I had hoped to spare you further sorrow, for the present Molly. Can you bear to know all !"

Molly suddenly paled to the hue of death Clasping her hands, she exclaimed—

" He is not killed !"

" Yes," said Hollis, the tears rushing to his eyes, notwithstanding his efforts to retain composure, " my father will never come to us again !"

A pause of heavy silence succeeded.

" And you kept this from me, all this time !" spoke Molly, at last.

" How could I think of adding to sorrow like yours, till, at least that deadful scene through which you passed, had in a measure subsided in your thought ?"

" But you suffered alone, Hollis. I am not selfish, whatever else I may be, and it would have been sweet to have comforted you."

Hollis' lips quivered, the tears rushed to his eyes anew.

" It would have been a satisfaction," continued Molly, fervently, " to have shared your grief as you have shared mine. In this way only, can I hope to repay you, in any degree, for all you have done for me."

This allusion, as usual, made Hollis wish to change the tenor of thought.

"My father," he renewed, "fell immediately after the American army had evacuated Ticonderoga. General St. Clair had gone forward with the main body of soldiery. The rear guard, in which my father held a post of command, was attacked by General Fraser. A desperate fight ensued, for we saw at once that the odds were against us. But we held our ground valiantly until the enemy was joined by General Reidisel with his division of Germans, and then the Americans were defeated. My father held out nobly to the last. I was by his side and urging him to retreat, when a ball took him through the breast. With the aid of another soldier I hurried him from the field. But he was dying. I knelt beside him and held his head in my arms, while it seemedto me that I should die also, for sorrow.

"'My dear boy, don't mourn for me ;' he murmured, 'we must all die once. Get your discharge. Go to Molly, and take her to Monmouth. See that no ill comes to her.'"

Hollis could not go on. The painful memory was too much to control.

"And those were his last words !" exclaimed Molly, amid many tears.

"No. There was evidently another and an important message, which he had upon his mind," Hollis continued, with an effort, "'tell Molly to find among my papers'—he began, but losing strength, said no more. In a few minutes he expired."

"What could that imply?" rejoined Molly, after a sorrowful silence.

"I have found among his effects," said Hollis, "a small sealed package, addressed to you. I left it undisturbed."

He then went for it. Molly received it with a strong emotion, requesting Hollis to remain and assist in its examination. The package was addressed— "For my dear Molly, if she survives me." The inclosure proved to be a small black book with a gold clasp, on which was engraven an armorial device. Its pages contained memoranda from the pen of Mr. Rushton. The first date was many years before, in his old English home. The record ran thus :—

"This is bliss deep, exquisite, heavenly—to be loved by those whom we love ! Alice, the lovely, the bewitching, is betrothed to me ! I must record the fact, that I may not imagine I have been dreaming. It appears that my father, shortly before his death, registered a vow with Lord Izlay, her father, that their children should wed together. Neither of us were aware of this, till after our betrothal, so we have loved with only the sweet impulses of our own wills. We are both motherless. I am an orphan. But my guardian is alike her father and mine. Izlay Castle is another home to me. The loss of the beloved dead is supplied by the completeness of our mutual love. She has ever been as a sister to me, and so I most often call her.

"Darling Alice ! I could live content with you, in a desert or howling willderness. A cup of water from the Witches'

Well of Izlay, if shared by your ruby lips, would be sweeter far than a goblet of golden nectar from Olympia, if drank alone. All the goddesses of Homer, the angels of Milton, or the loveliest maid of Circassia, are but dross compared to thee, my beautiful, my own ! My *own !* Is it really so ? Let me pause to revolve the certainty of these joyful words. Her whispered promise,—' I will be yours, dearest,' is graven upon my heart, to be erased nevermore. The thought makes my brain whirl with delight.

"Next week I shall enter Trinity College. Were it not for the explicit wish left me by my father, that I should go through a collegiate course of study, I would never think of leaving Rushton Hall. The absence from Alice will be an age. But we shall write often. I shall think of her continually."

"Cambridge.—I am now quietly established in my rooms in the great court of Trinity. Already the memory of Alice is associated with every new scene. Here, where so many of the illustrious dead have received instruction, I am inspired only with this love, which

> ———' Is not to be reasoned down, or lost,
> In high ambition, or a thirst of greatness.'

"In the college groves, the libraries, exercises, everywhere, this introversion of my thoughts upon the blissful past, will assert its power in the face of all efforts. Socrates inculcated the doctrine of the golden mean in all things— and ' A medium is best in everything,' was the saying of Cleobulus, one of the seven wise men of Greece ; but there is no medium in true love. It is either Heaven or Hell.

"I am disappointed in my expectation of a letter to-day, from Alice. Can she be ill, or dead ? Great Heavens ! Such thoughts are madness. This evening, to quiet the tumult of my breast, I took a sail upon the Cam. But all was stupid and inadequate to possess me with the least sense of pleasure. I wonder not that Milton complained of ' the shadeless fields and sedgy pools of Cambridge ;' or, that another author speaks of the ' dulness of the reedy Cam.' "

"Before I had dropt my pen last night, my gyp brought me a letter from Alice. It was like herself—short, loving, beautiful. Never before did I realize the blessedness of the invention of writing letters. Pope must have known something of this, when he wrote these words :

> ' Heaven first taught letters for some wretch's aid,
> Some banished lover, or some captive maid;
> They live, they speak, they breathe what love inspires.'

"Such pretty, fairy-like chirography as is this of Alice ! Were I a monk of the Middle Ages, I could retire to some cloister, and devote months to rare illuminations of this precious little missive. The first design should be an angel, lovely as a seraph, moving her lily fingers upon a harp, golden and heart-shaped! Her sentiments are coy, but they make me understand that she loves me.

> 'O love, requited love, how fine thy thrills,
> That shake the trembling frame with ecstacy!'

"By the way, how easily, of late, do delicious bits of sentimental verse fall from my pen, as it is said, honey dropt from the trees in the golden age! I could not sleep till I had written Alice a reply. *Scribere jussit amor.*—Ovid Ep. iv. 10."

———

"Affliction. Alice's father is dead. I, too, have lost a father, for Lord Izlay was the noblest of guardians and friends to me. Alice, dearest, mourning Alice, will also lose a home. It seems that the Izlay estate was heavily encumbered with debt, and a small sum, a mere trifle will only remain clear. But, thanks to a gracious fortune, I am wealthy, so that upon my arriving at the age of majority, the loss of her fortune will be fully recompensed. Alice goes to reside with a distant relative in London, for the present. I shall see her often.

"Would that it were possible to remove Alice to my home —the home of my ancestors. I like not her being in the vortex of town life. Her cousin, Lady Kintern, is wholly a lady of fashion, gay, heartless, and, I fear, unscrupulous. I have seen her only once, but I thoroughly dislike her. I tremble with foreboding of evil, when I think of the influence to which Alice is now habituated—so unlike that which she has known, hitherto! She has bloomed into womanhood like a blush rose-bud into flower, within the genial atmosphere of a conservatory, lined with an Oriental beauty and softness. She knows nothing of the world. God grant that its garish beams may not blight the fragrant freshness of her young life!"

***

"Alice does not write to me, or if she does, the letters are lost. Her last was very brief, and not satisfactory. It was not unloving, but I demanded more. Now I realize that even that is better than none. My brain is on fire with torturing conjecture. In my Greek exercise to-day, I read: 'The wise with hope support the pains of life.' Euripides advised well, though he were called a *woman-hater*. I am not wise, but without hope I should perish."

***

"At my hotel in London.—I have just returned from a visit to Kintern House. Alice met me with ill concealed sadness. A change! What can it portend? When I accused her of coldness, of constraint, she denied it; but by

Heavens ! it is true. I inquired the cause of my failure to receive letters. She hesitated, blushed, and was troubled. Lady Kintern assumed the matter, by saying in her own cutting manner : ' You can not be so unreasonable as .to expect Lady Alice to devote all her time to correspondence ! She has something else to do here, in town, I assure you, sir.' ' Indeed,' rejoined Alice, with tears in her sweet eyes, ' I would have written, but '—— She was again cut off by her ladyship, who seemed eager to crush down what Alice would say. I was enraged—too much so to open my lips in comment. Here, another visitor was announced, and I hastily took my departure, promising Alice to call on the morrow. I could not wait, however, and again went to see her this evening. She had gone to the opera. Thither I directed . my course immediately. Saw a young officer in Lady Kintern's suit. He was all devotion to Alice, and evidently her attendant. I heard nothing, saw nothing, after this. A torrent of burning lava deluged my heart ; to witness Alice's smiles upon another was madness."

———

" Repeated my visit at Kintern House. Was told that Alice was not in. When I sent to know at what hour I could see her, Lady Kintern came, unsolicited, on my part. She said—Oh ! ye gods ! curse that woman !—that my visits there were not agreeable. She considered it due to me to be informed of the fact.

"'But Alice,' I said, 'it is Alice whom I come to see.'

"'I tell you, sir, that she quite agrees with me,' said her ladyship.

"'Heavens! we are betrothed.'

"'But not wedded, nor ever will be.'

"'She is to me, as my own. Her father witnessed and sealed our mutual pledges with his favor.'

"'Her father is dead. Lady Alice is free to choose whom she prefers,' pursued her ladyship, with a fiendish smile.

"'She has chosen,' I reiterated, violently.

"'True ; and her choice is *not* yourself.'

"'Your words are false, madam."

"'Ask Lady Alice, yourself. I will engage that you see her this evening.'

"'I will see her. From her own lips, I will prove that you are at fault,' I concluded, leaving that woman as hastily as possible.

" Now, as the day wanes, and the hour appointed to meet Alice approaches, were I waiting to know if I shall be condemned to drink a bowl of hemlock, I could scarcely be more keenly tortured with suspense. But I cannot for a moment really believe that Alice is faithless to me."

———

" At Rushton Hall.—I am getting up from a long, severe illness. I could well nigh regret that I was not suffered to die. Then, this record would not be stained with words wrung from my heart's blood !

"I am deserted .

"God of mercy ! why did I ever know the sweets of bliss, so soon to have them change to gall, tenfold more bitter than any other ? With a heart crushed, almost broken, can I resume the burdens of life and go forward ? The rector of Rushton, kind, excellent old man, reads prayers in my room, morning and evening—the familiar prayers of the Church, but new and beautiful as they come from his hallowed lips. He reminds me that there is blessed consolation for all, even the most bruised and broken. The great Redeemer pities our sorrows. With his stripes, we are healed."

"I have become able to walk under the open sky, once more. A new feeling possessed my soul, so that I felt like uncovering my head for awe ! Now I believe I worship God ; hitherto, I have worshipped idols. This sickness, so weakening, humiliating, has been rich in good fruits to me. Life for me is changed. Nevermore will it be bright, or gay, or joyous as before, but more hallowed, consecrated to holier uses. I have passed the ordeal of fire, and have been sealed with the baptism of suffering. My soul is strengthened, not destroyed, as I have feared ; its vision purified, so that I can see farther, deeper, and higher.

"Yet, I must struggle long and mightily with my spirit, for there is no change which is wholly and at once salutary. A work is to be done. By strength and strength will I attempt to form a life wholly dedicated to Heaven, with the hope of acceptance at last, by the death and mediation of the Great Intercessor.

"Yesterday, I walked over the park. The deer started at the sight of me as though I had been a spectre. To-day, I was able to go as far as the rectory. The good rector was in his study, with his youngest daughter employed as his amanuensis. My presence affected her scarcely less than the deer; for she is timid and retiring as a fawn. The rector loaned me several books to read—ancient works of the Latin fathers of the Church; those of a later day of Elizabeth, the authors of which studied the Scriptures in exile, under the shadow of concealment and distress; and one or two, more modern, that my range of examination may be thorough and comprehensive. I shall diversify this reading by valuable works of general literature, for I hold that esthetics are necessary for the 'mind's mead,' as well as ethics, and what Tillotson calls scholastic theology."

———

"I have resolved to leave England for a temporary residence in America. My physician prescribes a change of air and scene, and as I have long regarded the colonies and their country with admiration, and a desire for personal knowledge, I shall take this opportunity to realize a boyish dream. Older and classic lands have less charms for me. I must leave these scenes; for hallowed and beautiful as they are with ancestral associations, one other memory, latest impressed on everything about me, renders me too unhappy for their peaceful enjoyment. Every tree and flower of the grounds is written over with her name. Every landscape has been admired with *her* eyes. From my windows I can see the turrets of Izlay Castle ; the lattice, where *she* used to sit and wave a light flag for me to come and see her.

"But, let me cease to write of this. I shall leave Rushton Hall in charge of the rector and my business agent, for I have no relative near me. My father's youngest brother, who alone survives him, is in a distant land. I shall regret to leave the rector and his amiable family, who have proved my invaluable friends."

———

"In America. One year has rapidly passed since I came to this new, and in many respects remarkable country. Increased strength of mind and body have been vouchsafed me. I bless God for it. I have travelled through all the principal cities and places of the colonies, and have thus formed several agreeable friendships with gentlemen of noble spirit and culture, in but few particulars inferior to some of the first noblemen of the realm—in many superior. They are not so trammelled by conventional laws or public restrictions. From the exigences of their peculiar situation, and possibly from the influence of the rough, but magnifi-cent, scenic features of their land, they have derived a grandeur of hardihood, a depth and compass of will to do and dare, which promise something more than is dreamed of in the philosophy of the mother country. I like these people vastly better than I expected ; and their homes, some of which are appointed in a style of luxury and liberality comparing favorably to that of domains in titled possession.

"Having at last taken up my abode in New York city, I set about systematically to engross my attention from the past. At first, I tried the life of a scholar ; I read and studied like a professor. But that would not do. Now, I have determined to devote my chief attention to commercial interests. The excitement of active business is the best specific I have tried. This, modified and intermingled with intellectual pursuits, shall be pursued faithfully, till the experiment is tested." .

"I have decided to make my permanent home in this country. The climate, my pursuits and surroundings, please me well. But the recent death of my old friend, the rector, renders it necessary for me to return to England, and make some new arrangements in regard to my affairs."

"When that great sorrow came over me, I thought I should never marry ; but the youngest daughter of the late rector returns with me to America, as my wife. She knew the history of my early love—therefore I have practised no deception. With her companionship I hope to banish unpleasant memories of the past; for she is gentle, truth-loving in all things, and possesses a mind of no common culture.

"A rural estate in Monmouth, coming to my ownership by the way of trade, and a handsome town house in New York, will divide our residence for the present."

"The birth of a son and the death of the mother! Alas! I knew not how truly, nay, reverently, I loved my wife, until she was taken from me. Her sound judgment and constant goodness were my dependence. What satisfaction is it now to me to reflect that no office of respect or kindness in my power was ever withheld from her! God grant to me the life of my son, and may he inherit the goodness of his mother. He shall bear her family name—Hollis."

"For the past few years I have devoted what leisure I could take from business to the establishment of a new Rushton Hall, on the Hudson. I selected this retired, but singularly beautiful location, that my son might be reared away from the world. If it be possible to educate him to love nature in all its varied forms, rather than society, false-hearted, fickle, frivolous, and in many other attributes, detestable, I shall be amply repaid for all my efforts."   *   *   *

Several pages here succeeded, detailing life at Rushton Hall on the Hudson, the plan of the education of Hollis, etc. With her usual impetuosity in the investigation of a mystery, Molly turned along, till her eye was newly arrested by the date of "Epps Hundred." She then resumed her reading aloud.

"Praise to the Father of mercies, my life has been spared from the hand of an assassin. And by whom? The miniature image of Alice! A little girl who is called Molly. Her origin is mysterious, but I cannot divest myself of the impression that this child is connected with her, whom I once passionately loved. She is in the charge of strangers, but it shall be my future care to protect her. As soon as it is possible, I intend to return to Epps Hundred, and get the permission of her present guardians to take her home with me, and make her as my own child."

———

"London. When I had planned to go for the child at Epps Hundred, I received news that my long-absent uncle had returned to England, and in humble circumstances, having endured a series of misfortunes. Wishing to make suitable provision for him in his old age, and to settle up all my affairs which remained in the charge of others, abroad, I determined to come thither without delay. Regarding our English law of descent of landed property as unjust, and preferring to continue my permanent residence in America, I have transferred Rushton Hall estate to my uncle.

"Another affair which I regarded of the last importance, remained for me to pursue before my return. This was to make inquiries for her whose name has been buried in my heart for long years, to learn, if possible, if my supposition respecting the child Molly, were, in any degree, justifiable. Lady Kintern and her family had gone to the Continent, and a long time supervened before I could fall upon any reliable clue to this history. I was about abandoning all hope of ever hearing from Alice again, when I accidentally traced her to the residence of a woman who furnished cheap lodgings, in a retired part of the town. She was not there, but that had been her last residence in London. For a sum of money, the woman told me all she knew. From this relation, long and often circuitous, and by frequent cross-questions, I gathered that Alice, soon after I last met her, had married a young nobleman of wealthy family, who was an officer in the army. The marriage had been secret, and Alice refused to discover her husband's name. Her relative, Lady Kintern, had spared no pains to bring about the marriage, having discovered that the young officer was deeply in love with Alice, that she might thus cancel the large sums which he had won from her in gaming. After her marriage, she had lived in strict retirement, but in a style suitable to her rank. All had proceeded without interruption, until her husband had been called to leave her and her infant child, to join his regiment. For some time after, letters from him arrived at regular intervals, containing ample supplies of money. But suddenly intelligence from him ceased, and this continued till Alice, in despair, ventured to address inquiries to some of her husband's family relatives, respecting him. She was informed that he had wedded a lady of rank and fortune, and with her was residing abroad. Then she struggled with her anguish alone ; for she had no friends to whom she could apply for advice or aid. Lady Kintern now refused to receive her, assuming to believe that her marriage had never taken place. With a small remnant of money, she retired with her child to the humble lodgings of this woman, and endeavored to earn a livelihood by giving instruction in music and drawing. In this she succeeded but poorly. Her bitter sorrows brought a disease ; and with no prospect but a brief life of suffering, she finally resolved to seek me, ask my forgiveness, and beg that I would care for her child, after her death. Learning that I was in America, she sold all her jewels save a gold case containing valuable papers, to enable her to go thither. With this provision, she embarked with her child for Boston, where she was told I resided, which information had probably originated from the fact of my spending the first month of my residence in America, in that city. Arriving at Boston, she wrote back to this woman, according to promise, stating that she had learned her mistake ; but, although her health was more miserable and her funds nearly exhausted, she hoped to reach New York, by great sacrifices. No farther tidings ever came from her.

"I had but one other question to ask—the name which the Lady Alice had called her child? I was told that it was Mary.

"Now, no doubt remains that the child who saved my life —the Molly of Epps Hundred—is also the child of Alice. Alas, for the delicate, unfortunate Alice, who died in a strange land, beneath the roof of strangers! Would that she could have lived to witness my forgiveness of the past— my vow to protect and love her child as my own!"

———

"Rushton Hall, on the Hudson. Molly, the dear child of Alice, is with me once more! Her face is so nearly a copy of her mother's, that when I look upon her, I am overcome with a strange, powerful emotion. But her spirit is not like what her mother's was; she is more daring, passionate, distinguished in her impulses. There are more of "Teucer's arrows" in her words. Her faults are numerous, but I believe that experience with her own innate perceptions, will aid in their correction; for their eradication, she must seek the grace of Heaven.

"God bless her! I have a new hope in my heart. Perhaps the sacred vow registered in Rushton Hall and Izlay Castle, years ago, will yet be fulfilled in the union of my son and the daughter of Alice!"

———

"War is declared between the colonies and Great Britain!

Having in heart become an American, I am fully responsive to this spirit which rebels against unjust extortion and oppression. My experience in mercantile affairs, testifies to the vexations resulting from the continued system of taxation. The regal powers will find that they have carried the iron rule too far. Cornelius Nepos said truly that—'No government is safe, unless fortified by good will.'

"I shall take up arms with the brave men who struggle for freedom under the yoke of tyranny. Should my life be sacrificed to the good cause, I trust that all will be well with me. One great wish of my later life alone remains uncertain of fulfillment—the marriage of Hollis and Molly. God grant that he be not reserved for a sorrow like that which clouded my earlier days! Retiring and distrustful of his own capacities, as was his mother, he fails to do himself justice, and I fear the sterling worth of his character will not be understood. Would that he could receive my past experience to fortify his soul against the disappointments of life! But he must learn wisdom for himself. Alas! I would even yield my life, if I might thus spare him the pain of crushed and fruitless hopes—those hopes which too often have a brief existence like Jonah's gourd! They spring up in a night, but when the morning rises, are smitten by a worm, to wither and perish. Then, the spirit is either faint or angry, as was the prophet; but a wise philosophy would inspire rather to the imitation of the snail, which, according to naturalists, when it has lost its head, has the power of reproducing another. Let those who lose the heart, thank

God it is no worse, and take courage for the reproduction of another !"

———

Thus the notes closed, evidently with the expectation of a sequel. But death had sealed the book. Both Molly and Hollis had been deeply moved by the record ; but the last words were so entirely unlike that for which they were previously prepared, their first impulse was to exchange a smile. Then Molly said, more soberly :

" The prayer of your father is answered, Hollis. His death was the means of disclosing to me your true character, and if I can spare you pain in the future, I shall be glad."

She paused, blushing deeply, suddenly reminded that she had spoken words of meaning.

" Is it possible, dearest Molly, that you can feel thus towards one so unworthy of your love, as myself ?" returned Hollis, tears of joy rushing to his eyes. .

Molly gave him her hand in reply, and Hollis realized that he was, at last, an accepted lover, with a sense of bliss, which made him well-nigh—

"A man too happy for mortality !"

CHAPTER XVII.

In the old parish church, Hollis and Molly were united in marriage. Molly was lovely, as are all brides ; she was very beautiful, as few are. Her face could scarcely have been more pallid, had she been the bride of death, but it contrasted almost startlingly with her dark, luminous eyes, exquisitely shading with their silken lashes, the unspoken thought of sorrow. From the topmost knot of her hair fell a profusion of curls over her head to her bosom, relieving the marble outline of her brow and cheek. Her dress of pearl white satin, such as Gaspar Netscher loved so often to paint among the figures of his groups ; the short gown or tunic of white flowered damask, with large sleeves deeply ruffled with rich lace and fastened back at the shoulder by a diamond clasp ; the wide, embroidered frill standing around the low neck, all corresponded with the elegance of attire, which was the mode of the wealthy classes of that time. From her white beaver hat, depended a long veil of black crape, and a shawl of the same material enveloped her figure like a pall, in respect to the recent death of him who had been a father to herself as well as Hollis.

In powdered hair, ruffles and long silk hose, Hollis looked scared and well-nigh overwhelmed. The rector delivered a discourse appropriate to the occasion, according to the custom, upon marriage occasions of distinction. His text was selected from Deut. xxiv., 5 : " When a man hath taken a new wife he shall not go out to war, neither shall he be charged with any business ; but he shall be free at home one year, and shall cheer up his wife which he hath taken."

Although Molly had been thoroughly sober and even dejected, the announcement of these words aroused her old propensity to mirth, and had it not been for the time and place, a choice sally would have escaped her. As it was, she ventured a single arch glance toward the old rector, whose face was very grave, and seemingly perfectly unaware of the magical power of his words.

The text, however, was more seasonable than the sermon. Like many others of his cloth, the rector was not in favor of rebellion to the mother country, and took every occasion to counsel not going to the war. Such was then the blind deference in which men of his profession were generally held; these sentiments were listened to respectfully, by men who would have replied to similar words from a common voice, with the bayonet and sword.

Although Hollis was among these, he profited by the argument. He resolved not to return to the military ranks at present, but to serve his country by opening his storehouses, filled with the products of the land, for the supplies of the army. The following winter, during which the American army quartered at Valley Forge, was the severest before experienced. Owing to defects in the provisions of Congress for the proper supplies of this department, the soldiers were, at times, almost in a state of starvation, suffering also extremely for the want of necessary clothing. Many persons, who had ample supplies of provisions, in the circuit of country which was foraged by the commissary-general, would sell them, if possible, to the British army, for better pay. But Hollis was indifferent on this point, and often refused to receive an equivalent for his valuable services. The settlement of his father's affairs left him in the possession of great wealth, and he took pleasure in thus disbursing it. Molly engaged herself and Mrs. Rogers in the making of coarse articles of clothing for the soldiers, and the preparation of lint for the sick ; often relieving the time by long excursions with Hollis upon horseback about the vicinity of their home. In her scarlet riding hood and cloak she would flit past the windows of the houses by the wayside, like a wandering comet, or a thing of supernatural wonder ; for she preferred the scene of a driving snow storm to any other.

The spring came and Hollis devoted himself to his home affairs and to the removal of his cabinet. His time passed swiftly and joyously, for he believed that he was beloved by her whom he proudly called his wife and loved, nay, worshiped with enthusiastic devotion. Molly was more thoughtful since coming to Monmouth. The trying scenes through which she had passed, and the great disappointment of her life had begun to deepen the beauty and mature the strength of her character. Never, for a moment, would she yield to that lackadaisical sentiment, which thrills the spirit into dejection before the triumph of another. But she had yet a masterly work to do, for when she thought of Reuben, which was often of late, she could not forgive him for the suffering he had caused her. The blessed spirit of faith in "whatever is, is right," and of forgiveness of injuries, had taken no root in her heart. It was inevitable that she could not thus be as happy as she might have been.

"At this time, Hollis unexpectedly found it necessary to go to Virginia for the final settlement of a branch of his father's affairs, and he proposed to Molly to accompany him. She assented to this arrangment with delight, for new scenes accorded with her mood. The necessary preparations being speedily accomplished, they left their home in charge of Mrs. Rogers and the faithful man servant who had been in their service for many years. Hollis upon his own horse Leo, the successor to Lucifer which had been shot in battle ; Molly upon Black Princess, and a servant upon another horse with the extra saddle-bags. The change of air and scene soon influenced Molly, so that she rallied a high flow of spirits and she was more like herself than she had been before for a long time. The roses came back to her cheeks in richer bloom and witty words gushed from her lips like crystals from a bubbling spring. The surrounding scenery, as they journeyed on, received a full share of her notice, often expressed in the drollest original comments ; and the children who ran out to see the lady in the red velvet riding-hood and cloak with rich white plumes depending to her shoulders, won many a graceful nod and pleasant words to treasure in their hearts like fragrant leaves in a drawer.

When she tired of deriving interest from her surroundings, Molly would whisper a significant hint to Black Princess to leave the other horses in the rear with all possible dispatch, which feat being sometimes successfully accomplished, contributed not a little to her gratification.

Day after day in favorable weather, they continued their route, now passing through long and gloomy forests, cities and villages, crossing rivers and mountainous country, with a variety of adventure, till they reached their place of destination. This was a place on the Appomatox river, distinguished in those palmy days of the cavaliers of the Old Dominion, for its society, who lived in a style of grandeur and profusion, borrowed from English associations, one of the most prominent features of which was that noble hospitality, which could be dispensed from only ample appointments. Molly was charmed with the scenes to which she was now introduced. The grand, old mansion houses, the retinues of servants, the ease and elegance of the people, chimed in with the strongest chords of her natural temperament, inherited from the blood of her proud, baronial ancestors. Balls and dinner parties were given in honor of these guests, whose family reputation secured them at once an *entrée* into the highest circles of society. Hollis had no tastes for such entertainments, but as Molly soon became the centre of their attraction, he kept his own preferences to himself and never refused to accompany her. Although Molly had mingled comparatively little in society heretofore, her rare beauty, wit and original manner made a decided impression. Proud gentlemen crowded around her with undisguised admiration, and the elegant, languishing ladies regarded her as a novelty whose words and acts bewildered and defied imitation. Envy could not call her ill-bred, for her ease was founded upon a perfect grace and that *savoir faire* which was too genuine to be mistaken. Neither was she coquettish, for the atmosphere of dignity with which she could surround herself at pleasure and the peculiar mould of her character, repelled undue familiarity.

Among the people whom Molly attracted about her, was an elderly gentleman, a judge in one of the courts and a *bon vivant* of princely fortune. He had no family ; but Cyprus, his beautiful villa, was ever open to the reception of such guests as he honored with his attentions. Judge Brockenbrough first met Hollis and Molly at the mansion of a friend. He had formerly known Mr. Rushton, and his interest was awakened at once. Molly pleased him unusually, so that he declared to some of his gentlemen friends, that of all the women in the world whom he had ever seen, Mrs. Rushton was the most beautiful and sensible. A half hour's conversation with her, he said, was more exhilarating than the best old wine of merrie England.

After this, he lavished upon them the most distinguished attentions. Immediately before their departure from that vicinity, they attended a grand ball at Cyprus, given by the Judge in their honor, at which were present, the beauty and chivalry of all the most aristocratic families in that section of the province. In a lofty, oaken-panelled hall, rich with solid mahogany, damask and silver, the entertainment opened by the Judge, with Molly for his partner, in a minuet. As, in those times, nearly everybody was expected to dance, ordinary dancing attracted little notice. But Molly moved through this most graceful dance with such surpassing ease and elegance of carriage, she won the admiration of every gentleman present, and the envy of many ladies who listened to the praises which she elicited. She had never looked lovelier, even in her bridal hour ; the exercise heightened the beauty of her cheeks, and the expressive radiance of her dark eyes. Her spirits were in the most admirable repose, and not a simper or smile betrayed a feminine consciousness of her triumph. This, indeed, was the chief secret of the rare charm which she threw around her. Her handsomely moulded figure was arrayed in a close bodice of green velvet, wreathed at the neck, and short sleeves, with delicate white flowers and red buds. From her belt depended a tunic of richly embroidered muslin, threaded with spangles, over a skirt of rose-colored satin. A string of pearls, set in gold, encircled her neck and arms, else shaded with exquisite lace. Long gloves of white silk, edged with pointed lace, incased her small, finely shaped hands. And a sprig of flowers, composed of jewels, which had been brought from abroad, flashed among the dark curls of her abundant hair.

The effect of her appearance was by no means decreased by her contrast with the Judge, who danced with a good-natured carelessness, approaching near to awkwardness. He was very tall, corpulent and unwieldly, with a dark, oriental face, surrounded by a highly powdered wig, and his full ruffles, large gold buttons and buckles, made every move-ment particularly conspicuous.

When the music ceased, the Judge led Molly to Hollis, remarking :

"Mrs. Rushton brings out so much beauty from every step she reminds me of the humming-bird, which in the prettiest of motions, extracts nectar from the sweetest flowers."

Hollis bowed with a smile of pleasure, for nothing delighted him more than to hear praises of Molly.

"I prefer the contra-dance ; there is some life in that," said Molly.

"But not half the grace," returned the Judge ; "Lully, the Frenchman, surpassed himself, when he invented the minuet."

"At this moment a servant came to announce to the Judge, the arrival of a stranger from a distance, and Molly's hand was immediately solicited to join the next dance. The Judge paused to introduce Hollis to one of his guests who was a noted scientific man, and then obeyed the new summons.

The merry hours of the evening sped on rapidly.—Molly, somewhat wearied with dancing at length, stood apart, and entered into conversation with some of her new acquaintances, when Judge Brockenbrough came up again.

"Mrs. Rushton," he said, "I think you told me that you had formerly resided in an eastern province—which was it ?"

"Massachusetts," she returned, with her curiosity slightly aroused.

"Indeed ! I have the unexpected good fortune to welcome a guest this evening, who has just arrived from that province. He is a young man of superior abilities, if he is my nephew ; and I will introduce him to you, if agreeable."

Molly assented, and the Judge directly after appeared with the gentleman. As they advanced through the crowd, Molly started as though she had been shot ; the color fled from her face, and her whole being seemed held in abeyance. She looked once more. Yes, the stranger was Reuben Epps ! He had become tall and noble looking : his clustering hair was a shade darker ; his eyes deeper and more thoughtful ; but he was too like what he was when Molly had last seen him, for her to doubt his identity, for a moment. Fortunately, at this moment, Judge Brockenbrough paused on his way, to exchange a few words with one of his guests, and Molly took the opportunity to regain her self-possession before the dreaded ordeal came.

All the innate spirit of her passionate nature was keenly aroused by the reaction. The remembrance of the bitterness through which she had struggled, by reason of his neglect, and finally cruel desertion of herself, inspired her with scorn and a will to triumph. The effort was a masterly one, but it was fully accomplished.

In reply to the bland presentation of the Judge, she met Reuben with a perfect dignity and tranquillity of nerve, to outward seeming.

"Great Heavens!" he exclaimed, after a second searching glance,—"Is this"—— he faltered, drew back a step and turned deadly pale.

"I am the wife of Hollis Rushton, Mr. Epps," returned Molly, with an icy politeness ; then added to her host, by way of explanation :

"This gentleman I once knew. It was when we were children. His father and mother were the earliest friends of my remembrance."

"A mutual and pleasant surprise then!" returned the Judge ; "his father is my half brother, and was a native of Bermuda Hundred, near this place."

"He shows his guilt of soul before me," thought Molly, as she perceived Reuben looking worse. and worse every moment, as if he would sink at her feet ; "I will perfect my triumph and show him that the spirit of a true woman cannot be crushed by the heartlessness of man."

She then inquired with interest for the several members of his family, and from his brief and nearly incoherent replies, managed to elicit that no important change had transpired since her departure from Epps Hundred. Opportunely for the preservation of the Judge's pride, he had turned aside to answer some other call, which prevented him from noticing the confusion of his nephew.

"I should like to have you meet my husband. I will speak to him."

But when she returned to make the presentation, Reuben was not there, nor was he seen again that evening.

Throughout the remainder of that brilliant festivity, Molly held her queenly priority, undisputed. None would have suspected that she was suffering an unspeakable misery— that her heart was bleeding anew at its immortal depths! For the thought that Reuben, the companion of her childhood, the long and ardently beloved, the object of her brightest dreams, was near her—under that very roof, came also with the memory of her wrongs, and gave a sharper point to her tantalizing torture.

The next day, Hollis and Molly were to leave for their return home. Judge Brockenbrough called upon them early, and fain would have persuaded them to defer their departure. But when he found that they must go, he compromised by promising to visit them in the following autumn, on his way to Epps Hundred. Molly made no inquiries respecting Reuben, and the Judge was utterly unaware of the real truth of the matter.

And so the chivalric Virginian and his new friends parted with mutual regret.

CHAPTER XVIII.

It was a very warm and sultry morning in the last of June. The inhabitants of Monmouth were all astir with the knowledge that the two armies were in their midst, and by their motions sustaining the probability that a general action was about to be hazarded. The British army, now commanded by Sir Henry Clinton, had assumed one of the strongest situations. Upon the high grounds about Monmouth Court House they lay, their right flank in the border of a small wood, the left guarded by a deeper one and the rear running towards a morass.

The American army was disposed by General Washington in such an adjacent position as to be able to harass the enemy in the rear, and take advantage of their first movement. The other generals, Lafayette, Greene, Wayne, Stewart, and Scott were directed to hold their troops in readiness to support the front.

Early in the morning, notice was given that the van of the enemy was in motion. General Lee immediately prepared to make an attack upon them, and he was soon joined by Generals Dickenson and Morgan with their spirited troops.

In full view of the home of Hollis and Molly, this action commenced. Hollis put on his military suit at once. The spirit which animated every true American was newly aroused at this spectacle, and he was impatient to mingle in the strife.

"Will you go, Hollis?" asked Molly, anxiously.

"Yes, dearest. Can I remain here tamely and not offer my assistance in the defence of my country? I shall be only a private, but there will be work enough for me to do."

"Remember the fate of your father," faltered Molly.

"I thought you were brave, my own wife," said Hollis, with a smile of affectionate pride.

"Battle scenes have not lost their charms for me yet, though I confess to unusual misgivings this morning," replied Molly.

"I shall return at night, darling, it may be with new glory attached to the honorable name which my father has transmitted to me. I must fight those red-coats, Molly. God bless you, and good-bye for the present," returned Hollis, bringing her to his heart with a parting caress.

"A blessing go with you, my husband," said Molly, as Hollis sped rapidly from the door.

The enemy advanced so near Molly's home, that she could plainly distinguish their motions.

"Oh that I were a man!" she exclaimed, "I would give

those British tyrants free doses of death. To think of their approach to our very doors ! Of their burning the beautiful homes of some of our neighbors because they would not turn traitors !"

She soon discovered Hollis engaged in the duty of cannonier, and she watched his motions with the deepest interest. As the morning deepened into day, the weather became intensely warm ; not a leaf of the trees moved, and the sun poured down such volumes of heat, the earth seemed brazen and parched to a painful endurance.

" Hollis will suffer with thirst !" Molly bethought herself ; " I will go and carry him a pitcher of water from the cold spring."

She hastily communicated her intention to Mrs. Rogers, the housekeeper and threw on her hat.

" I would advise you," remonstrated Mrs. Rogers, " to keep within house to-day. The Britishers will kill you, like as any way, if you go out there."

" I shall go," replied Molly. " How good the water will taste to him, when he is struggling so hard in this heat !"

Her glance now fell upon Hollis again ; his hair was thrown back from his forehead, he had cast aside his coat, and he was loading and discharging the cannon with an admirable coolness, while the balls of the enemy whizzed about his head. Molly was strongly impressed by the picture ; he had never looked so glorious to her before, save when he was about to sacrifice his life at the pine tree, the central object of savage ire. She could not be restrained

longer   Skipping away to the cold spring, a few yards distant, she filled her pitcher, and remembering Hollis' liking
for spearmint, paused a moment to break off a few leaves of
the rich bed, fringing the bank at her feet.   These she settled in the pitcher, as she ran up to Hollis.   He received her
offering gladly, blessing her for the thought in a low voice,
and drank the whole before he resumed his duty.

Molly ran away again, regardless of the many eyes which
had been attracted by the strange sight of her white muslin dress amid the bloody strife.   She returned to her post
of watching with a breathless anxiety, for the battle waged
closer and fiercer.   Unconsciously she would break forth
into words of encouragement for her favorite generals, as
she distinguished their uniforms, or the noble horses which
they rode, falling dead beneath them.

Once more she ventured out to carry water to Hollis, for
he nobly and unremittingly worked on in the very face of
the foe.   She had refilled her pitcher, when turning, she saw
Hollis fall to the ground.   With a blanched cheek and with
a terrible foreboding rushing over her heart, she lost no time
in reaching the spot.

Alas ! he was dead !   A shot of the enemy had killed him
instantly.

"Take that cannon away," said General Wayne, to one
of the soldiers ; " we cannot fill the post by as brave a man
as has been killed."

" No," returned Molly, looking upon the General with a
face like death, yet calm in its inspiration of bravery height-

ened to heroism ; "the cannon shall not be removed for the want of some one to serve it ; since my brave husband is no more, I will use my utmost exertions to avenge his death."

Molly was now fairly aroused. She loaded and discharged the cannon, while the officers beheld her with undisguised admiration.

"There !" she exclaimed after the first fire ; " take that, ye remorseless Englishmen, and wait for the next."

Again and again, she discharged the cannon, dealing death and destruction at every shot.

"Whom have we here ?" inquired General Washington, attracted to the spot by the singular spectacle.

"An angel of the hosts of Michael. The powers of hell would drop before her !" replied General Wayne.

Molly now determined on a *coup de maitre.* Accordingly, she reloaded the cannon with double the ordinary quota ; then charged. A terrible crash succeeded. Molly was thrown into the air several feet, then she fell to the ground with violence. Three British soldiers were killed, and an officer of high rank was apparently mortally wounded.— Many who stood by were thrown down and general confusion prevailed.

This last discharge had broken the cannon into fragments !

For a few minutes Molly was insensible, but she soon rallied and rose with a steady eye. The soldiers loudly applauded her, notwithstanding which she immediately withdrew to her home, followed by two soldiers with the body of her husband.

On the following morning, Molly was surprised by a visit from Generals Washington, Wayne, and Lafayette, who had witnessed her brave conduct at the late battle-ground.—Molly retained her self-command.

"Our army, madam, being about to leave Monmouth, we took this early opportunity to express to you our entire approval of your action of yesterday," said General Washington.

"Sir," replied Molly, "I only wished to serve my country; the death of my husband made me almost frantic."

"You merit a coat of arms like our Joan of Arc," observed Lafayette; "hers contained two golden lilies, and a sword pointing upward, bearing a crown."

"I should prefer eagles in place of the lilies," said Molly.

"You shall have an epaulette for your coat of arms," said General Washington, rising in his accustomed dignity of manner; "I here confer upon you the rank of Captain, as a testimonial of my regard for your services."

The other Generals arose, and crossing their arms upon their breasts, beheld the scene with a smile of gratification.

"Many thanks, General," said Molly; the tears rushing to her eyes; "but would that my husband had been spared to have received this honor instead of myself."

"I trust that you will come to a glorious end,"—— remarked Lafayette, "unlike the Maid of Orleans, who was burned at the stake."

"I have come to that already," returned Molly "at least

I have been taken prisoner by the Indians, and confined to
a tree, where I should have been burned alive, had not he
who afterwards was my husband, nobly offered his life for
mine."

"Are you indeed that young girl who figured so conspicuously at the murder of Miss McCrea ?" inquired General
Wayne.

Molly bowed.

"Brave Madame !" exclaimed Lafayette ; "before we
leave, permit me to salute you after the custom of my country, when we would honor noble ladies like yourself."

A blush suddenly overspread Molly's cheek, as the chival-
rous general imprinted a kiss upon her brow. A few calm,
earnest words, like a benediction, General Washington added
to Molly, and the distinguished visitors took their departure.

"Mercy on us !" exclaimed Mrs. Rogers, who had partially witnessed this scene ; " you are now really a captain !
This is the most wonderful thing I ever heard of in all my
life."

The good woman quickly took occasion to circulate this
circumstance over all the vicinity. Many came to see the
epaulette which General Washington had bestowed upon
Molly, and henceforth she was called " Captain Molly" by
the people of Monmouth.

On the evening after Molly had followed the remains of
her husband to the grave, she sat in her parlor, without
lights and alone, sadly communing with her own heart, while

Mrs. Rogers and the servants were talking in low voices in the next room. The moon shone brightly in long spectral shadows upon the cabinet which Hollis had so much prized, upon his books—everything, which reminded her of her loss. As she thus sat, the picture was a study for a master ; and, even then, it was being studied by a master, though not by a painter. Molly was in black crape, her fine hair plainly wreathed her pale forehead, and her clear, dark eyes, suffused with tears, were looking away upon the trees which were swiftly swaying their branches against the window-panes, and softly defining their outlines upon the sky. The room was old-fashioned and luxurious, suggestive of deep thought and hidden memories. It was low, with a smoke-browned beam or summer, stretching across the middle of the ceiling, and a post in each corner. The windows were narrow, with diamond-shaped panes ; and the hearth wide before the deep chimney, in which were set boughs of cedar and pine. A carpet, which Mr. Rushton had brought from England covered the centre of the floor. The cumbrous chairs of solid mahogany were lined with richly embroidered cushions fringed stiffly. A buffet, the shelves of which were adorned with ancient goblets of cut glass, silver plate, and a service of china in small dainty pieces, quaintly figured, stood in one corner. Opposite this, was a long clock, surmounted by brass knobs, and displaying a tiny ship, upon a brazen sea, swinging perpetually just over the dial ; this ticked so loudly it seemed to tell off the moments between time and eternity with a startling emphasis.

13*

When it had slowly and solemnly struck the hour of nine, Mrs. Rogers entered, and told Molly that a poor woman was at the door, who begged a lodging and a morsel of food. Molly desired that she should be brought in, and went out herself to give directions to supply the mendicant.

She was never void of curiosity, and the wretched, singular looking being who appeared before her, at once awakened her interest. So large and coarse were the woman's features, and so oddly repulsive was her face in the shadow of an enormous old calash, Molly was reminded of powerful witches in chimney-corner tales. As the woman ate, she rallied extra courage before saying —

"How came you in this condition, my poor woman."

"Oh, my old man was killed in the battle of Garmantown. He died a fightin' for his country like all possessed. Ye can't tell how brave he was, but he was poor in purse as Job's cat, and arter he died I had myself and fifteen children to take care on ;" she rejoined, between large mouthfuls, in a low, whining tone.

"But your eldest children must be old enough to take care of themselves, and assist you," said Molly.

"My eldest boy is a cripple from the day he was born ; my next is a fool ; the next two are e'en a most as bad off, and so on through the whole so that I'm dreadful hard on't all together."

"I should think so," remarked Molly, suppressing a smile.

"I've got my livin' a tellin' fortins some," the woman continued, casting up a strange eye toward Molly, "now I'll tell yourn, ef you'll let a poor woman have a place on the floor, big enough to sleep on."

"You may remain here over night without the trouble of telling my fortune," said Molly.

"O lor! how good ye are, ma'am! Heaven bless your soul here and herearter, for your charity to a lone cretur, like me."

"How have you contrived to get along thus far?" asked Molly.

"These ere war times are pesky tight," grumbled the woman, bestirring herself to take from her deep pockets various parcels. "Here I've been up and down the country this great while, a tryin' to sell yarbs to folks and I've made but a poor livin' at best."

"True," said Molly, "these times are trying for the poor," and she inwardly chided herself for her late feeling of mirth. To make amends, she promised to supply the woman bountifully on the next morning.

Molly designated a bed for the woman, but this she refused ; on no condition could she be prevailed upon to take any better quarters than a mat upon the floor. In the adjoining bedroom slept her most faithful man-servant, Dick ; she therefore saw no particular objection to the arrangement.

Accordingly, all the household soon after retired for the night. Molly went to her chamber, and weary with the excitement of that day, directly fell into a deep sleep. When the old house clock struck the hour of midnight, she awoke from the thrall of a distressing dream. Trembling with nervous apprehension, she opened her eyes and looked over the room. The moon was still shining, all was at rest, but she durst not stir ; she could not. What was her consternation, shortly after, on discovering her door open very softly and slowly. Her first thought was that Mrs. Rogers had come to her for medicine ; but she held her breath anxiously. The door opened wider, and the figure of the beggar-woman glided in !

Fortunately, Molly lay in the shadow, so that her face was not distinctly visible, but she could see the woman look hurriedly and fiercely toward her, then advance to her bed with a tread of catlike stealth.

"Oh, God ! what can I do ?" thought Molly.

She had not strength to scream to arouse assistance, and this she would not have dared to do, for a long knife in the hand of the woman glittered in the light of the moon ! Molly closed her eyes ; she believed her hour had now indeed come. She had been spared many perils for this, the last ! She heard the garments of the wretch brush the side of her bed, she felt her hot breath fall upon her face as she bent over her. Molly had still sufficient presence of mind to breathe regularly and give an appearance of deep sleep. Satisfied with her examination, the woman turned away, and stepped softly towards the chest of drawers which were in the chamber. Molly partially unclosed her eyes. Yes ! she was about to be robbed ! She thought of the loaded gun which Hollis had always kept at the bed's head, but she durst not bring that knife to her throat. The woman continued her work, steadily and swiftly ; drawer after drawer was carefully opened, while she examined the contents, and removed such articles as she wished to the huge pockets on either side of her dress. When the drawers were sufficiently rifled, the hag went out, leaving the door partially open behind her.

Now, no time was to be lost, for Molly was not one to remain inactive in such a case. With extreme care, she left her bed, and taking the gun, was determined to charge upon the robber, before she could leave the house ; hastening to the head of the stairs, she could see by the moonlight that the woman was near the landing. Molly aimed upon her without demur ; her gun clicked, but did not go off. The woman hearing a sound, turned, and instantly comprehended her danger. She darted for a back door, to make her escape, but, unaccustomed to the house, opened a door leading to the cellar, and plunged headlong down a flight of steps.

Molly bethought herself of her plan in a moment. She flew down stairs, turned the button over the cellar door, and sought the aid of her man-servant, Dick. No answer was returned to her hurried announcement of danger, and she found that he was gagged and bound hand and foot. Mrs. Rogers and the other servants were soon aroused, and Dick being extricated, she prepared to make the robber capitulate. On opening the cellar nothing unusual was to be seen ; but when the servants proceeded, they found the body of the robber lying on the ground, and the blood flowing profusely from a wound in the head. She was insensible, if not dead.

Molly gave directions that exertions should be made to restore her to life, and the wretched person was promptly cared for. A physician, who was a neighbor and a friend to Molly, was called in, and restoratives were effectually applied.

"Your robber is not a woman," said the doctor, at length, to Molly. "A man's garments are discovered beneath these outward tatters."

"It may be some famous man in disguise," returned Molly.

"Some famous rascal, undoubtedly. I had better let him die !"

"No," said Molly, "he has been punished sufficiently already. Perhaps he has done some good deed in his life, which merits mercy at our hands ; if not, we will be merciful."

The robber now murmured brokenly. Molly listened attentively, and caught the words :

"No, Goody, I didn't do it. There's no blood upon Button's soul yet."

A new, wild thought struck Molly, and she studied more attentively the countenance of the robber.

It was Button Husley ! An old feeling of kindness stole over her, notwithstanding all the wickedness she had known to be connected with his history. If possible, his life must be saved once more, for she had not forgotten that years ago he had saved hers. Her plea with the doctor was not unavailing, and in time Button slowly revived to consciousness.

As soon as his wounds were dressed, and the doctor gone out, Molly sought to speak with him.

"Button Husley!" she said sternly.

"Great Heavens!" he cried, vainly attempting to spring up; "who is this?"

"I am your friend," returned Molly, "and yet you came to rob me!"

"I did not intend any mischief, the Lord knows. I was only walking over the house, as I sometimes do in my sleep; and I believe I fell," he answered, with his old skill at expedients in difficulty.

"Attempt not to deceive me more," said Molly, impatiently, "lest you next fall into the bottomless pit, Button."

"You mistake my name," he continued, in a low voice. "It is Pinkle Van Horn, and I belong ter York State. But who, in the name of Heaven are you?"

"Don't you remember Molly, who used to live at Epps Hundred?" she replied.

Button gazed upon her as one in a dream; his sluggish mind recalled the long-forgotten past with an effort. But he broke out at last with an oath:

"Is this you, the little, lively Molly I thought so much on in them days! And I saved yer life, too, down there by Cave Rock; don't you 'member? Arter all that, you won't have a heart to bring me to justice, jest for a feller gettin' up in his sleep ?   Then, if you'll let me go safe, I'll tell you all about that are gold case that was once yourn."

"Tell me !" said Molly, imperatively, and betraying her intense interest.

"Then promise to let me go when I get over this infernal fall."

"I promise to do so," replied Molly.

"Ye see," began Button, "sence that are day you saw me last, when I made off for Witch Hazel woods, I've ben through a 'mazin' sight, some pesky hard luck, too ; I've found that nothing's truer than what old parson Willowday used to preach up—'the way of the transgressor is hard.' But what I've 'scaped and edged through all this long time is neither here nor there.   It's the gold case I'm to let on about.   Ye see, arter I got the case (and, I may as well own up to the trick now, I s'pose), I went off to York State, and meddled with one thing and another till the war broke out, and somehow I got into the ranks of the Britishers.   But I didn't sell the case, cause I didn't want the thing to bring me out ; but at last, I had a good chance, and I sold it to a feller soldier that cum from London with one of our big ginerals.   Some months arter this, he comes to me one day, and said to me :—Sir John Montrose, that are high, red-coat gineral who kept him, ordered me to go to him for a confab.   I was kind o' skeered, but I went. Then he axed me where I got that are gold case that I sold t'other day.   His eye had lighted on it somehow, and I see

he was in arnest and no mistake. But ketch Button Husley asleep, and you may ketch a bird with putting salt on
its tail "——

"I thought so last night," interrupted Molly, quietly.

"Oh, I was asleep then, or I shouldn't ha' been walking
about, you may depend upon that," said Button, somewhat
nonplussed.

"Go on about the case."

"Well, I made up some sort of a story to hand over to the
gineral ; but he wouldn't be gummed, and he said ef I'd tell
him jest where that are case come from and every hooter of
a thing I knew about it, h'd give me a thousand pound. I
told him ef he wouldn't let on 'bout it to any livin' soul I'd
out with it. So I did, leaving out the bad part of course.
I told him 'bout you, Molly, and yer mother that died at
Epps Hundred. He asked where you was then, and I told
him I'd heerd once, a good while ago, that you was gone
inter York State. I didn't tell nothin' 'bout that are Rushton man, lest I should git found out. I could see he was
mightly taken aback, with all his grand ways, and bought
the gold case and seemed to set his life on't. Arter that he
told me ef I'd find out where you was, he'd give me jest
what I axed. Now I reckon I shall make money, ef the
gineral don't die afore I get to him."

"Who is this Sir John Montrose?" inquired Molly, hanging breathless upon his words.

"Why, all I know is, he's a great English lord or sum-
thin ; and he's a regular fighter. I kind o' reckon he's some

relation to you and yer mother, by the way he took to that are gold case."

" Where is he, now ?" Molly continued.

"In a bad fix over to Middletown, where Sir Henry Clinton lies with his army. T'other day at the battle, arter fightin' famously, he got shockingly wounded."

Molly was thoughtful for some time, but at length she said : "How came you here as a robber, Button ?"

"I didn't come for that bizness," said Button, with an air of injured innocence. * But I heard 'em tell 'bout a rich widder that lived here, and ye see I was hungry and kind o' tired, and I thought it would be a good place to turn in for the night."

" I will forgive all," concluded Molly ;" if you will conduct me safely to this British officer, Sir John Montrose, so soon as you are able."

"I reckon that are gold case will make my fortin arter all," murmured Button to himself.

CHAPTER XIX.

Button did not purposely delay his recovery ; indeed, he was impatient to be gone, for the eventual gain, which he hoped to derive from the gold case, was uppermost in his mind. He was severely and lastingly injured by his late accident, but such was the nature of the injury, he was soon enabled to move, and on the following day, declared his intention to leave for the British camp.

For other reasons Molly was likewise anxious to go thither, but it being decidedly hazardous for her to do so, she communicated her plans to no one of her household. But a few days previous to the death of Hollis, he had concluded the disposition of his father's estate, so as to convert it all into money, save the house at Monmouth, which course, in the present uncertain state of the country, he deemed the wisest remaining for him. This money was designed as a loan for Congress to aid in carrying forward the war, but was now in Molly's house, and, rejoiced that it had escaped Button's search she took the precaution before leaving, to put it with all her jewels, in a small box, which she carefully deposited in a secret place.

Then, remembering a poniard which Mr. Rushton had once given her, she concealed it about her person ; and, telling Mrs. Rogers that she was going out to visit a sick person and would return before morning, she started off upon Black Princess, a short time after Button had left her house. In the dusk of the evening, she had agreed to join him at a place about a mile distant, and they were to proceed to Middletown with as much caution and dispatch as possible. Molly found Button true to his post, but with some misgivings, as she committed her horse to his guidance, said :—

"You will not prove treacherous in this affair, I hope ?"

"As sartain as the stars are out," replied Button, "not a hair of your head shall fall to the ground, while you are long o'me ; for ye see I'm true as death when I take a notion. Ef I wa'n't, my chief wouldn't send me off from the ranks to navigate 'round 'mong the rebels a makin' diskiveries and sich like. They know I don't desart sarvice when I'm likely to git good pay. You're an old friend to me, Molly, and there's a spot in my heart, bad as it is, that knows what's about right in sich a case."

"You know too, Button," said Molly, cunningly, " that if you conduct me safely to this officer, you will probably receive a handsome reward."

" Trust me for seein' which side my bread is buttered on,"
returned Button, with a shake of his and a droll twinkle of
his round eyes

Upon reaching the British camp, it was with no little difficulty that Molly gained admission to an officer of the rank
of Sir John Montrose.   But when he had discovered who
wished to see him, he ordered that she should be admitted
immediately, notwithstanding he was suffering severely from
his wounds.   When about to enter his presence, Molly faltered, and, for the first time in her life, yielded to a mastering sensation of awe for a human being.   A solemn mystery was embodied before her, and had she come there to
consult the Delphic oracle, she could not have been pervaded
by a deeper impression.

She found the British officer stretched upon a camp-bed
with the close attendance of the surgeon and one or two of
his generals. A lantern, suspended by a chain from the centre
of the tent shed a dull light over the scene, so that Molly
comprehended all its features at a glance.   She saw the pale
face of the wounded officer with his keen grey eyes, riveted
upon hers with an emotion, new and powerful, thrilling her
to the depths of her soul.   She paused irresolutely, and
drooped low the long lashes of her eyes.

Sir John desired the officers to retire, and motioned Molly
to his side.   Taking her hand between both his own he
looked long upon her face till a new light shone in his
eyes.

" Yes ; it is her child !   I doubt it no longer.   I thank

God that I have lived to see this hour. You do not remember your mother ?" he added.

Molly shook her head, too much moved to speak.

" The past all comes up before me as it were but yesterday ;" he continued, in a hollow, mournful voice, "I can scarcely believe that you are not Alice, herself ; though you are unlike her, in some respects."

"Can you tell me aught of my father ?" murmured Molly.

"First repeat what you have heard of him," replied Sir John.

"I know not his name. I only know that he was married to my mother in England and afterward, left her and her child to struggle on in life alone."

"The tale is too true," said the officer, suddenly reviving a little ; "the beautiful Alice was poor and her husband was a younger son of a proud family of rank. It was expected of him to contract a wealthy alliance. After he had left her to join his regiment and go abroad, the news of his marriage reached the ears of his family. His titled father was angry with him to the extent of swearing his disinheritance, if he did not wholly desert his wife. I have not strength to explain more than that they succeeded in alienating his affections, and a natural tendency to dissipation banished every remaining scruple.

" Years after, he returned to England repentant, desolate and broken in health and spirits. Then, he would have given life itself to have found those whom he had wronged ; but it was too late. All traces of them were lost. He then rejoined the Royal army and won distinction in various engagements.   In this war with the colonies, he has been active and conspicuous.   But it is all over now."

He paused, apparently exhausted and overcome with the strong effort which he had made.

"Is my father now living," asked Molly.

"Yes, but he is soon to die. I am he !"

"My father !   Have I found a father at last !" exclaimed Molly, with a rapt devotion which smote the officer to the heart.   Then, with a new thought, she added :

"How know you that I am your child ?"

"By the gold case which one of my servants obtained of the private, Pinkle Vanhorn, who has found you at last and brought you to me.   That case was my bridal gift to Alice, your mother ; it could only be opened by a secret spring, and within it were the old pictures of her and myself."

He then drew forth the case from his bosom and unclosed it to Molly's astonished gaze.

There was the face of a young and surpassingly lovely woman.   The clear, hazel eyes, with their expression of sad sweetness, were beautiful as those of love itself ; her rich, small lips were a rose-bud twined with a smile ; soft, brown ringlets clustered about the face, which was of a perfect oval symmetry and just tinged with bloom like a delicate sunset-cloud.   The sweet femininity and almost childlike beauty of that face made Molly weep for regretful love.

Opposite this, was the picture of a young man in military

dress, with a proud, sensuous cast of couutenance, and with the same keen, grey eyes that had at first affected Molly so strongly.

"Within that case," the officer continued, "I found the papers which certified my marriage to Alice, and scraps of verse which I had once written to her. They are here," he concluded, "put them within the case once more and keep it for yourself, henceforth."

"I trust that you will live," said Molly.

"No ; I am fatally wounded. Before the rise of another sun, I shall be gone. Shall I die, my child, without your forgiveness ?"

Molly knelt by his side and pressed his cold hand to her lips.

"My father, I have nothing to forgive. That God before whom you are soon to appear, knoweth all hearts. If you have sinned. He can pardon."

"I know not God. I cannot approach his presence as I would that of my king. Would that my life had been less made up of errors. There is the sting of death," groaned the dying man.

"The blood of Christ cleanseth from all sin ;" said Molly, "I cannot have you die, unreconciled to Him. Will you not pray for mercy in this solemn hour ?'

"It is too late to begin now," he replied.

"Then I will pray for you," said Molly, bowing her head and placing her father's hand upon it.

In words of simple faith, yet most fervent supplication,

Molly cried before God from the uttermost depths of her soul. Before she had concluded, her father exclaimed :

"See ! There is new light here, golden and glorious ! There is your mother ! Oh, Alice !" he continued, out-stretching his arms, while the tears dimmed his glassy eyes.

"My beautiful ! My beloved ! I hear music, but not martial strains ; 'tis the sound of heavenly hosts. Do you not hear it, my child ?"

His eyes closed and he uttered broken words of supplica-tion. After this, he gradually fell into a slumber. Molly re-mained by his side and watched him carefully, while the sur-geon having re-entered, reported that he had but few hours longer to live.

Toward morning, a British officer entered and announced himself as Sir Henry Clinton.

"Madam," he said to Molly ; "Sir John Montrose is about to die. Do you propose to return to Monmouth, to-day ?"

"I do," she replied.

She had scarcely spoken this, when she heard a low groan, and turning, saw that her father was in the agonies of death.

"God have mercy ! My child, forgive !" he murmured, and expired.

Well was it for Molly, that she knew not, nor ever knew, that her last discharge of cannon at the late engagement, had caused Sir John Montrose to be fatally wounded. Thus, accidentally and unconsciously, her wrongs and those of her mother were avenged !

When Molly had become sufficiently composed to speak, she requested of Sir Henry Clinton that the body of her father might be given her to convey to Monmouth for burial. He evaded her request, and directed a servant to conduct her to another tent. There she found one of the officers who had stood by the side of Sir John Montrose, at the time of her entrance into his presence. So much had she been pre-occupied with the thought of the wounded man whom she had come to see, she had not observed this person's attention directed closely upon herself. It was General Boscawen, an evil, unscrupulous man ; but who possessed such influence with Sir Henry Clinton, he had only mentioned that Molly was too dangerous a rebel to allow her freedom, and per-mission had been accorded him to detain her for the present.

He evidently regarded her with passionate admiration, and spared no pains to divert her notice to himself and make a favorable impression. She conceived at once a strong dis-like toward him, and only demanded anew permission to re-turn to Monmouth.

"That cannot be granted you, my fair lady, for you are a rebel, and too rare a prize to let thus easily escape ;" he replied, with an attempt to gallantry.

"What !" exclaimed Molly ; " I am not to be detained as a prisoner, when I came here only to witness the death of my father ! Is there not sufficient honor in the soul of a British officer to scorn to take advantage of a woman !"

"A British officer may have a warm heart as well as a

cool head. I will tell you now that you are my prisoner (and, I trust, for life) most beautiful of women !" he replied, with a suavity, which quickly aroused Molly to desperation.

" You—base, British tyrant have no power over me. I defy your threats," she returned, rising and attempting to escape.

" You will find it not so easy, my pretty bird, to get out of the cage as to get in," he said, triumphantly. When she discovered that all egress was closely barred, she burst into tears. This wholly unexpected event overwhelmed her with anger and grief. Her request to see Sir Henry Clinton once more was granted ; but her entreaties and denunciations, were alike unavailing. He promised her upon his honor that she should be treated in all respects in a manner due to a lady of rank, save the liberty to leave the camp. This promise was strictly fulfilled.

When Molly found that her release was impossible at present, she requested Boscawen to allow her to dispatch a note to her housekeeper, which, to her astonishment, he readily granted. She then wrote to Mrs. Rogers that she was a prisoner in the British camp, and charged her to take the strictest care of the box which she would find hidden under the pillows of the bed that she usually occupied, concluding with the hope that her release would soon take place. This note she carefully sealed and gave it to Boscawen, who averred that it should be safely delivered by his own servant.

The following day, the British army left Middletown

and proceeded to Sandy-Hook, where they passed over to New York. Here, the headquarters of the British were situated, so that they could be supplied with the necessaries of life, amounting to luxuries.

No effort was spared by General Boscawen to surround Molly with every thing which he thought could win her heart and banish the memory of her sorrows. She was made to attend sumptuous dinners and balls, at which the beauty and high rank of the British and Tories were present; but she remained gloomy and silent, repeating her request for liberty on every possibly occasion.

" Confound these rebel women !" exclaimed her lover, impatiently, to Sir Henry Clinton, after one of his fruitless attempts to ingratiate himself in her favor ; " they hate us English officers as they would the very d— himself. But this one is a diamond among common stones, too rare and brilliant to let slip from my possession."

" Remember," returned his commander ; " that I tolerate no unfair movement in my ranks. You must make her your bride, for my word, which is never broken, has passed that. the lady be protected."

" I shall soon make the citadel capitulate in one way or another," said Boscawen with a chuckle ; " for I have not the patience of Job."

Unknown to them, Molly overheard these words, and with an apprehension falling upon her heart like lead, she made one more effort to revolve a plan of escape.

Since coming to New York, she had several times caught

a glimpse of Button in the service of British officers, but had been unable to communicate with him. Now, she most carefully sought her opportunity, and, on the next evening, when she attended a ball given by Sir Henry Clinton, she did not return to her room at an early hour, as had been her custom ; but waited till Boscawen was partially stupified with liquor, as he invariably became after a protracted carousal. She then signed to Button to follow her to an adjoining ante-room.

"Lord ! Molly !" he broke out, "how pale and poor you have grown, since you got in this 'ere den of Britishers ! a feller would think, now, you'd lost every friend you'd ever had, except me—Button Husley, otherwise Pinkle Vanhorn."

"Hush !" whispered Molly ; "take care, or we shall be discovered. I have lost all my friends," she continued, "but, Button, I hope to prove whether you will befriend me so far as to lend me your aid."

He eyed her with curiosity.

"I wish to escape from here," said Molly, in a very low tone.

"Well, you know, 'if wishes were horses, beggars might ride,'" returned Button.

"You cannot have it in your heart to betray me ?"

Button shook his head and whispered :

"I guess as how I'm too good for that. You've saved my life, Molly, more'n once."

"Then can you devise any means to enable me to leave

here ?" Molly continued, anxiously ; "I will reward you well, Button."

" Ye see, I've never got my pay yit for that are chore I did for ye 'bout the gold case. It turned out so bad, I was mighty sorry : howsomever, I can't run the risk of my head, without good pay."

" Here is a ring with a diamond of great value," replied Molly ; "if you will help me to escape, this ring shall be your own."

"I can't work on credit ; let me be sure of that are diamond fast thing, and then I'll set my noddle to work a contriving'," said Button, with glowing eyes.

Molly took the ring from her finger, and gave it to him.

"It was a gift from my husband," she said with a sigh, "but my liberty is dearer than all now."

Button remained thoughtful, then inquired if she were kept locked within her room ?

She replied that she was not, save at night, though she was kept under guard.

"Day arter to-morrow morning," whispered Button ; "there's a review and the ginerals will all be away. Then I'll contrive some way to cheat your guard off from his post. Then I'll come under yer winder and make a low whistle. When ye hear that, slip down to the mess-room and I'll help ye rig up so that ye shall pass for an old market-woman. I'll show ye the way to the line and give ye the pass-word. But we must'nt talk any more, now ; them ere red eyes will diskiver us."

Molly gave him a grateful look, and glided away to her room.

"The intervening time before the morning on which it was planned for Molly to escape dragged away heavily. But it came at last, and to her unspeakable joy, she heard the low whistle. She went to her door. No guard stood there as usual ; and she hastened to the appointed spot. Button met her, gladly informing her that he had sent her guard on "Tom Fool's arrant," for the moment that she left her room, and he had now returned to his post, not imagining but that all was right.

Molly quickly threw on her disguise of the old cloak and hat of a market-woman, and announced herself prepared to go.

"Let what will come," said Button, when he had conducted her out by a retired way and they were comparatively secure, "don't you let me out."

Molly gave him the desired assurance, and hastened him forward with all possible dispatch. They escaped observation, to Molly's infinite relief.

"This 'ere is a peculiar time," said Button ; "any other mornin', when there warn't a review, ye see, our business wouldn't be so easy."

Just before they reached the guard-house at the line, Button gave her the pass-word, charging her to speak it in a low, grumbling tone ; and, adding some further directions how to proceed, slipped aside to watch if she were successful.

She spoke the word to the guard without discovery. Oh, joy ! she had escaped !

Button now returned rapidly, while Molly went forward on her way, inspired by a hope which filled her heart with an exultant delight. She felt like flying over the ground, but she did not dare to walk in more than a moderate pace, lest she should be observed and detected.

She had proceeded some distance, and begun to consider herself safe, when she espied two horsemen approaching upon the road. Her heart throbbed violently, for she soon perceived that they were British officers. For a moment, she looked about her to devise some plan of secreting herself, but she saw that her only alternative was to proceed straight forward, trusting to her fortune to escape their notice.

Her courage fell when she saw that they were Sir Henry Clinton and Boscawen. The strength which had hitherto nerved her every motion, now fled, and she would have sunk to the ground, had she not recalled that there was yet a possibility of escape. With a masterly effort, she tried to appear as unconcernedly as possible.

They came up ; she averted her head and drooped it low, when a light breeze swept up the wide brim of her hat, and thus let escape a shower of curls, which had been carefully confined from view. She drew forth her ungloved hand from the cloak and quickly restored the hat ; but the keen eyes of the British officers had detected the brown curls and the small, lily hand, which contrasted strangely with her tattered and uncouth garments.

They immediately halted.

"Whither bound, my bonnie lass ?" inquired Clinton.

Molly hung her head, and replied in a low, tremulous voice, as if her soul were escaping from her body—

"I've been to market, and—I'm going home."

"You don't look much like a market-woman," said Clinton.

"They havn't such hair as that ;" said Boscawen, in a low tone to Clinton. "I'll be shot, if I don't see the face which is under that old hat."

Molly attempted flight, but the odds were sadly against her. Although she ran as for her life, she was quickly overtaken and encircled in the strong arms of Boscawen.

"This is my bird, after all !" he exclaimed, recognizing her with astonishment.

Molly struck him broadly in the face, while she struggled to escape.

"Now, be easy ; that's a good girl," continued Boscawen, rudely kissing her under her hat. Notwithstanding her violent struggles, he bore her to his horse and placed her upon the saddle before himself. As they continued their way, Bascawen said to Clinton :

"You now see how fortunate was the appointment with Lord Howe to review the fleet. If we had remained upon the parade ground as we had first planned, we should have missed the recapture of this prize."

"Which is more valuable in your eyes, than any frigate on our seas," returned Clinton, with a smile.

14*

Molly listened with despair in her heart, for she now seemed utterly forsaken of hope.

When they reached head-quarters, Boscawen reconducted her to her room and paused to say :—

"You see, lady, its of no use for you to try to escape from me. As sure as death, you are mine. Let me also add for your consolation, that if you had really escaped and reached Monmouth, you would have been sorry ; for you have no home and all the money which was once yours, is in my possession.

As wretched as Molly now was, these words, so incomprehensible, caused her to look upon him with curiosity.

"I had no idea of taking a bride without seeing what I could get with her," he continued.

"So, instead of sending the note which you wrote to your house-keeper, I used it for my private advantage. That box which you directed to be so nicely kept, I was determined to have, and in the disguise of a rebel officer, I went over to Monmouth, before we left Middletown By a fine little stratagem I got all of your people out of the house :

"Tis false," interrupted Molly.

"No ; I had only to tell them that on your return you had met with a serious accident a mile or two back, and they all scampered off without delay, I pretending to follow. After I had found the box of money and jewels, I thought it prudent to fire the house and then make good my escape."

"Tyrant !" exclaimed Molly ; "this story is planned by you within this hour, but you cannot deceive me."

" Come with me and I will prove the truth of what I have said."

" I command you," he added, as he saw her hesitate.

She arose mechanically and followed him. There, indeed, in his room was her box !

No word could she say more. She returned to her room.

"Henceforth you will be kept locked within this room and the key will be in my own pocket," concluded Boscawen as he fastened the door upon her.

By one of those mysterious habits of the mind which brings up a marked contrast, in a time of intense emotion, the long past—its hours of happiness and peace—now arose distinctly in Molly's memory. She was again at Epps Hundred, with the blessed friends of her early life. She heard their cheerful voices and remembered their words of love, which had filled her young heart with gladness. But when she thought of Reuben, she exclaimed :

" Could he see me now, even if he has learned to hate me, he would pity this, my wretched fate. Alas ! I shall never meet him more !"

She then drew forth the gold case and looked long at the picture of her mother. The mild, beautiful eyes seemed to suffuse with sorrow, till Molly's tears flowed so fast, she closed the case.

At last, she remembered the old habit which the mother of Reuben had first taught her. She knelt and prayed to

God ; and, from her desolate, broken spirit, flowed the words of the Psalmist :

" My flesh and my heart faileth ; but God is the strength of my heart, and my portion forever.

CHAPTER XX.

MOLLY saw no more of Boscawen for several days after she was remanded to the prison, being strictly confined within her room, and, as before, was served only by a female domestic, who now refused all communication with her. But, at length, the heavy step which she had learned so much to dread, she heard at her door, and the key turned within the lock, causing her to shudder with new apprehension.

Boscawen entered with a smile, and accosting her gaily, seated himself at her side.

Molly shrank from his presence, as from that of a venomous reptile.

"I have come," he said, "upon business of importance to you and me. If you will be gracious, fair lady, you will find it greatly to your advantage."

"God help me," murmured Molly to herself.

"Yesterday," continued Boscawen, " Sir Henry Clinton discovered a spy in our ranks—one of those accursed rebels who deserve to be hung between the heavens and earth, till the birds of the air have left their bones as a monument of justice. He is now in a dungeon and to-morrow he will meet his death. He has inquired for you and calls himself your friend."

" My friend," exclaimed Molly.

" He gives his name as Reuben Epps."

" Reuben near me !" she cried, springing to her feet ; " let me go to him this moment."

" Stop," said Boscawen, " you forget that he is a prisoner as well as yourself."

" Oh, my God !" groaned Molly, " can I do nothing to save him ?"

" Yes," replied Boscawen ; " I have the keys to all the dungeons. It is in my power to let him escape."

Molly fell on her knees before him while she exclaimed—

" Save him ! You must not—will not let him come to death ?"

Her face was deadly pale, and her large dark eyes were so full of passionate entreaty, Boscawen regarded her with awe and new admiration.

" I will save him," he replied, taking her hand and pressing it to his lips.

" Generous man !" exclaimed Molly ; " blessings be upon you, evermore, for this noble deed !"

" Spare your thanks for the present," returned Boscawen with a sinister laugh :

"I shall not do this, without conditions."

"Name them," said Molly, eagerly.

"He offered to give up his life for yours, but I am able to spare that sacrifice."

Molly heard these words with a keen sensation of happiness. Reuben did not hate her after all !

"If I do not help him to escape," he went on, coolly ; "he will be tried by a court-martial, condemned and shot dead by a dozen bullets before the set of to-morrow's sun."

"He may be acquitted," she said, huskily.

"Impossible," declared Boscawen, producing a copy of the articles of war ; "a spy must be punished with death."

"But Sir Henry Clinton may be induced to show mercy. Let me go to him."

"He will show no mercy to the rebels ; they show none to us. Not long since that old, death-dealing, hell-daring rebel, General Putnam, detected a loyal lieutenant in the American camp, and when his release was demanded by Gov. Tyron, he sent back this reply : ' Sir, a lieutenant in your king's service, was taken in my camp as a spy ; he was tried as a spy ; he was condemned as a spy ; and you may rest assured, sir, he shall be hanged as a spy. P. S.—Afternoon. He is hanged.' It cannot then be supposed that we are fools enough to show mercy under like circumstances."

"You have promised to save him. Name your conditions," said Molly, breathlessly.

"That you make no resistance to the bans of our marriage to-morrow morning."

Molly started back as if she had been suddenly shot to the heart.

"I cannot, oh, I cannot promise that! It is too much to ask!" she groaned.

"Then," said Boscawen, sternly, "so sure as I am a live man, you shall behold with your own eyes, the corpse of your friend by another day; and, what is more, you shall be my bride, willingly or not."

"This is dreadful!" returned Molly, clasping her fingers so tightly that they were stained with blood. "Great Heavens! what shall I do?"

"Only what I require, and this spy shall go free."

"I believe it not in your power to give him freedom;" said Molly, struck with a new suspicion that he had taken this means to deceive her.

"I pledge my honor," replied Boscawen.

"Your honor!" Molly repeated, scornfully.

"If that is not sufficient, Pinkle Vanhorn, whom you know, shall under my directions secretly release the prisoner, and to-morrow, bring from him to you, in my presence, a written declaration of his release. I will send him a suit of my own uniform, that he may leave in disguise, and give him a pass in my own hand."

"Let me have time to think of this," said Molly, mournfully. "It is so sudden, so overwhelming!"

"There is no time for delay," said Boscawen. "Remember, if you will do what I have said, freedom for your friend. Refuse, death for the spy, and our marriage to take place, without your compliance."

He rose to go. Molly raised her eyes to Heaven in supplication, then said :

"Spare him, and I obey—if I live till that hour."

"Very well," said Boscawen, triumphantly ; "so soon as it is evening, the prisoner shall be released."

"One more request," said Molly. "You will not refuse me the last ? Allow me to see him—the prisoner—before he leaves this place."

"No," he returned, "my sweet bride must not be exposed to the rude gaze of an accursed rebel. She is too lovely, too precious a pearl to be cast before swine."

Molly bowed her head and sobbed aloud. Boscawen went out, carefully locking the door behind him.

Despair, the dark ministrant of the soul when the last hope has fled, now brooded over Molly like a cloud of the wrathful storm. Life had no more charms for her. She could look backward, and, with calm gratitude remember that she had saved the life of Reuben, but for the future there was no hope. To marry a man like Boscawen was worse than death and she resolved that the event should never take place. The poniard which she had placed in her bosom on leaving Monmouth was still there, and this could prove her deliverer in her latest extremity.

Hour after hour she remained motionless, as if her heart were stricken to stone, revolving the awful and overwhelming events with which a mysterious Providence had surrounded her, and determining what remained for her to do. She took no note of time or the objects around her. Evening stole on, the clear, cold stars of the December night illumined the heavens, and the silvery beams of the moon rested across her room, but the night had no light or beauty for her.

It was very late, when her attention was attracted by a tread approaching her door. Although she had never been disturbed before at such an hour, she recalled whom it could only be. Nerved to desperation, she stood up erect in the remotest corner of her room, and drawing forth her poniard, awaited the entrance of Boscawen.

"God have mercy on my soul!" she exclaimed. "I will die rather than become his prey! The moment has come!"

The key turned in the lock, the door opened. She looked hurriedly around and saw—not Boscawen, but the face which had haunted her dreams both sleeping and waking, for long, troubled years! Yes, it was Reuben Epps!

She was speechless and would have sunk to the floor had he not rushed forward and caught her to his breast. The reaction was too overwhelming, for a moment she seemed to have swooned.

"Molly! dearest Molly!" he whispered; "arouse yourself for the sake of your life. I have come to save you. We shall fly from here this night."

"Where is he—Boscawen?" murmured Molly, in her affright.

"Fear nothing from him. I must not pause to tell you all now ;" he replied, throwing a large cloak over her shoulders, the hood of which concealed her head. "Enough that he is in a distant part of the building, at a late carousal, and so entirely overcome with intoxication that Button Husley obtained his keys from his pocket without any difficulty. He then conducted me hither, and in my disguise of Boscawen's own uniform, I was not suspected."

"His keys," said Molly, under her breath, as they went out and locked the door behind them ; "go with me to his room ; there is something which belongs to me I will have."

Without asking an explanation, Reuben followed her to Boscawen's door ; the key was applied successfully, and Molly perceiving her box, motioned Reuben to conceal it under his cloak. They then quickly passed out, relocked the door, and hastened to the yard below, where they found Button awaiting them with horses.

"If here isn't my own Black Princess !" said Molly, springing to the saddle.

"I've taken good care of her since she came to these ere quarters, along o' you," Button replied.

"Be cautious, or we shall be discovered," whispered Reuben.

"They are too drunk up there to know their right from their left," said Button ; "much less to know what's going on with us."

"Do not forget to restore the keys to Boscawen's

pocket," added Reuben, " and for your good services accept this piece of gold."

Button gladly received the gift, spurred the horses, and Reuben and Molly rode off at a rapid pace.

When they reached the guard-house at the line, Reuben presented his pass which had been furnished him by Boscawen.

" All right so far," said the sentinel, as he examined it by his lantern ; " but there's nothing said about the person that is with you."

Molly quickly recalled the pass-word which Button had told her at the time of her former attempt to escape, and pronouncing it to the sentinel, she was permitted to go forward.

The night was cold, frosty and sparkling, and they rode rapidly without pausing to exchange a word until the dawn. They had now left New York far behind them, and comparatively out of danger of discovery, they halted in an obscure spot at a small tavern.

For some time, both were so overcome that neither could inquire of the other what was uppermost in their hearts. But at length, when they were comfortably seated before a bright fire of huge hickory logs and began to breakfast, Reuben said :

"You may wonder, Molly, why I was taken as a spy, a character which I have always detested. But I was willing to make any sacrifice if thus I could discover you."

" Was it, then, to find me that you risked your life, dear Reuben ?" asked Molly.

"Oh, Molly ! it is perfect bliss to hear you thus address me once more ;" he replied, gazing into her eyes in earnest devotion.

"I cannot understand this," said Molly ; "you are now the Reuben of olden days, but in that time when you ceased to write me "——

Her voice faltered and the tears rushed to her eyes.

Reuben drew nearer to her, and taking her hand in both his own, said :   "Dear Molly, it is due to you that I explain now.   When I last saw you at my uncle's in Virginia I was so overwhelmed with what I thought was your indifference, I could not remain in your presence.   To know that you were the wife of another, seemed but the black seal of all the written misery I had endured from the time of our separation.   For some time after that, I suffered so severely, that I could not pursue the study of my profession as I had proposed to do with a distinguished physician for whose instruction I had been invited to Cyprus, especially, by my uncle. But when, sometime after, I received a letter from home, detailing the death-bed scene of Hazor Wilkhurst—(you remember him as our old teacher and brother of our housekeeper)—a new leaf was opened, explaining the one, trying mystery of my life.   It seemed that he had long cherished his old grudge against both you and me, and had carried out his spirit of revenge.   In his last hours, his guilt arose before him in dread accusation, and he confessed that when he held the situation which my father had obtained for him in a post-office, through which all our letters passed, he had destroyed them and written others to deceive us and alienate our affections."

"Is it possible," exclaimed Molly, "that you did not write that sad letter which almost broke my heart?"

"I wrote nothing but that which repeated my love, and entreated you, by all that had been dear to us in the past, to answer me, if but one line."

"Alas! how much pain would the knowledge of this have spared me!" said Molly;" and you never received one of my many letters to you?"

"Yes; one only. After waiting for more than a year, there came a letter, as I supposed from you, telling me of your love for Hollis Rushton, and that, in future, I must regard you as only a friend. Then, I was almost distracted, for I loved you, Molly, as I shall never love another."

"Let us be grateful to God that this sad mystery has at last been explained," returned Molly, much moved,

"After I heard this confession of Hazor Wilkhurst," Reuben continued, "we received news of the battle of Monmouth and the death of your husband. I then resolved to seek you and ask your forgiveness. I started immediately for Epps Hundred, intending to take Monmouth on my way. But, there, I discovered that your home had been burned to ashes and that you were retained as a prisoner by the British. To find you and assist you to escape, was my next purpose, and assuming the character of a British soldier, I made my entrance into New York. There I was discovered and you know the rest."

" O dear !" exclaimed Molly, in one of her characteristic moods," this is the oddest affair, take it all through, that ever I read of—though I don't ever read much, as you remember, Reuben. That makes me think of old times at dear Epps Hundred. How I wish I could see Mary ! Was your father well, when you last heard ?"

" My father is dead," replied Reuben, sadly ; " I am pained to say that his habit of intemperance overcame him at last." " He did not marry Mrs. Dyke, I hope ?" she continued, anxiously.

" No ; thanks to Heaven ! that woman failed of her object, though she effected great misery for us all."

" And Mary ?"

" She is still at home and married, I suppose, before this. But you must return with me to Epps Hundred, Molly, and learn the rest for yourself. I will not tell you more."

" My money has all been stolen from me," said Molly ; " would you wish a penniless friend to burden you ?"

" Talk not thus," replied Reuben, " after all that we have suffered. I, too, am poor ; the estate which was once my mother's is now greatly decreased in value ; and, in these times of war, there is but little money circulating in the land. But I have still a home : you have none. While you choose, that home shall be also yours. If you have finished breakfast, let us proceed on our way with all possible dispatch."

"Be sure and take care of that box we brought from Boscawen's room, for it contains some family relics, which I should regret to lose," concluded Molly, as they went out to resume their journey.

CHAPTER XXI.

CONCLUSION.

YEARS passed, bringing many important changes in the history of the country. After peace was established between Great Britain and America, the business interests throughout the country gradually revived, and new villages, towns and cities were built up, dotting hill and vale with beauty. Epps Hundred gathered around and within its borders many homes and places of business, so that, under another name, it came to rank as a place of importance. Reuben was there established as a physcian, and in due time, Molly became his happy wife. On opening the box which had accompanied them thither, she found that it contained not only the jewels and money of her own, but several rouleaux of gold, which had been there deposited by Boscawen for safe keeping. This, she revealed to Reuben after their marriage, and desired him to use the money which had been Boscawen's in the erection of a new and handsome mansion at Epps Hundred, that she might thus be repaid for the destruction of her home at Monmouth. Accordingly, the old house was appropriated to the use of their numerous servants, and, but a few rods distant, upon the apex of a hill commanding an extensive prospect on all sides, arose a noble substantial building, adorned with the English colonnade. A few ancient, forest trees of gigantic growth, overshadowed the spot, and careful cultivation soon made the surrounding slopes display varied points of attraction.

Mrs. Rogers and Dick had been sent for by Molly and became members of her household at Epps Hundred.

Mary, the sister of Reuben, was the wife of the minister, who had succeeded Parson Willowday. His seven children, by a former marriage, were dear to her as her own ; and her daily life, her care and self-sacrifice for their sakes afforded a striking example of the kindness of a step-mother. A neat parsonage, with a small farm attached, about a mile from the old homestead, was Molly's bridal gift to Mary. Frequent were the visits exchanged between them, and long hours of quiet delight they spent together, reverting to the scenes of the past, and relating details of their several lives from the time of their separation.

When Mary spoke of that long, gloomy period which succeeded Molly's departure from Epps Hundred ; of the suffering of Reuben and herself by reason of receiving no intelligence, save the most distressing, from her ; and the dark shadows which deepened over their lives, year after year, the tears would rush to Molly's eyes, and she could only return —" Let us thank Heaven that a brighter day has dawned !"

All this affluent experience of trial and joy did not pass Molly without leaving a strong influence upon her character. Maturity of thought and a new tenderness, born of maternal love, gradually moulded her womanhood into a lovelier type. Not now, by the wild impulsion of her own will did she seek to regulate her life, but by that faith of the heart which has truly profited by affliction, she trusted in Heaven for all wisdom and guidance.

With the people in the vicinity of her home, she was a great favorite. Devoid of the arrogance sometimes attendant upon superior fortune, her unaffected, sprightly manner and her discriminating benevolence, could not fail to win the love of all. But in her own home, was she especially beloved, nay, reverenced. A devoted wife and mother, a kind mistress and a clever manager, she was the central life of the whole household.

Thus assisted, Reuben found no obstacles in the way of his public pursuits. Conscientious, benevolent and skillful, his life was a continued service in the aid of others, and he became one of the most eminent physicans of his time.

After the invasion of Virginia by Arnold, Judge Brockenbrough was induced to accept the invitation of his nephew to make Epps Hundred his future home.

The beautiful Cypress had been partially laid waste in the general depredations of the traitor, but the remnants of its former appointments, he brought hither, and also a few negro servants for his personal service. These, at Molly's particular request, he was soon induced to liberate from bondage.

Not less to gratify his own taste for luxurious surroundings, than to contribute to the comfort of his friend's rare household, decorations and imported works of art were introduced at Epps Hundred, till it was transformed to a villa scarcely inferior in beauty and magnificence to Cypress. A prominent feature of the new régime of the judge, and one decidedly novel in that vicinity, was a chariot and four noble horses, with liveried driver and footman, after the custom of wealthy gentlemen of the Old Dominion.

Notwithstanding this, Molly often chose to ride on horseback in company with her husband in his daily round of business. Reuben delighted in nothing so much as in her society. Whether she were serious or gay, her words moved his soul, as could no other. He had never loved her most for her rare beauty ; and now, though her cheek wore its richest bloom, her eyes a deeper shade of loveliness, exquisitely fringed, as it were, with sweetest emotions, and the grace of her figure was more perfectly developed, she was dear to him for something higher and holier than this ;— even for the truth and purity of her character, the indescribable attraction of her manner, and for her measureless affection for himself.

One morning, when Molly had accompanied him on a professional visit, she proposed they should return by the way of Witch Hazel House. She had not forgotten her old associations connected with the spot, and occasionally preferred to pass that lonely and deserted way, instead of taking· the new and improved road. The grass had grown tall and rank in the ridges between the paths ; unpruned branches of the trees hung low, so as to obstruct the course ; the bridges were broken aud scarcely safe ; and on all sides, were evidences of desolation and neglect.

The old house had not been inhabited since the death of Goody Wythe, and had now crumbled down to little else than a ruin. There still remained, however, rooms, though without windows and doors, through which, at night, great bats flew with their dusky wings, disturbing the dust and mould, and breaking the silvery threads of the nests of spiders. The owls perched on the broken chimney and hooted mournful tales of the dark, ominous past. In the dark cellar, stood slimy pools of water ; adders crept in and out its wall, and other reptiles gathered there as to a place of trust.

As they approached the spot, Molly exclaimed to her husband :—

" See ! there is a faint smoke curling up from the old chimney ! What can it mean ?"

" If I were superstitious I would credit it to the supernatural, for certainly no human being would think of inhabiting a place like this ;" returned the Doctor, not less astonished than herself.

Spurring forward his horse, he resolved to penetrate the mystery.

Through one of the open windows, the wretched face of an old man, half-hidden with long white hair and beard was thrust forth, as they halted before the house. The Doctor motioned him to come out, whispering to Molly that he was curious to ascertain for a certainty if such a looking being did not flourish cloven feet.

The old man obeyed, hobbling forward with crutches and but one leg. He looked upon them carefully for a moment, then said :—

" If this ain't Reuben Epps and Molly, as sure as I'm alive and hoppin.' You haven't come to bring me into any trouble, have ye ?"

They exchanged glances of surprise, when the Doctor exclaimed :—

" Is it possible ! Indeed, Button, we did not know you,"

" Even now," added Molly ; "I can hardly be persuaded that it is not a spirit, that I see here."

" Well ; ye know I've got to be an old man, and I've been through amazin' hard fortin. It's time, I spose, that I was kivered up under the sile of the arth," Button returned.

" But what has brought you round to this old place at last ?" inquired the Doctor.

" Oh !" said Button ; " arter the war was over, I dodged round from one spot to 'nother, through more hair-breadth 'scapes than you can shake a stick at. Ye see I'm e'enamost broke to pieces, and I never could tell why it was I was born for sich a many hard knocks. At last, I thought I'd crawl back here to the old spot and die."

" When did you come ?" asked Molly.

" Why, I got here only last night, and sich a night as it was I never seed afore. If all the imps of hell had been tuggin' at my heart, I couldn't ha gone through any more. Ye see I couldn't keep it out of my head—all them are old times when Goody lived here with me. They say she's dead now, but I see her last night as plain as ever I did."

" I shouldn't suppose you would have slept in the old house at all with any comfort," said the Doctor.

"It was amazin' hard work to try at it, but I'm so pesky poor, I've nowhere else to go. I wish I could die, for nobody can be more miserable than I be."

The tears came to Molly's eyes

"Button," she said, kindly ; "you shall not want hereafter ; at least, if you continue to live near us."

" No," said the Doctor, " we will take care that you are provided for."

" O, God bless you," said Button, while for the first time since his boyhood, he yielded to tears. " I know I saved yer lives from them ere Britishers, but I 'spected I'd done sich a lot of left hand tricks, you wouldn't take much pity on me, arter all."

> " But in that instant o'er his soul
> Winters of memory seemed to roll,
> And gather in that drop of time,
> A life of pain, an age of crime."

"We must hasten away, for I have an engagement," said the Doctor ; " but I will see you again before night. Here is some money, you can take for the present. Go down to the Hotel where the Bald Eagle used to stand, and get a good dinner."

"Yes," said Molly, "make yourself comfortable, till we can fix upon some place for your future home."

They now rode away, while Button stood and looked after them till they were out of sight. Then, putting on his old three-cornered hat, he started off to the Hotel.

It was such an occasion of joy to him, he not only order-ed dinner, but plentiful supplies of liquor. After he had eaten and drank till he began to consider it were wisest for him to take his departure, he secured another bottle in his pocket and started on his return. Every step augmented the giddiness resulting from his potations, so that when he came to the cross-road which branched off to Witch Hazel House, he forgot to strike into it, as he intended, but proceeded for-ward, pitching and rolling from one side of the way to the other, in a most circuitous manner.

At length, nearly overcome by the fumes of intoxication, he resolved to halt by an old saw-mill, to which he had come on the way. Just above the mill, by the side of the stream, he sat down upon a huge log. The sun came out and shed new warmth upon him, which added languor to his stupe-faction. It was a bland, delicious day of the Indian sum-mer ; the ground was strewn thickly with crimson and golden leaves ; the woods directly opposite him, with their varied tinges, cast long shadows into the stream. Button looked down into the water upon the inverted trees, and muttered broken exclamations of transported sense ; then, spying a few nice chips at his feet, he cast a sidelong glance at a man engaged at work a few steps distant, and believing himself unobserved, slyly tucked them into the pocket of his coat for future use.

The man whom he had seen, now returned to the mill and set the wheel in motion, which continuous sound soon lulled Button into a sound sleep.

But, suddenly, the mill wheel stopped. The attendant astonished at the event in which he had no agency, ran forward to ascertain the cause. There, crushed among the spokes of the great wheel, he saw the mangled and broken limbs of a human body !

It was Button, who had fallen from the log into the water and been carried swiftly into the flume, to meet this awful death !

No one could mourn for him, when it became known that he was dead, for his life had been so marked with evil deeds, as to be scarcely more than a record of crime. Molly saw that he was decently buried by the side of Goody Wythe ; and repeating his history to her children, in illustration of the consequences of a sinful career, did not omit to notice his few good deeds, to which she had been indebted for her life.

The tenth anniversary of the marriage of Reuben and Molly came round ; it being also the day of public thanksgiving, they resolved to honor it with even more than the accustomed celebration.

Molly's three children, a triad of beauty and love, made her daily life, else imperfect, harmonious, like the ancient, three-stringed lyre. The oldest, named Montrose, an intelligent boy of eight years; Alice, a thoughtful blue-eyed girl, of six summers; and Reuben, a little curly-headed boy of three, whose pet name was "little Ben," composed the group. For these children and their young friends, the festivities were partly to wear the character of a holiday, and they were by no means inactive in the preparations. Indeed, for weeks previous, the whole household of Epps Hundred actively bestirred themselves in their various departments to accomplish suitable arrangements for the anticipated day.

The festive day came. A light snow had fallen on the night previous, clothing all the earth with white, making it in its calm beauty, kissed by the rosy dawn, a fitting bride for the clear, cold sky.

From the windows of the mansion at Epps Hundred, could be seen, coming up from the buildings in the surrounding vales below, graceful wreaths of smoke, suggestive of the varied good cheer which was in preparation. Young people were out upon the hill-sides engaged in sports with the new snow; and others were hurrying to and fro in the streets upon errands laden with plenty. In due time, the church bell rang for the accustomed religious service, and the Judge with Molly and her children repairred thither in the chariot, while the Doctor chose to ride on his horse by their side.

The words of the psalm of thanksgiving as they were solemnly read by the good minister, had never fallen more deeply upon Molly's heart. The text—"He maketh peace in thy borders and filleth thee with the finest of the wheat"—

with its illustration, was particularly impressive at this time. And, when the singing commenced, the Deacon giving out the lines as usual, Molly united her voice with the great congregation in fervent strains of praise.

When they returned from church, accompanied by their guests, all the rooms of the mansion were thrown open. In every fire-place burned huge, hickory logs, sending forth a cheerful glow upon the gay paper on the walls, and over the rich antique furniture.

In the dining room, the long oaken table was spread with pewter plates, large dishes of apple-sauce, boiled vegetables, platters of joints and surloins, fine geese and turkeys, while in the centre was a whole pig of a delicious, brown roast, with a lemon in its mouth and graced with sprigs of parsley and sage. Upon the sideboard, were tankards filled to their brim, services of china and silver, smoking urns of tea and coffee, sweet meats, doughnuts, plethoric pumpkin and meat pies, plum puddings, apples and nuts ; all composing a feast worthy to be compared with the symposia of the ancients.

Opposite each other, at the centre of the table, sat Molly and the Doctor, with a youthful guest on either side ; at one end the Judge and his prime favorite, little Ben ; while at the other were the parson and the matronly Mary, with her step-children, and several other numerous families from the vicinity, completed the merry group.

When an appropriate grace was said by the minister, the servants commenced active service, and the bountiful repast began to be discussed. The meal was not a silent one ;

pleasant words and rapartee were interchanged with sparkling variety.

When the business of dining was concluded, the company
retired to the drawing-rooms and amused themselves as their
various tastes dictated. Some of the gentlemen drew together and told humorous stories connected with the late war,
often pausing to laugh heartily, thus widening their rubicund
visages to the utmost. Others engaged themselves closely
at games of draughts and chess. The children were amused
with the brisk sports of " blind man's buff," " roll the plate,"
" hull gull," etc.

Molly was the life of the whole company, now interspersing a lively anecdote, now frolicking with the children, im-
provising riddles and exchanging sallies of wit on all sides.

Some of the guests half smothered little Ben with kisses,
and had many things to say to each of the children. They
also bestowed due praise upon the exhibited sampler of
Alice's own work with its gay border of angular flowers and
bipeds, inclosing the scene of Eden in striking distinctness,
and also her name and age, with four lines of quaint verse.

When all these diversions were somewhat exhausted,
dancing was introduced according to the universal custom,
and thus the hours flew by on golden wings, till the shadows
of evening began to fall. For the childrens' sake, at a comparatively early hour, the guests spoke of dispersing to their
homes.

Molly then proposed singing, to which all cheerfully assented.
The good old tunes of that day in the words of, " As shep-

herds in Jewry were guarding their sheep," " His hoary frost, his fleecy snow," " Blow ye the trumpet, blow," " Gabriel the herald of the skies," etc., were sung with great impressiveness, and by even more than ordinary unction, by the elder people. The children sat composed and attentive, and little Ben nestled in his mother's lap with a subdued air, while she twined his flaxen curls over her fingers, as she sang.

At length, to conclude, it was requested that they should all unite in singing Old Hundred. Then from those happy, grateful hearts, arose, as a solemn acclamation to Heaven, the time honored words,

" Be thou, O God! exalted high ;
And, as thy glory fills the sky,
So let it be on earth displayed,
Till thou art here as there obeyed."

THE END.

MISCELLANEOUS.

A. S. ROE'S WORKS.

The Star and the Cloud; or, A Daughter's Love, by A. S. Roe, 12mo. ....Cloth, 1 25

A Long Look Ahead; or, The First Stroke and the Last, by A. S. Roe, 12mo..Cloth, 1 25

I've Been Thinking; or, The Secret of Success, by A. S. Roe, 12mo............Cloth, 1 00

To Love and to be Loved, and Time and Tide; or, Strive to Win, by A. S. Roe, two volumes in one, 12mo... Cloth, 1 25

—

Mary and Hugo. A Christmas Legend, by Mrs. E. Oakes Smith, Illustrations by Darley, 12mo. Cloth 75

Bertha and Lily; or, The Parsonage of Beech Glen, by Mrs. E. Oakes Smith, 4th edition, 12mo. illustrated, Cloth, 1 00

The Newsboy, by Mrs. E. Oakes Smith, 12th edition, 12mo. illustrated, ...Cloth, 1 00

Isora's Child, by Harriet A. Olcott, 6th edition, 12mo...... Cloth, 1 25

The Torchlight; or, Through the Wood, by H. A. Olcott, 12mo.........Cloth, 1 25

Alone, by Marion Harland, 24th edition, 12mo.. ....Cloth, 1 25

The Hidden Path, by Marion Harland, Author of "Alone," 23d edition, 12mo. ....Cloth, 1 25

Victoria; or, The World Overcome, by Caroline Chesebro' 12mo. ....Cloth, 1 25

Susan, The Fisherman's Daughter; or, Getting Along. A book of Illustrations, by Caroline Chesebro', 12mo. Cloth, 1 25

The Last of the Foresters; or, Humors of the Border. A Story of the old Virginia Frontier, by John Esten Cooke, author of "The Virginia Comedians," 12mo...................... 1 25

The Green Mountain Girls. A Tale of Vermont, by Blythe White, Jr., illustrated, 12mo. Cloth, 1 25

Toiling and Hoping. The Story of Little Hunchback, by Jenny Marsh, 12mo................ 1 00

The Heart of Mabel Ware. A Romance, 12mo......Neat cloth, 1 25

My Confession. The Story of a Woman's Life, 12mo. 75

Silverwood. A Book of Memories, by a Lady of Virginia,..Cloth, 1 00

Daisy's Necklace; and What Came of it, by T. B. Aldrich, author of "Babie Bell and other Poems," 12mo. 75

Married, not Mated; or, How they lived at Woodside and Throckmorton Hall, by Alice Cary, 12mo. Cloth, 1 00

The Lost Hunter. A Tale of Early Times, 12mo..........Cloth, 1 25

Knight of the Golden Melice. A Historical Romance, by the author of "The Lost Hunter," 12mo. ....,...... 1 25

The American Gentleman's Guide to Politeness and Fashion, by Harry Lunettes, 12mo. ....Cloth, 1 25

The Rainbow Around the Tomb A Book for Mourners, by Emily Thornwell, 12mo...Cloth, 75

Young Lady's Guide to Perfect Gentility. A New Book of Etiquette, by Emily Thornwell, 12mo. ....Cloth, gilt back, 75

Young Lady's Own Book. An Offering of Love and Sympathy, by Emily Thornwell, illustrated, 12mo. ....Cloth, gilt back, 1 00

Stephen's Egypt and the Holy Land. With Maps and Engravings. 8vo. ....Cloth, 2 00

. One of the most brilliant and fascinating books of travel ever published. The account of the visit to the city of Petræa, which is excavated in the solid rock, and had not before been visited for centuries by any European traveller, is most deeply interesting.

The Merchant's and Banker's Annual Register for 1857, by J. Smith Homans, editor of "The Banker's Magazine," 8vo. 1 00

Cotton is King. The Culture of Cotton and its relation to Agriculture, Manufactures and Commerce, and also to the Free Colored People of the United States, and those who hold that Slavery is in itself sinful, by David Christy. Second and revised and enlarged edition, with Tables, 12mo.................... 75

The Rifle, Axe, and Saddle-Bags, and other lectures, by Rev. W. H. Milburn, the eloquent blind Preacher. With an Introduction by Rev. John McClintock, D.D. With a portrait on steel, 12mo.....Cloth, 1 00

MISCELLANEOUS.

Star Papers; or, Experiences of Art and Nature, by Henry Ward Beecher, 26th edition, 12mo.................Cloth, 1 25

Turkey morocco, antique, portrait, 8 50

Lectures to Young Men on various Important Subjects, by Henry Ward Beecher, 26th thousand, 12mo. Cloth 75

An Encyclopedia of Instruction on Man and Manners, by A. B. Johnson, author of "Physiology of the Senses," 12mo................... 1 25

Physiology of the Senses; or, How and What we Hear, See, Taste, Feel and Smell, by A. B. Johnson, 12mo. 75

Webster's Family Encyclopædia of Useful Knowledge; or, Book of 7,223 Receipts and Facts. A whole library of subjects useful to every individual, illustrated with nearly one thousand engravings, 1,238 pages, 8vo. illuminated backs or sides in gilt, ... 3 00

This is a valuable and truly useful work, comprising everything needful to be known in domestic economy essential to the comfort, convenience, utility, and enjoyment of a family. In fact, there is nothing in the entire range of the domestic economy of a family that cannot be found in this book. It contains nearly 1250 pages, with a copious index, and is profusely illustrated. It is a work which every husband should buy for his wife, and every father for his daughter.

Wau Bun; or, The "Early Day" in the Northwest, by Mrs. John H. Kinzie, of Chicago, Illustrated, 8vo................... 2 25

Country Margins and Summer Rambles, by S. H. Hammond, and L. W. Mansfield, 12mo. Neat cloth, 1 00

Ewbank's Hydraulics and Mechanics, containing Descriptive and Historical Accounts of Hydraulic and other Machines for raising Water, with Observations on various subjects connected with the Mechanic Arts, Illustrated by nearly 300 engravings, 8vo. Cloth, gilt back, 2 50

Spirit Rappings Unveiled, by Rev. H. Mattison, 12mo. Cloth, 75

The Enchanted Beauty; or, Tales, Essays and Sketches, by William Elder, 12mo......................Cloth, 1 00

Camp Fires of the Red Men; or, A Hundred Years Ago, by J. R. Orton, illustrated 12mo. ....Cloth, 1 25

My Courtship and its Consequences, by Henry Wikoff. A true account of the Author's Adventures in England, Switzerland, and Italy, with Miss J. C. Gamble, of Portland Place, London, 12mo. Cloth, 1 25

The House I Live In; or, The Human Body, by Wm. A. Alcott, M.D., 1 vol. 18mo....... 63

The American Gift Book. A Perpetual Souvenir, with six elegant steel engravings, 12mo. Cloth, 1 00

The Sultan and His People, by C. Oscanyan, with numerous illustrations, 12mo......Cloth, 1 25

The American Revolution and Beauties of American History, 12mo.....Cloth, 1 00

The Husband in Utah, edited by Maria Ward, author of "Female Life among the Mormons," 12mo.................... ...Cloth, 1 00

The Philosophy of Skepticism and Ultraism, by Rev. J. B. Walker, author of "The Philosophy of the Plan of Salvation," 12mo.................Cloth, 1 25

Buchan's Domestic Medicine and Family Physician, 12mo... ....Cloth, 1 25

Walker on Female Beauty, 12mo......................Cloth, 1 00

Fox's Book of Martyrs, illustrated, 12mo................... 1 25

Captain Molly. The Story of a Brave Woman, by Thrace Talmon, 12mo. 1 00

The Prisoner of the Border, by P. Hamilton Myers, author of "The Last of the Hurons," &c., 12mo. 1 25

POPULAR BIOGRAPHY.

GENERALS OF THE REVOLUTION.

Six Vols., 12mo. Illustrated, $1 25 each.

Life of George Washington, by John Marshall.

Life of General Francis Marion, by W. Gilmore Simms.

Life of General Nathaniel Greene, by W. Gilmore Simms.

Life of General Lafayette, by Wm. Cutter.

Life of General Israel Putnam, by O. L. Holley.

Life of General Daniel Morgan, by James Graham.

———

Life of the Emperor Napoleon Bonaparte, by P. C. Headley, 12mo. ....Cloth   1 25

Life of the Empress Josephine Bonaparte, by P. C. Headley, 12mo. 1 25

Pictorial Life of Benjamin Franklin, including his Autobiography, 8vo. 2 00

Lives of the Discoverers and Pioneers of America, containing Columbus, Vespucius, De Soto, Raleigh, Hudson, Smith, Standish, Arabella Stuart, Elliott, and Penn, 1 elegant volume, illustrated, over 12mo. ......Cloth,   1 00

Life of Gen. Sam Houston. The only Authentic Memoir of him ever published, illus., 12mo...Cloth,   1 00

Lives of Eminent Mechanics, together with a Collection of Anecdotes, Descriptions, &c., relating to the Mechanic Arts, illustrated with fifty Engravings, 12mo. Cloth, gilt back,   1 00

Lives of the Signers of the Declaration of American Independence, with a Sketch of the Leading Events connected with the Adoption of the Articles of Confederation, and the Federal Constitution, by B. J. Lossing, steel frontispiece, and fifty portraits, 12mo. ....Cloth,   1 00

Life of General Andrew Jackson, including an Authentic History of the Memorable Achievements of the American Army, under General Jackson, before New Orleans, in the Winter of 1814-15, by Alexander Walker, with a frontispiece, 12mo.........Cloth,   1 25

Life of James Buchanan, by R. G. Horton, 12mo......Cloth,   1 00

Life of John C. Fremont, by John Bigelow, 12mo......Cloth,   1 00

Life of Patrick Henry, by William Wirt, with portraits on steel, 12mo. ....Cloth,   1 25

Life of Charles XII., King of Sweden, by Voltaire, 12mo. Cloth,   75

LIBRARY OF TRAVELS AND ADVENTURE.

Adventures of Gerard the Lion Killer, comprising a History of his Ten Years' Campaigns among the Wild Animals of Northern Africa, translated from the French, by Charles E. Whitehead, illustrated, 12mo...........Cloth,   1 25

Travels and Adventures in the Far West, by S. L. Carvalho, illustrated, 12mo. ....Cloth,   1 00

The War in Kansas; or, a Rough Trip to the Border, among New Homes and a Strange People, by George Douglas Brewerton, author of "A Ride with Kit Carson," &c., illustrated, 12mo. Cloth,   1 00

Bell Smith's Travels Abroad illustrated, 12mo. Cloth   1 00

Hunting Adventures in the Northern Wilds; or, a Tramp in the Chateauguay Woods, over Hills, Lakes, and Forest Streams, by S. H. Hammond, with 4 colored illustrations, 12mo...Cloth,   1 00

Indian Battles, Captivities, and Adventures, from the earliest periods to the present time, by John Frost, LL. D., with illustrations, 12mo. .... Cloth,   1 00

Cumming's Hunter's Life among Lions, Elephants and other Wild Animals, edited by Bayard Taylor, colored illustrations, thick 12mo...........Cloth,   1 00

Female Life Among the Mormons, with illustrations, 12mo.....................Cloth,   1 00

Layard's Popular Discoveries at Nineveh. illustrated, 12mo.... .... Cloth,   1 00

The Green Mountain Traveller's Entertainment, by Josiah Barnes, Sen., colored frontispiece, 12mo. ....Cloth,   1 00

Travels in Greece and Turkey, by the late Stephen Olin, D.D., illustrated, 12mo. Cloth,   1 00

Humboldt's Travels in Cuba, with an Essay, by J. S. Thrasher, 12mo. ....Cloth,   1 25

THE STANDARD BRITISH CLASSICS.

⁎ The following beautiful and desirable editions of the celebrated English Classic Authors, are printed from new stereotype plates, clear open type, and bound in uniform binding; they are the most desirable and convenient editions of these great and popular authors, whose works are so indispensable to every well-selected library. They are now ready, except "Smollett" and "Johnson," which will follow later in the season.

The Works of Joseph Addison including the whole Contents of Bishop Hurd's edition, with Letters and other Pieces not found in any previous collection, and Macaulay's Essay on his Life and Works. Edited, with Critical and Explanatory Notes, by G. Washington Greene, with portrait and plates, complete in 6 vols. 12mo. ...Cloth, 7 50
Sheep, library style, 9 00
Half calf, extra or antique, 13 50

The Works of Oliver Goldsmith comprising a variety of pieces now first collected, with copious Notes, by James Prior. Steel portrait and vignettes, complete in 4 vols. 12mo. ....Cloth, 5 00
Sheep, library style, 6 00
Half calf, extra or antique, 9 00

The Works of Samuel Johnson, including his "Lives of the Poets," "Rasselas," &c., with the new Biography by Macaulay, complete in 6 vols. 12mo. ...Cloth, 7 50
Library style, 9 00
Half calf, extra or antique 13 50

The Works of Henry Fielding, with a Memoir of his Life and Writings, by Thomas Roscoe. These volumes contain "Tom Jones," "Joseph Andrews," "Amelia," "Jonathan Wild," &c. First complete American edition, with portrait on steel, 4 vols. 12mo.
Cloth, 5 00
Sheep, library style, 6 00
Half calf, extra or antique, 9 00

The Works of Tobias Smollett, with a Memoir of his Life and Works, by Thomas Roscoe. These volumes contain "Roderick Random," "Humphrey Clinker," "Peregrine Pickle," "Count Fathom," &c. First complete American edition, with portrait on steel, 6 vols. 12mo.................Cloth, 7 50
Sheep, library style, 9 00
Half calf, extra or antique, 13 50

The Works of Laurence Sterne, comprising "Tristram Shandy,""Sentimental Journey," "Sermons and Letters." First complete American edition, with a Life of the Author and portrait on steel, 2 vols. 12mo. ....Cloth, 2 50
Sheep, library style, 3 00
Half calf, extra or antique, 4 50

The Works of Dean Swift, including "Gulliver's Travels," "Tale of a Tub," "Battle of the Books," and his Thoughts and Essays on various subjects, with a Life of the Author, by Rev. John Mitford, and copious Notes, by W. C. Taylor, LL. D., portrait on steel, 2 vols. 12mo. ....Cloth, 2 50
Sheep, library style, 3 00
Half calf, extra or antique, 4 50

The Works of Charles Lamb, comprising his Letters, Poems, Essays of Elia, Essays upon Shakspeare, Hogarth, &c., and a Sketch of his Life, with the Final Memorials, by T. Noon Talfourd with a portrait, 2 vols. 12mo. cloth, 2 50
Sheep, library style, 3 00
Half calf, extra or antique, 4 50

MARRYATT'S NOVELS,

Twelve volumes, 12mo. Cloth, ... 12 00
Library, sheep, ... 15 00
Half calf, gilt, ... 24 00

⁎ This is the first Complete American Edition of Capt. Marryatt's popular works, printed from new stereotype plates, long primer leaded, matching in size the popular 12mo. edition of Irving, Cooper, Dickens, &c.

Jacob Faithful. 2. Peter Simple. 3. Naval Officer, 4. King's Own. 5. Japhet in Search of a Father. 6. Midshipman Easy. 7. Newton Forster. 8. Pacha of Many Tales. 9. The Poacher. 10. The Phantom Ship. 11. Snarleyyow. 12. Percival Keene.

"Captain Marryatt is the best painter of sea characters, since Smollett."—*Chambers's Cyclopædia of English Literature.*

STANDARD FEMALE NOVELISTS.

The Works of Jane Austen, comprising "Pride and Prejudice," "Sense and Sensibility," "Mansfield Park," "Northanger Abbey," "Emma," "Persuasion." First American edition, with portrait, complete in 4 vols. 12mo.
Cloth, 4 00
Half calf, extra or antique, 8 00

The Works of Hannah More, comprising "Cœlebs in Search of a Wife," and her Tales and Allegories Complete. Portrait on steel, 2 vols. 12mo. ......Cloth, 2 00
Half calf, extra or antique, 4 00

Works of Charlotte Bronte (Currer Bell), comprising "Jane Eyre," "Shirley," and "Villette," 3 vols. 12mo. ....Cloth, 3 00
Half calf, extra or antique, 6 00

The Works of Jane Porter, comprising "The Scottish Chiefs," and "Thaddeus of Warsaw." With steel portrait, 2 vols. 12mo...Cloth, 2 00
Half calf. extra or antique, 4 00

The Works of Anne Radcliffe, comprising "The Mysteries of Udolpho," and "Romance of the Forest." With steel portrait, 2 vols. 12mo........................Cloth, 2 00
Half calf, extra or antique, 4 00

The Works of Frances Burney (Madame D'Arblay), comprising "Evelina," and "Cecilia," with a copious Biography of the Author by T. Babington Macaulay. Complete in 2 vols. 12mo. with portrait ....Cloth, 2 00
Half calf, extra or antique, 4 00

"Familiar as Household Words."

RE-PUBLICATION OF THE OLD NOVELISTS.

NEW LIBRARY OF CLASSIC AUTHORS.

Standard Fiction—People's 12mo. Edition.

*** Each volume is embellished with one or more illustrations, and all are bound in neat uniform binding, red or black cloth, full gilt backs, and sold for *One Dollar*, or in gilt sides and edges *Two Dollars*.

The Scottish Chiefs,........	1 00	The Mysteries of Udolpho,	1 00
Thaddeus of Warsaw, ...	1 00	Tristram Shandy,....	1 00
Children of the Abbey,....	1 00	Cœlebs in Search of a Wife,	1 00
Gil Blas, by Le Sage,..........	1 00	Tom Jones, by Fielding,..... ..	1 00
Don Quixote, by Cervantes,...	1 00	Amelia, by Fielding, ...	1 00
Arabian Nights,.............	1 00	Roderick Random, ...	1 00
Robinson Crusoe, by Defoe,	1 00	Humphrey Clinker,........	1 00
Swiss Family Robinson,..	1 00	Evelina, by Miss Burney, ...	1 00
Pilgrim's Progress, ...	1 00	Cecilia, by Miss Burney,....... ..	1 00
Holy War, by John Bunyan,..	1 00	Emma, by Jane Austen, ...	1 00
Vicar of Wakefield, and Rasselas (two in one), ...	1 00	Sense and Sensibility, and Persuasion (in one volume),...	1 00
Paul and Virginia, and The Exiles of Siberia (two in one)	1 00	Pride and Prejudice, and Northanger Abbey (two in one), ...	1 00
Gulliver's Travels, ...	1 00		
Romance of the Forest, ...	1 00	Mansfield Park, ...	1 00

LIBRARY OF POPULAR TALES.

Ten Volumes, each volume with Colored Frontispiece. 12mo., Cloth, gilt back $1.

Perils of Fast Living. A Warning to Young Men, by Charles Burdett.

Lights and Shadows of a Pastor's Life, by S. H. Elliott.

The Young Lady at Home, by T. S. Arthur.

American Evening Entertainments, by J. C. Campbell.

The Orphan Boy; or, Lights and Shadows of Northern Life.

The Orphan Girls; or, Lights and Shadows of Southern Life.

The Beauty of Woman's Faith. A Tale of Southern Life.

The Joys and Sorrows of Home. An Autobiography, by Anna Leland.

New England Boys; or, The Three Apprentices, by A. L. Stimson.

Prose and Poetry of Rural Life, by H. Penciller.

NEW LIBRARY OF WIT AND HUMOR.

The Widow Bedott Papers, by Francis M. Whitcher, with an introduction by Alice B. Neal, with eight spirited illustrations, 12mo. cloth, gilt back, ... 1 25

'Way Down East; or, Portraiture of Yankee Life, by Jack Downing (Seba Smith), 12mo., illustrated, ...Cloth, 1 00

The Life and Sayings of Mrs. Partington, by B. P. Shillaber, forty-three illustrations, 12mo.....................Cloth, 1 25

The Sparrowgrass Papers, by F. S. Cozzens, illustrated by Darley, 12mo. ....Cloth, 1 00

The Puddleford Papers; or, Humors of the West, 12mo. illustrated,...........Cloth, 1 00

The Bunsby Papers; or, Irish Echoes, by John Brougham, 12mo. illustrated, ...Cloth, 1 00

Lord Chesterfield's Letters to his Son. With a portrait on steel, 12mo,..................... 1 25

Essays of Elia, by Charles Lamb, 12mo.. .... 1 00

Addison's Spectator, complete in 2 volumes,............... 2 50

Foster's Essay on Decision of Character, and Gems of Thought, 12mo. ....Cloth, 1 00

Doddridge's Rise and Progress, 12mo.... .... 1 00

Baxter's Saints' Rest, 12mo. 1 00

Pen Pictures of the Bible, by Rev. Charles Beecher, 18mo. Cloth, gilt back, 50 Full gilt sides and edges, 75

Rhymes with Reason and without, by B. P. Shillaber (Mrs. Partington), 12mo. portrait, Neat cloth, 1 00

Gerald Massey's Poems, 12mo....... ....Neat cloth, 75

The Balloon Travels of Robert Merry and his Young Friends over various Countries of Europe, by Peter Parley, with eight illustrations, 12mo. Cloth, gilt back, 1 00 Full gilt sides and edges, 1 50

Gilbert Go-Ahead's Adventures and Travels in Foreign Parts, by Peter Parley, eight illustrations, 12mo. Cloth, gilt back, 1 00 Full gilt sides and edges, 1 50

www.ingramcontent.com/pod-product-compliance
Lightning Source LLC
Chambersburg PA
CBHW051113120726
47905CB00005B/1263